MW00655758

CHRISTMAS IN CAMBRIA

AN OTTER BLUFF ROMANCE

LINDA SEED

Linda Seed

This is a work of fiction. Any characters, organizations, places, or events portrayed in this novel are either products of the author's imagination or are used fictitiously.

CHRISTMAS IN CAMBRIA
Copyright © 2020 by Linda Seed

All rights reserved. No part of this book may be reproduced in any form or by any means without the prior written consent of the author, excepting brief quotes used in reviews.

ISBN: 978-1-7343453-5-3

The author is available for book signings, book club discussions, conferences, and other appearances.
Linda Seed may be contacted via e-mail at linda@lindaseed.com or on Facebook at www.facebook.com/LindaSeedAuthor. Learn more about Linda Seed's novels at www.lindaseed.com.

Cover design by Kari March.

Created with Vellum

BY LINDA SEED

The Main Street Merchants

Moonstone Beach

Cambria Sky

Nearly Wild

Fire and Glass

The Delaneys of Cambria

A Long, Cool Rain

The Promise of Lightning

Loving the Storm

Searching for Sunshine

The Russo Sisters

Saving Sofia

First Crush

Fixer-Upper

Loving Benny

Otter Bluff

The Icing on the Cake

Christmas in Cambria

SIGN UP TO GET A FREE LINDA SEED STARTER LIBRARY

Sign up for Linda's twice-monthly newsletter and get her free ebook starter library: three full-length romances and a bonus short story available only to newsletter subscribers. Your information will never be shared or sold, and you can unsubscribe at any time.

To subscribe and get your free ebooks, go to the following address:
https://claims.prolificworks.com/free/hDF1LvnI

CHAPTER 1

The very thought of Christmas—up to and including Santa, elves, reindeer, the colors red and green, and poinsettias—made Delilah's bowels clench and her stomach roil as though she were suffering from food poisoning.

Still, she was determined to create a happy and festive holiday for her kids or die trying.

That was what she told herself as she drove up Main Street in Cambria and turned left on Burton Drive, headed toward the ocean. The kids were strapped into their booster seats in the back of the rental car, cranky from the long drive north from LAX.

"Are we almost there?" Jesse, her six-year-old, had been asking the same question for more than an hour, and Delilah was happy to finally answer in the affirmative.

"Just another couple of minutes, I think."

"I'm hungry." Gavin, her four-year-old, was always hungry. They'd eaten on the way, but that hadn't gone far toward filling the bottomless void that was his appetite.

"I know, sweetie. When we get there, I'll make you a snack."

She had two bags of groceries in the trunk that she'd picked up in Morro Bay. The way her kids ate, it wouldn't last long, but it would be enough to get them settled. She made her way down Burton, turned on Ardath Drive, and headed toward the Marine Terrace neighborhood. She'd already stopped at the rental office and picked up the key.

Minutes later, she was pulling into the driveway of Otter Bluff, a single-story oceanfront house with blue siding and white trim. Three bedrooms and 1,400 square feet, most of it in need of renovation but all of it hers for two months. The pictures she'd seen online had called to her.

This was a place where she could stay for a while to plan her next move. This was a place where she and her boys could have Thanksgiving and Christmas without the memories of what Mitch had done to them.

This was a place she had chosen, not him.

"Okay, guys. We're here. Let's go in and see what we've got."

~

DELILAH'S HATRED of Christmas was a fairly new development. She'd loved it until her husband abandoned her for another woman the year before on December 24, leaving her and their two children alone, devastated, and broke, despite the fact that Delilah's ex earned an annual income in the high six figures.

He'd continued paying the mortgage, so at least they weren't put out on the street. But the bank accounts had been in his name, and that money had magically vanished when he'd announced he was leaving her.

She'd gotten a job, of course, but it hadn't paid nearly enough, especially given the high cost of child care.

Delilah had been an idiot—she could see that now. She'd married young, before she'd earned any real job experience, and she'd agreed when Mitch had insisted she stay home.

He'd wanted her to be a stay-at-home mother to their children, a stay-at-home wife to him, and she'd agreed, because why not? It had seemed like a luxury at the time.

As soon as he passed the bar exam, Mitch had landed a job at a high-paying firm, and they hadn't needed whatever income she might have brought in. He worked long hours—twelve, sometimes sixteen in a day—and who could blame him for wanting someone at home to take care of things? He'd needed hot meals, clean suits, a home that was in order and running smoothly during those brief times when he was in it.

They'd gone that way through the birth of two sons and through two moves, each into a house larger than the last. Cocktail parties with the partners, interviews to get the kids into a top preschool and kindergarten, Delilah dressed in clothes Mitch's secretary picked out for her because he couldn't have her wearing anything that made him look like less of a success.

She'd never been able to keep up with his standard of who she should be, but God, she'd tried. It bothered him when she'd put on weight during the pregnancies. She'd worked to take it off, but she'd never gotten her old body back.

She hadn't thought he'd leave her, though, not really.

And then he had, on Christmas Eve, while the gifts were still wrapped under the tree, the kids asleep upstairs waiting for Santa.

So, yes, she hated Christmas. Her love of the holiday was yet another thing he'd taken away from her.

This year, though, she was determined to get it back.

QUINN STOOD atop a bluff overlooking the Pacific Ocean—the vast blue expanse stretching out to the horizon, the surf crashing far below his feet, gulls cawing overhead, a gentle breeze rustling his hair—and thought, *I am sick to death of this crap.*

He'd told his clients what to bring and what to wear. He'd told them verbally, then he'd e-mailed them a written list. He'd told them again on the phone when he'd called to confirm their booking.

They hadn't paid attention to a goddamned thing he'd said. All four of them would be sunburned to a crisp if Quinn hadn't brought extra sunscreen. All of them would be bitten to hell if he hadn't brought extra bug repellent. And all of them were suffering from blisters because they'd worn flip-flops instead of the hiking boots he'd recommended.

Flip-flops, for fuck's sake.

The blisters weren't his problem, of course, but in a way, they were, because they'd been bitching about the pain for the last two miles.

Was it his fault they couldn't follow instructions? Was it his fault not a damned one of them had been smart enough to wear comfortable, supportive shoes on an all-day hike?

"Oh, God." The mother, a woman in her forties, sat on a rock, rubbing her feet with her hands. "I'm bleeding. My feet are bleeding."

"We're looking at the Point Sur State Marine Reserve, which protects all of the marine life within its boundaries," Quinn recited as though she hadn't said anything. "Sea otters, sea lions, and harbor seals are common in this area."

"I'm going to die." The father, a pudgy guy in his fifties, sat on the rock next to his wife and put his head between his knees as though trying not to faint.

"Take my picture." The teenage girl handed her brother her phone. She climbed on top of a boulder with the ocean in the background and struck a pose.

"Suck my ass." The brother set the phone on the ground and walked away.

The girl, pouting, climbed down, retrieved the phone, and offered it to Quinn. "Will you do it?"

He took the phone. "Yeah, but only if you stay off that boulder. The last thing I need is for you to plummet to your death so you can look good on Instagram."

She rolled her eyes extravagantly.

God help him.

Ten minutes later he unloaded the tourists at their rental car, collected a tip that should have been more, and stashed his gear in the passenger seat of his van. He thought about making the drive back to his place in Cambria, then decided against it.

No matter how often he did it, a six-hour hike was still a lot, and a two-hour drive afterward didn't have much appeal. Instead, he drove into Big Sur, went to a diner, and ordered a cheeseburger, fries, and a beer from a waitress in jeans and a T-shirt, a white apron around her waist.

While he was waiting, the owner spotted him from behind the counter and gave him a wave. "Hey, Quinn. You just back from a hike?"

"Yeah. Mom, Dad, and two teenage kids, all of whom were a pain in the ass. How you been?"

"Good. Good." Otto bobbed his head. He grabbed Quinn's food from the pass, brought it to the table, and slid into the booth across from him. Otto was a big guy, about six foot four and 250 pounds, and sliding into the booth wasn't as easy for him as it had been for Quinn.

They chatted a little about Otto's wife and kids, Quinn's business, the tourism situation in Big Sur, the weather, and how the 49ers were doing. As they talked, Otto stole the occasional fry from Quinn's plate.

"Listen, I better get back to work. You staying tonight?" Otto maneuvered himself out of the booth and brushed fry salt off his hands.

"I thought I'd go back in the morning. You mind if I park in the lot?"

"Hey. My place is your place."

"Appreciate it."

Quinn finished his food and his beer and went out to his van just as the sun was dipping below the trees.

The van was outfitted with a bed, a space heater, a mini refrigerator, a tiny sink with a pump faucet, and a single-burner stove with an electric cooktop. Quinn had converted it himself in his spare time, and it had become his second home when his job kept him from getting to the first one.

It didn't have a bathroom, but that usually worked out okay—Otto left a key under the backdoor mat when Quinn was there so he could use the employee restroom at the diner. And then there were campgrounds, gas stations, or, hell, even the woods. He could always find somewhere to take care of business.

He climbed into the back of the van and stretched out on the bed with a book—the pages illuminated by a battery-operated lamp—just as the rain began to fall. Lying there in the dry warmth of the van with the book and his comfortable mattress as the rain drummed on the roof made him feel cozy and serene.

He'd have been tempted to live in the van full-time if it weren't for things like showers and storage space. Plus, he liked to eat, and van cooking usually amounted to heating up a can of chili. Also, when he wanted to bring a woman home, they usually reacted better to his house than they did to the van. So, there was that.

Quinn drifted off to sleep with the book open on his chest and the soothing wet patter singing to him.

"I don't like this bed."

Delilah had just gotten Gavin tucked in with his stuffed bear, Waffles. She sat on the edge of the bed and brushed the hair from his forehead with her hand. "Why not? Isn't it comfortable?"

"It's just weird."

She interpreted that to mean the bed was different—that it wasn't his. She leaned forward and kissed him on the cheek.

"I know you like your bed at home," she told him. "But this is vacation. It's an adventure. You like adventures."

"I guess." He pulled Waffles closer.

"Tomorrow we'll go to the beach. That'll be fun, right?"

"It's too cold for the beach."

The weather had been cold in Cambria lately, according to the online forecasts. But Delilah was determined to pursue fun for her children as though all of their lives depended on it.

"It's too cold to swim, maybe, but it's not too cold to build sandcastles," she said.

"I guess."

She kissed him again, then kissed Waffles. She got up, went to the door, and turned out the light. "Sweet dreams, Boo." She hadn't called him by that nickname in more than a year, but she hoped it would comfort him to hear it.

Hell, she hoped it would comfort her to say it.

She checked on Jesse, who insisted he was too old to be tucked in and had taken care of his own bedtime routine, then she went into the kitchen, poured herself a glass of white wine, and sat down on the sofa in the living room.

God, she felt like hell.

The whole time she'd been unpacking, making dinner, cleaning up, then supervising bath time, she'd kept an upbeat patter with her boys about how much fun they were going to have here, how many things they were going to do in Cambria, and how they were going to make exciting Christmas memories here.

Privately, though, she wanted to sit down somewhere alone and cry.

Instead, she called her sister.

"How's the house?" Roxanne asked her when she picked up.

"It's good. The house is good. I mean, everything except the kitchen is outdated, but you should see the view. The ocean is just outside the sliding glass door. You can hear seals barking."

"Wow. That's great."

"Yeah. Great."

"So why do you sound like you want to strangle someone?"

Delilah considered that. "Not someone. Mitch. That's who I want to strangle."

"Oh, Delilah."

"We're supposed to be home right now. Together. As a family."

But she no longer had a home. Her house—the one she'd raised her kids in for the last five years—had been sold in the divorce settlement. Her half of the proceeds, a substantial amount, had allowed her to come here to take some time to sort out what she wanted before she built a new life for herself and her boys.

"I told Jesse and Gavin we'd have fun," she said.

"And you will."

"They will, anyway, if it's the last thing I do."

"You could come stay with us," Roxanne said. "Joey wouldn't mind. We've got the spare bedroom, and the boys could stay in Kyle's room. It would be fun. It would be like a sleepover."

But Delilah didn't want to do that—didn't want to bring her sorrow and her relentless, hopeless gloom into someone else's home. "That's sweet, Roxanne. Really. But I can't."

"Of course you can."

"We're okay. You don't have to worry."

She wasn't okay—not yet—but she knew she would be.

How long that would take, she didn't know.

CHAPTER 2

On Delilah's second day at Otter Bluff, she was in the kitchen making a snack for the boys when someone knocked on the door. She opened it to find a grandmotherly woman holding a cloth-covered basket and smiling at her.

"Oh. Good morning. May I help you?" Delilah was still wearing her bathrobe at ten a.m., and she pulled the robe more closely around her body.

"I just wanted to come by and say hello. I'm Dolly. My husband and I live in the gray house across the street. I noticed you have some adorable boys."

"I . . . yes. Jesse and Gavin. They're six and four."

"Oh, that's lovely. Would you like some muffins? I baked them myself." She thrust the basket at Delilah, who accepted it.

"Thank you. That's so nice of you. Would you like to come in?"

Dolly waved her off. "Oh, no, I can see that you're not expecting company. But if you come by later I can tell you all of the things there are to do in Cambria with kids. People think this is just a community for grownups, but no. There's so much for the little ones. I can make a list."

Delilah had been in a bad mood, as she was so often these days, but now she couldn't help smiling—and not just the polite, sociable smile that came to her lips in situations that required it. She couldn't remember ever encountering this kind of neighborliness in her old neighborhood. There, if someone came to your door, they were selling something.

Gavin came up beside Delilah and clung to her thigh, his thumb in his mouth. He'd given up thumb-sucking when he was three, but the stress of the divorce had brought the habit back.

Delilah smoothed his hair with her hand. "This is our neighbor—her name is Dolly. Say hello, sweetheart."

Gavin waved at Dolly with three fingers of the hand that wasn't busy with the thumb-sucking.

"Why, hello. And what's your name?" Dolly leaned down, her hands on her thighs.

Gavin didn't answer, so Delilah stepped in. "This is Gavin. He's a little shy."

"Oh, that's just fine. I have a grandson about your age, and he's shy, too."

Gavin allowed her a smile around the thumb.

After a little more chitchat, Delilah said her goodbyes, closed the door, and brought the basket into the kitchen. Jesse was just emerging from his bedroom, where he'd been watching a show on his iPad.

"We need to invite Dolly over for tea," she told the boys.

"How come?" Gavin wanted to know.

"Because it's polite. When somebody does something nice for you, it's polite to invite them over for tea."

"Could there be cookies, too?" Jesse asked.

"Well, I suppose so," Delilah told him.

"Okay." He shrugged.

She put two of Dolly's muffins on plates for the boys' snack, feeling a tiny stirring whisper of something she hadn't felt in some time.

Optimism.

~

QUINN WOKE to the sound of birds in the trees outside his van. The sun had just risen, and the cool dawn air was soft with fog. He dragged himself out of bed, found the hidden key, and used the diner's bathroom. He washed his hands and splashed water on his face.

It was just after six, and the diner didn't open until eight. He couldn't wait that long for coffee, so he locked up, put the key back where he'd found it, and went to his van.

He fired up the stove, boiled some water in a kettle, then used his single-cup pour-over setup to make coffee.

When it was done, he took his mug to an Adirondack chair set up on the diner's patio and drank the hot, strong brew while watching the fog move through the pines.

Not a bad life, all things considered.

Sure, the tourists could be a pain in the ass sometimes, and his work didn't pay enough. But he got to wake up to this in the morning instead of putting on a suit and driving to some generic office building where he'd spend eight hours in a cubicle.

And, hell, even the tourists were okay sometimes. Every now and then he got one—somebody who was so moved by the natural beauty they were seeing that they practically buzzed with excitement.

Knowing he was the one who brought them that? Yeah, that was all right.

He finished his coffee, put his van back in order, ate a PowerBar, then started the drive south.

DELILAH BAKED a batch of chocolate chip cookies, brewed a pot of tea, and invited Dolly over to share them, partly because of courtesy and partly because she was so starved for adult interaction she thought she might start howling at the moon.

They'd been in Cambria two days, and Delilah was still so wound up over everything that had been happening in her life that she felt like her shoulders had been permanently relocated to a spot just beside her ears. She'd been trying to hide it for the boys' sake, but she snapped at them too often, and they were probably so used to seeing a fake smile on her face that they no longer knew what a real one looked like.

Maybe a chat over tea with someone who wasn't under ten years old would raise her spirits. It certainly couldn't bring them any lower than they already were.

"Can I have a cookie?" Jesse hovered over the plate Delilah was arranging in anticipation of her neighbor's visit.

"Me too," Gavin said.

"We have company coming," she told them. "It's polite to wait."

They both looked so horrified that she relented.

"All right. Take one each and save the rest until Dolly gets here." Jesse extended a hand toward the plate, but Delilah raised it out of his reach. "Wash your hands first."

"Aw, Mom."

"Both of you."

When the boys' hands were clean, Delilah sent them off with their cookies. They both ran into Delilah's room because it had a television. Delilah knew she should get them out of the house, limit their screen time—but sometimes she needed that distraction just to get through the day.

She'd thought she would feel better once her divorce was finalized, but she'd never felt more exhausted, more defeated.

For now, she was faking being okay. And part of faking it involved socializing with others the way people did when they hadn't been emotionally traumatized.

She arranged the tea and cookies on the table and waited for Dolly's knock.

~

"You're here until the first of the year, then? Oh, that's marvelous." Dolly was sitting at the kitchen table at Otter Bluff with a cup of tea and a small plate bearing a cookie in front of her. She'd brought Delilah some fresh basil she'd transplanted from her garden into a small terra cotta pot. The basil sat on the kitchen counter looking green and cheerful.

"The thing is ... I'm not sure where we're going after this." She hadn't wanted to blurt out her troubles, but she couldn't seem to help it. "Our house was sold in the divorce, and we don't have anywhere to go come January first."

"Oh." Dolly's brow furrowed. "What do you think you'll do?"

"I don't want to think at all." Delilah sipped from her mug and set it back down on the table, wrapping her hands around it. "I just want to take some time and not think. The divorce was awful. It was a year of ... of emotional torture. And now it's over, and I just need to take some time to not feel that way anymore. If I don't have something figured out by the first of the year, we can stay with my family. My sister has already offered. Until then ... I just want to pretend everything's okay until it is."

Dolly reached out a hand and squeezed Delilah's arm. "Well, then you do that. What about your ex and the boys? Is he in the picture?"

That was a long story, one she didn't want to get into in detail. She stuck to the basics. "He moved to Paris. He'll have the boys for two weeks in the summer."

"And how are the kids dealing with that?"

"They're doing the best they can. We all are."

~

BY THE TIME DOLLY LEFT, Delilah had her new basil plant, a plan to have lunch with Dolly on Saturday, and a list of local activities for children, ranging from beach-going to parks, libraries, and museums —ideas Dolly had gleaned from years of visits by her grandchildren.

She got started that day.

Delilah packed snacks along with the beach towels, sand toys, beach chairs, and Frisbee she'd found in the garage at Otter Bluff, and she took the boys to the beach at San Simeon Cove.

It was a chilly November day—too cold for the boys to go swimming—but coming from Connecticut, they were used to much harsher weather than this. Delilah set herself up in a chair near the pier while Jesse and Gavin ran around chasing each other and looking for interesting rocks and shells.

The overcast sky brooded overhead, and tendrils of fog moved through the tops of the trees that lined the bluffs. A flock of pelicans glided above the water, looking for their next meal.

Don't think about what's next, Delilah reminded herself. *Just think about today.*

She closed her eyes and breathed in the ocean air. Over the whoosh of the waves, she heard Gavin's laugh, and that was one thing she could focus on.

One good thing.

Sometimes that was enough.

~

QUINN WAS TRYING NOT to think about the holidays, but the town of Cambria was making it damned hard.

First there had been the Scarecrow Festival, which, thankfully, had ended October 31. Now, he couldn't turn his head sideways without seeing some kind of Thanksgiving decoration, ranging from decorative metal turkeys to paper-mache cornucopias to banners proclaiming the community Thanksgiving dinner or some holiday-themed art show.

For God's sake, couldn't a man live in peace without the pressure of having to give thanks or bring goodwill to mankind?

As he browsed the aisles of the Cookie Crock for his weekly grocery run, the upcoming holidays continued to taunt him.

Turkeys on sale! Get your premade mashed potatoes and stuffing, just place your order now! Canned pumpkin, two for four dollars! Marshmallow fluff, on special!

Don't even get him started on the goddamned cranberry sauce.

He hadn't always been this way. He hadn't always hated the holidays with the fiery passion of a true convert. He hadn't really loved them since he was a kid—Christmas and Thanksgiving and all of that were for kids, after all—but the hatred had come later. After everything had gone to hell with his family.

First there'd been his uncle's death. Then there'd been the reading of the will. Then, finally, the explosion of anger, resentment, and recrimination that came when Quinn had inherited the bulk of his uncle's estate.

And, hell, it hadn't even been that much. He'd been able to make a nice down payment on his house in Cambria, but that was about it. It wasn't like he'd been set for life.

His two brothers had insisted that he split the money with them, and his mom and stepfather had sided with them. Quinn had refused, mainly because his two brothers were assholes.

Quinn's uncle Nate had thought so, too, and that's why he'd written them out of his will.

Why should Quinn give them anything after the way they'd treated Nate? After the way they'd shown their asses?

They'd threatened a lawsuit that hadn't materialized. The lack of legal entanglement was good, but it hadn't stopped Quinn's family from turning on him.

Most of the time, having them out of his life was okay. Things were more peaceful that way. But at certain times, it was hard. At certain times, it hurt like hell. And those times tended to coincide with the entire damned holiday season, starting with Halloween and stretching right on through New Year's.

Well, he'd do what he always did around this time of year. He'd stay home a lot, and when he did go out, he'd drink too much and find someone to bring home with him.

It had worked in the past. Why mess with a winning formula?

He was picking up some Granny Smith apples in the produce section when someone called his name.

"Hey, Quinn. How you doin'?" Jerry, the produce guy, was coming toward him with a cart full of romaine lettuce ready to be put on display.

"Not bad. You?"

They chatted a little bit about football—Jerry was a 49ers fan, and they'd crapped the bed in their last game—and then a little bit about Jerry's wife, who was expecting their third child.

One nice thing about a small town was you could always find someone to shoot the shit with, even when all you were doing was buying apples.

When that was done, Quinn thought he was going to make a clean getaway, but Jerry ruined everything.

"You gonna be seeing family for Thanksgiving?" he asked.

Jerry was an acquaintance—Quinn wouldn't really call him a friend—so he didn't know about Quinn's circumstances, and Quinn wasn't about to tell him now. Instead, he made some noncommittal noises.

"I'm just gonna see how it goes." Which didn't mean anything—that was the very beauty of the sentence.

"You need somewhere to go, you can come to our place," Jerry offered. "We're having Emma's family, my family, the next-door neighbors, and the next-door neighbor's family. We're gonna have so many people one more won't make a difference."

Quinn was simultaneously touched and horrified. It was genuinely kind of Jerry to make the offer, and the idea that someone wanted him at their Thanksgiving table made him feel unexpectedly emotional—a feeling he mercilessly suppressed as soon as it emerged. At the same time, he couldn't imagine himself actually sitting there eating sweet potato casserole with a crowd of people who were probably far more emotionally functional than he was.

"That's nice of you, man," he said. "Really. But I think I'm gonna just keep it loose and see what happens." Another sentence that conveniently didn't mean anything.

He said goodbye, paid for his groceries, and got out of there before he could admit something embarrassing—like the fact that he was lonely.

He'd rather drive nails into his kneecaps than pour out his heart to Jerry, or to anyone else, for that matter.

As far as he was concerned, January first couldn't come soon enough.

CHAPTER 3

The idea of hiking had been Delilah's. Well, Dolly's, really. It had been on the list of things to do that Dolly had offered Delilah during their get-together. Neither of the boys had been interested, but Delilah had pushed the issue.

Which made her feel even worse when everything went wrong.

They'd been in Cambria four days, and Jesse and Gavin were already complaining about being bored.

When their house had sold, Delilah had pulled Jesse out of kindergarten—something that was allowed in the state of Connecticut with a signed parental waiver—and at first he'd thought it was a fun novelty that he wouldn't have to go to school. But it hadn't taken long for him to start protesting the lack of things to do, and Gavin had soon joined in.

So, Delilah had researched hiking trails, packed snacks, water bottles, and bug spray, and ordered her two reluctant and whining kids to get in the car.

"I don't want to go." Jesse shoved his lower lip out in a pout.

"Me neither." Gavin tended to agree with Jesse on most things, especially when he was in opposition to whatever it was Delilah wanted.

"Why not?" She kept her tone upbeat, her face open and enthusiastic. "It'll be fun. The article on the Internet says there's a waterfall at the end of the trail."

Jesse rolled his eyes. "It's water. I've seen water."

"Well, you haven't seen this water. Besides, we all need the exercise." She shooed them out of the house and into the car, her day pack full of supplies.

"You said this trip was going to be fun. It's not fun. I miss Dad," Jesse said.

All at once, Delilah's composure slipped, and she felt her throat clog with emotion. She blinked her eyes to hold off tears, cleared her throat, and forced her lips into a smile. "I know you do, honey. I do, too. But we have each other. So, let's try to have a good time, all right?"

~

It started okay, despite the kids' protests. Delilah drove north to where the map indicated, parked at a turnout off Highway 1, slung her pack over her shoulders, and got the kids out of their booster seats.

The first part of the trail was wide and relatively level, and the landscape was lovely, with towering pines, dramatic hills, and the ocean stretched out into eternity below the bluffs. The boys chatted happily as they walked, and Delilah breathed in the clean fall air, congratulating herself on her excellent plan for a wholesome family outing.

Things were still okay as the trail narrowed and began to climb into the hills. Delilah wasn't in the best shape—she could admit that—but the exertion felt good. The boys had forgotten to be opposed to the outing and were exclaiming over the squirrels, the birds, even a small, harmless snake that slithered over the path.

As it turned out, she was worried about the wrong things. She was worried about sunburn, poison oak, bug bites, possible dehydration if they went too far and too long without remembering to drink their water.

She wasn't worried that one of her boys would leave the trail and fall into a ravine, but that was what happened.

Jesse had brought a small rubber ball that he'd gotten from a vending machine in Morro Bay. He was tossing it into the air and catching it as they walked—something Delilah had thought nothing of, never imagining that it might lead to potential disaster.

"Throw it to me," Gavin said. Jesse threw it to him, and Gavin caught it.

Then Gavin threw the ball back to Jesse, but it went high, sailing over Jesse's head and off the path.

They could see it from where they were—the ball, a bright, neon orange, lay in a clump of bushes a few feet down the hill from where they stood.

Jesse stepped off the path to get it, and Delilah warned him to be careful. At the time, getting the ball seemed like a reasonable thing to do, as the incline wasn't too steep where it lay, and it was only a few feet away.

Jesse picked up the ball, and it seemed like the whole thing was going to be a momentary, easily forgettable blip in their day.

Then his feet slipped, and Delilah watched helplessly as her son slid down to where the earth fell away. He plummeted, screaming, into a brush-filled ravine so far below the path that Delilah could no longer see him.

Her heart pounded so hard that her vision blurred and her head filled with buzzing panic.

"Jesse! Jesse!"

"Mom!" he called back.

Okay. He can hear me, and he can answer. Okay.

"Are you hurt?" she called down to him.

"Uh … no. I'm scratched a little, that's all."

Thank God. Oh, thank God.

The buzzing in her ears began to subside, and her heart slowed a little, though it was still beating way too fast. She took a deep breath, let it out, and told herself to stay calm. He'd fallen, but he was okay. Kids fell all the time.

"Can you climb back up?" she asked him.

She heard sounds—a rustling in the brush far below her—as he tried.

She heard him drawing closer, then, horrified, she heard the sound of him sliding back down to where he'd started. "Mom, I fell again," he told her.

"Jesse, are you okay?"

"Yeah. I just can't get up there."

She assessed her situation. She could climb down to him, but then what if they both were stuck down there with Gavin up here on the trail alone? He was only four years old. She couldn't take the risk that he'd be left up here on his own.

"Okay. Just sit tight, honey, I'm going to call for help." She pulled out her cell phone, but the screen said NO SERVICE. She could feel herself starting to panic, but she couldn't do that. The boys would follow her lead. She needed to be calm, confident, in control.

"Why aren't you calling?" Gavin asked, his face a mask of fear.

"Sweetie, there's no cell service here." She kept her voice matter-of-fact for his sake. "Don't worry, though, we're going to figure this out." She and Gavin could go get help, but that would mean leaving Jesse.

She looked at her phone again and walked a short distance up the trail, hoping to find a pocket of service.

No luck.

He's okay. We're all okay. There's no need to panic. I'll just think and figure this out.

And she would, she knew that. She just had no idea how.

~

Quinn couldn't have said why he picked that particular trail on that particular day. Hiking was like breathing for him. He did it when he needed to clear his head, when he needed to think. He did it when he was sad or lonely or happy or bored. Something about being out there in nature amid the trees and the wind and the birds made him feel right, as though he were in exactly the right place at the right time.

As it happened, he *was* in the right place at the right time, as far as the family on the trail were concerned.

He'd been walking for a couple of hours, and he was descending the trail on the way back to his van when he heard some kind of commotion up ahead. He couldn't determine the nature of the commotion, but it sounded like someone was upset.

He rounded a curve in the trail and saw a woman and a kid up ahead. The woman was kneeling on the ground and peering off the side of the trail, and the kid was hanging back, sucking his thumb and crying.

"I want Jesse!" the kid wailed as the woman said something Quinn couldn't hear.

"Need some help?" Quinn asked.

The woman looked up, and both surprise and relief washed over her—he could see it as clearly as if she had been wearing a costume that she'd now removed.

"Oh, my God. Yes. My son fell into the ravine. He's six years old. He's okay, he's not hurt, but he can't get back up, and I can't go down there and leave Gavin alone, and my cell phone isn't getting a signal, and ... I'm rambling. Yes, I need some help. Are you going down to the highway? Could you call the police or somebody when you get there? There should be a signal down there. Call 9-1-1 or the park rangers, or ... I don't know who. Just somebody who can rescue my son?"

Had he thought she'd seemed relieved? Now that she was babbling at him at a thousand miles a minute, it was clear that she was still in mid-panic.

His impressions of the woman hit him in quick bursts: short, maybe no more than five foot three. Late twenties, early thirties. Dark hair in a ponytail, blue eyes, a sprinkling of freckles across her nose that made a person think of the kid she had once been. Her V-neck T-shirt showed an inch of cleavage, and he tried not to look directly at it. Her jeans showed off some lush and extravagant curves—ditto the part about not looking.

At least, not too obviously.

He willed himself to focus. *Kid in jeopardy. Right.*

He stepped off the trail, peered down toward the drop-off, and called to the kid. "Hey down there. Jesse, is it?"

"Who are you?" The kid sounded scared, so Quinn tried to be soothing.

"I'm Quinn. How far did you fall?" From the sound of his voice, it was maybe twenty feet. Probably no more than that.

"I don't know," the kid said. "I didn't really fall. I just kind of slid." His voice had taken on a whining quality, probably from fear.

"Okay. You're not hurt, though?"

"Not really. I scraped my knees."

"All right."

"Can you please go down to the highway and call someone?" the woman asked.

"You don't need me to call someone. I'm someone." He began climbing down the side of the ravine to get the kid.

"You're going down there? Oh, my God. Okay. Okay." The woman was still freaking out, and he let her. If that was what she needed to do, where was the harm?

He climbed down, watching his footing, using tree roots and clumps of bushes to anchor his hands and feet. The thought of poison oak occurred to him, but he didn't see any, so that was good.

When he got down there, the kid was sitting on the ground, his eyes round with fear. He was wearing shorts, and his knees were bleeding a little, but it didn't look too bad.

"You must be Jesse." Quinn offered his hand for the kid to shake. "I don't see any other six-year-old boys down here, so I'm assuming."

The kid's hand felt small and fragile in his. He shook it manfully, then bent down and hooked a finger at his own back. "Here. Climb on."

"You want me to get on your back?"

"Yeah. Like a piggyback ride. You've done piggyback rides, right?"

"Yeah."

"Okay. Up you go."

The kid climbed onto his back and grasped him around the neck, nearly choking him. He repositioned the kid's hands to his shoulders. "Hold on there. Otherwise I'm going to pass out from lack of oxygen before we get up there."

"Okay. Sorry."

Once that was settled, he told the boy to hang on and started climbing. While he climbed, going slowly, taking one careful step at a time to avoid falling, he made small talk to keep the kid calm.

"You're in, what, first grade?"

"I'm supposed to be in kindergarten, but I'm not going because we're on vacation."

"You're skipping school for vacation? That's gotta be pretty sweet."

"I guess."

"How about your brother? Is he skipping school, too?" Quinn kept up the patter to keep the kid calm, and it seemed to be working. They'd made it halfway up to the trail, and the boy was chatting amiably with him.

"He's only in preschool, but he knows his letters and stuff. His teacher called my mom in for a conference because he's really quiet and he doesn't have any friends."

"Huh. You must like it that he's quiet, though. No little brother annoying you, yapping about this and that."

"He talks at home. Just not at school," Jesse said.

"You know what? I was the opposite."

The kid was slipping a little on Quinn's back, so he took a moment to shift him a little higher.

"You were?"

"Oh, sure. I couldn't keep my trap shut. My teacher had to move my desk away from everyone else's just so I wouldn't have anybody to talk to."

"How's it coming down there?" The mom's voice sounded shaky, a little shrill.

"Good. We're almost there," Quinn told her.

When he hefted himself and the boy up onto level ground and then onto the trail, the woman gasped in relief and snatched the kid off of

Quinn's back and into her arms so fast the boy's feet probably never touched the ground.

"Jesse. Thank God. I didn't know how I was going to get you up from there." She clutched him to her.

"Mom. Let go. You're hugging me too hard."

She let go of him with a laugh, then hugged his brother as though she were taking inventory of her offspring.

"Did you get your ball?" Gavin wanted to know.

Jesse pulled the ball out of his pocket and held it up triumphantly.

"At least it wasn't all for nothing." The woman ruffled Jesse's light brown hair with her hand. Then she turned to Quinn. "I can't thank you enough. You're a hero." She held out her hand to him. "I'm Delilah Ballard. You've met Jesse. And this is Gavin."

He shook her hand, feeling a little puffed up about the hero thing. It wasn't every day he got to rescue a kid and get the gratitude of a pretty woman—though, in his line of work leading wilderness hikes, it wasn't unprecedented.

"Quinn Monroe. And it was my pleasure."

She turned her attention to her son's knees, which were bleeding lightly. She made a fuss over his injuries, pulled a packet of wet wipes out of her day pack, then started dabbing at the boy's scraped knees. As she worked, Quinn noticed her hands and the fact that her left one didn't have a ring.

"Mom, ow!"

"I'm sorry if it hurts, but I have to clean this." She wiped away the blood and gingerly removed bits of dirt and gravel. "Doesn't look too bad."

She straightened up, balled up the wipe in her hand, and looked at Quinn. "We wanted to go hiking. It seemed like a simple enough thing to do, but I guess it wasn't. We're not exactly outdoorsy."

That was his cue. He reached into his pocket and pulled out a business card. "If you want to try again, let me know. I lead nature hikes tailored to your needs. Overnight, all day, a few hours—whatever works for you. I know the most scenic spots, and I know the difficulty level of the trails so I can steer you away from potential problems." He held out the card to her, and she took it.

~

DELILAH HELD the card in her hand, read it, then tucked it into her back pocket. Under other circumstances when a man offered her his card, she might have thought he was making a move—giving her his contact information not so she could hire him, but so she could give him a call, maybe see him again sometime.

But in this case, she dismissed the thought. The man standing in front of her was stupidly handsome. At no time in her life had Delilah ever attracted the interest of anyone who looked like this.

Dark hair that was thick and wavy, just long enough to curl over his ears. Eyes a mesmerizing green. Facial features that belonged on a marble bust of some Roman general. He was tall—over six feet—with broad shoulders and a trim waist. And that smile—oh, God. He had a way of smiling that said he was imagining what you might look like naked.

But Delilah was just ... well, she was just Delilah. She was someone her ex-husband had criticized for being too chubby, too plain, too lacking in sophistication. Too much a mother and not enough a woman. So the card obviously was just business.

"Thanks. I'll keep that in mind," she told him. "If we go hiking again. Which, at the moment, I'll be happy if we never do."

He laughed amiably. "Fair enough. You want me to walk you three back to your car?"

~

QUINN DELIVERED them to the turnout where their car was parked without further incident. He stood by while Delilah supervised the buckling of seatbelts and the distribution of snacks and water.

He was particularly attentive when she bent over to pick up a packaged cheese stick that she'd dropped. He couldn't help admiring the fit of her jeans, which hugged an ass so round and tantalizing that he felt an almost irresistible urge to reach out and caress it.

Since that might ruin his image as a hero to women and children in distress, he shoved his hands in his pockets to keep them from doing anything untoward.

"You guys all set?" he asked.

She turned to him and smiled. He liked her smile, and he liked how small she was in comparison to him—how she had to tip her neck back to look at him. It made him feel like a big, strong man, God help him.

"Thank you again. So much."

"No problem. You drive safe, now."

What kind of a lame pickup line was that? *You drive safe, now?* Was that the state of his game, that he couldn't think of anything better?

As she drove off, he thought it was better that she was leaving him in her rearview mirror. Just because she wasn't wearing a ring didn't mean she wasn't married. Some married women didn't wear rings. And even if she was single, she had kids, and Quinn wasn't the type for that. He didn't have the interest, and he didn't have the patience to deal with someone else's children.

He'd liked Jesse, though, and that Gavin kid had been cute as hell.

Still. He wasn't going there. If she called, he would offer to lead a hike, as he would for any other client.

That was all.

CHAPTER 4

"I'm telling you, he was like some mythical god emerging from the woods to rescue Jesse," Delilah told Roxanne later that evening when the kids had been fed and bathed and were watching TV before bed. "If it weren't for the scratches on Jesse's knees, I would think I imagined the whole thing."

"So, he gave you his card? Are you going to call him?" Roxanne asked.

"Well, maybe to lead a hike for us, since we obviously can't be trusted to go on our own. But I'm not going to *call him*, call him."

"Was he wearing a ring?"

"No."

"Were you?"

Delilah hesitated. "No. I finally put it in my drawer a few weeks ago."

"Okay, then. How do you know he didn't give you his card because he wants to go out with you? How do you know it was just business?"

Delilah barked out a bitter laugh. "You didn't see him. There's no way that man gave me his card because he wants to go out with me."

"How can you be sure?"

"Because he was so hot it was absurd. I mean really ridiculous. He probably dates underwear models. You know, ones who are working on their advanced degrees in astrophysics in their spare time. What would he want with me?"

Roxanne was quiet for a moment, and Delilah felt the lecture coming before she even started to speak.

"Mitch did this to you," she said.

"Roxanne ..."

"He did. He convinced you that weren't beautiful enough, that you weren't smart enough or sophisticated enough or ... just enough of anything for him. But you are all those things. He was the one who failed the relationship, not you."

And, damn it, Delilah felt tears spring to her eyes, felt the heat and the pressure of it. She rubbed her eyes with her fingers and took in a shaky breath. "Yeah, well. I don't want to date anyone, anyway. I'm just ... I can't imagine putting myself through that again."

"I'm not saying you should marry the guy. Just maybe call him and see what happens."

"No, thank you."

"Well."

"I can't think about men when I'm still so fucking mad at Mitch. You know? What he did to me is one thing, but abandoning the boys? You should have seen the way they looked at the guy on the trail. Like he was some kind of miracle. They're so starved for a father—or at least for some strong male figure—that it makes me want to scream or cry or throw something. Jesse can't stop talking about him."

"Aww. Poor kid."

"He keeps saying we should invite this guy over because he did us a favor, and that's what you do when someone does you a favor. You invite them over. The neighbor brought us some muffins, so I invited her over for tea, and now Jesse's fixated on it."

"*Hmm,*" Roxanne said. "How hot did you say he is?"

"Like Chris Hemsworth if Chris Hemsworth were maybe ten percent hotter."

"Maybe inviting him over isn't the worst idea in the world. But maybe wait long enough for me to fly out there first."

"You're hilarious."

"Who says I'm joking?"

"I'm hanging up now."

She did, but she felt a little better than she had before she'd called. A little lighter. Talking to her sister always helped.

She set her phone aside and went into the living room to herd her sons to bed.

QUINN SPENT the rest of the day alone in his house, working.

Cambria—like any other coastal California town—was an expensive place to live. That meant he couldn't make a living just from guiding tourists on wilderness adventures. He refused to work a nine-to-five job, though—he'd done it before, and he'd hated it with the fiery intensity of a nuclear explosion. Instead, he'd cobbled together multiple freelance gigs to support himself.

He wrote articles for outdoors magazines when he could get the work. The rest of the time, he built websites for a wide range of clients including small businesses, restaurants, even authors and artists.

After rescuing the kid, he'd come home, showered, and started working on a review of backpacking equipment: "ten things to leave out of your pack, and ten things you shouldn't leave home without." Everything was lists these days. Or, when he was writing copy for a website, those damned slide shows. Slide shows were the bane of his existence.

When he'd gotten a good start on that, he set it aside and put in some time on a website for a local furniture store. They already had a site, but it was crap. They needed it to be more functional, more intuitive for the user. And, of course, they needed it not to look like hell.

He sat at his desk in front of his computer nursing a beer, his shirt off, his music up loud. He liked something low-key while he was writing—acoustic indie, maybe, or some soft R&B—and something high-presence for website work. Right now, he was blasting Green Day and formatting the Sofas and Sectionals page.

He lived in a two-bedroom cottage on Lodge Hill with only one neighbor in his immediate vicinity—a woman in her seventies whose husband had died the year before. He had an agreement with her that he would play his music as loud as he wanted between the hours of ten a.m. and six p.m., then he would cut the volume by half or use his earbuds the rest of the time.

He checked the clock and saw that he only had a few minutes left. Of course, that would be moot if she wasn't home. He peeked out the window to see if her car was in the driveway, and he saw that she'd just arrived and was struggling to get a large bag of groceries out of the back of her car.

Quinn went outside, trotted down the street to Mrs. Foster's house, and called out to her. "You need some help with that?"

"Oh, Quinn. Yes, please. How nice of you."

Mrs. Foster was a tiny woman with fluffy white hair and thick-framed glasses that dwarfed her face. She was wearing a cardigan sweater, some kind of stretch pants, and a pair of athletic shoes that looked too big for her.

He peeked into the bag. "Cake mix. You doing some baking?"

They chatted about that—her grandkids were planning a visit, and she wanted to make cupcakes—as he hefted the bag and brought it up the stairs to her house.

Inside, he put the bag down on the kitchen counter, which was as tidy as if it had been staged for a Realtor.

They talked a bit about this and that—his work, what she'd been reading lately, the gossip she'd heard at the Cookie Crock—and by the time he got out of there, he wasn't in the mood for working anymore.

He tried to get back to it, this time with his earbuds in and the stereo speakers off, but his mind wandered away from sofas and sectionals and toward the woman he'd met earlier in the day.

Delilah. Hmm.

No way was he going there. For one thing, single mother. For another, she might be married, even if she didn't wear a ring. And anyway, he didn't even have her contact information.

She had his, though, which opened up an array of tantalizing possibilities.

Except that he absolutely wasn't going to avail himself of those possibilities, even if she did happen to call him.

The idea of women and the possibilities of which he might avail himself led him to wonder who might be hanging out at Ted's tonight, and whether anyone might be amenable to having a drink with him, or having other, more interesting things, with him.

Hell, it was worth a try.

~

AT OTTER BLUFF, Jesse would not drop the topic of Quinn Monroe and whether Delilah would call him.

"Why not? He gave you his card. He said you could."

It was just past seven a.m. the day after the hiking incident, and Delilah had barely gotten the boys set up at the dining room table with their cereal and a plate of cut fruit. She'd only had one cup of coffee, and she wasn't in the mood for requests.

"Eat your breakfast," she told her sons.

Jesse and Gavin were still in their pajamas, their hair mussed and their skin smelling like sleep. She wanted to clasp both of them to her, but only Gavin accepted that these days—Jesse had announced that he was too grown up for his mother's embraces.

Impulsively, she put her arms around Gavin, gave him a squeeze, and inhaled his sweet scent.

"That's not an answer," Jesse said.

"No, it isn't." Delilah pulled her robe around her and sat down in the chair opposite them. "The answer is, I'm not going to call him because … well, because he's probably very busy and doesn't have time to chat with us."

"If he didn't want us to call him, he wouldn't have given us his phone number," Jesse said, not unreasonably.

"We didn't even get to hike very far," Gavin put in. "We had to stop when Jesse fell. And Quinn keeps people safe on hikes. He said."

Jesse, who'd been looking at his brother, turned his gaze to Delilah in triumph. "Yeah. Plus, you said it's polite to invite people over when they do something nice for you."

"You said," Gavin insisted.

"We are not inviting Quinn Monroe over. He was just being nice when he gave us his card. We *might* book one of his guided hikes, but I'm not promising anything. Now, that's the last I want to hear about it. Eat." She got up from the table and went into the kitchen to wash the cutting board she'd used for the fruit.

Delilah poured herself a second cup of coffee, added milk and sugar, and took her mug out to the back patio. She sat in an Adirondack chair and watched the waves crash into the bluffs below her. The day was foggy and overcast with a chill in the air, and she pulled her fuzzy robe tightly around her body.

Out in the distance, a pair of otters floated on their backs and twirled in the water.

She sipped her coffee and thought about the boys and their fixation with Quinn Monroe.

When he'd rescued Jesse, the poor guy had unwittingly positioned himself as everything the boys had been missing since their father left: a strong man, a benevolent male authority figure whom they could admire.

Of course they wanted more of that. They were starved for it.

She wasn't going to call him—of course not—but that didn't mean she couldn't find someone to fill that void in the kids' lives. She needed to spend more time around her own father, her own brothers. If Jesse and Gavin could just get more attention from their grandfather and uncles, maybe that would go a long way toward fulfilling that need.

She sighed. Maybe she shouldn't have run away from the East Coast when everything had happened. Maybe she should have stayed so the boys could soak up family, immerse themselves in the men who still were around in their lives.

Well, this was only temporary. Only two months, until the holidays were over. She needed to get through Thanksgiving and Christmas in a place where she wouldn't constantly be thinking about Mitch. And she needed to do it away from her family and their constant, oppressive concern. Away from their constant, oppressive questions about what had gone wrong and what her role in it might have been.

He'd left her for another woman. It was a story so old it was probably represented in cave paintings. But that didn't stop her family from hinting that maybe if she'd been a more attentive wife, maybe if she'd been more careful to fulfill his needs ...

Now that she thought about it, her family might not be the best influences for Jesse and Gavin.

She looked out at the horizon, smelled the ocean air, and reminded herself to live in the moment, at least for a while. She was in a beautiful place, and she and her boys were safe and well.

That was all she could manage.

For now, it would just have to be enough.

CHAPTER 5

Quinn had pretty much convinced himself that he wasn't going to hear from Delilah. Then he got her text message.

It was just a text message. Nothing special. It wasn't like she'd sent him a picture of her breasts. And yet, seeing it made him feel all tingly, as though he'd gotten a mild electrical shock.

You are invited to our house today at ten in the morning.

Then it gave the address and her name—Delilah Ballard.

Something about the message was off. It was weirdly formal, and it was so abrupt, with none of the usual friendly chitchat one usually saw in text messages. Plus, it didn't say why he was invited to the house. What for? So they could talk about a possible wilderness excursion? Or was it personal?

He thought about it, then responded, *I'll be there.*

Why not? He didn't have anything else on his schedule that morning, and he was intrigued. And, who knew? If he played his cards right, maybe a photo of breasts would come later.

Delilah's kids were acting weird—which was to say, even weirder than usual.

She'd been trying to get out of the house for half an hour to go to the grocery store, but Jesse and Gavin seemed dead set on preventing her from doing it. She needed to get things for lunch, and it was already late morning. Why the hell were they making it so hard?

"Jesse, come on!" She had her purse and her keys in her hand, and she'd thought they were all ready, but Jesse had claimed he needed something from his room, and now he wasn't coming out.

"Just a minute, Mom! I can't find my bracelet."

Delilah had bought him a braided leather bracelet from one of the boutiques in town the day before. He hadn't seemed all that interested in it until now.

"You can find it when we get back," she called to him.

"But I want to wear it!"

Gavin stood by, sucking his thumb. She ran a hand through his hair, tousling it playfully. Then she spotted something on a side table next to the sofa: Jesse's bracelet.

"Jesse, it's out here! I found it."

He came out, accepted the bracelet from her, then asked her to tie it on his wrist. While she was doing that, Gavin vanished into his room.

"Gavin, honey, come on. We're ready."

"I need Waffles!" he called to her. Lately, in addition to sucking his thumb, Gavin had taken to carrying the stuffed bear around with him. Delilah was worried about it—as a mother, she tended to worry about everything—but she told herself that if he needed the comfort, if it helped him get through all they were navigating in their lives, then it was fine. It was good.

"Honey, do you want me to help you look?"

"No, I can do it."

She checked the time on her phone. Ten a.m. Ah, well. There was still plenty of time before lunch. She could wait.

She was still waiting when someone knocked on the door.

At the sound, Jesse's eyes widened and he dashed off to join Gavin in his bedroom.

And what the hell was that about?

She went to the door expecting Dolly or maybe the mail carrier. Could be someone from the property management company, she thought.

The last person she expected was Quinn Monroe, who was standing on the doorstep looking at her expectantly, that shockingly handsome face of his arranged in a half grin.

"Oh. Hi." Delilah just stood there.

"Hi." Quinn just stood there, too.

After an uncomfortable moment of both of them looking at each other, Quinn said, "The invitation was for ten, right? Am I early?"

"Invitation?" she said.

"Yeah. You know, when someone asks you over, and you come. Invitation."

"I'm sorry. I'm still not—"

"You texted me." He pulled out his phone, called up the text, and held the phone out to her. "See?"

Suddenly, she knew exactly what had happened and why. Embarrassment made her cheeks hot, and she pressed her hand to her forehead. "Oh, my God. I'm so sorry about this. Come in."

He came into the foyer, and she closed the door behind him. Then she called her sons. "Jesse. Gavin. Come out here."

They didn't.

"I said, come out here. Right now."

When they still didn't come out, Delilah turned to Quinn. "Come in. Please. I'll be right back."

She went into the room where the boys were both sitting on the bed. She closed the door behind her and crouched down to face them both at eye level.

"All right. Whose idea was it to invite him?"

Gavin, his eyes wide, plugged his thumb into his mouth. Jesse squirmed a little under his mother's scrutiny.

"Look, Jesse. I know you wrote the text, because Gavin doesn't write that well yet. Quinn's here now, and if you two don't confess, I'm going to have to send him home in the assumption that my phone was hacked by some deranged matchmaker. Now, are you going to come clean?"

Jesse assumed the manner of one who was being unfairly persecuted. "Mom, you said! You told us that when somebody does you a favor it's nice to invite them over for tea! But then he did us a favor, and you didn't invite him! And somebody had to, so I borrowed your phone and texted him."

"You borrowed my phone," she said.

"Yeah. Because I don't have one, even though everybody in my class did."

"That's enough, Jesse." Delilah sighed and regarded her oldest boy. "You signed my name to the text."

"That's because he wouldn't come if he thought it was me. He'd ask if my mom knew I was texting him, and then he wouldn't come, and then we wouldn't see him again, and ... and I like him!"

Jesse's lower lip was starting to wobble, and Delilah felt her resolve melt.

"All right. Well, this is your little get-together, so come on out and say hello."

She led the boys into the living room where Quinn was standing.

"Hey, guys." Quinn gave them a little wave.

Delilah didn't want to embarrass the boys, but she didn't want to take charge of this gathering, either, since none of it had been her idea. So she put on a bright voice and said, "The boys wanted to invite you over to say thank you for rescuing Jesse. And they didn't tell me because they wanted to surprise me. We really are, all three, very grateful. Would you like some tea? Or coffee?"

Delilah saw Jesse relax visibly. The poor kid was probably afraid she was going to tear into him in front of Quinn, who was, apparently, his new idol.

"Sure. I'd love some coffee," Quinn said.

Delilah could always tear into Jesse later, in private. For now, she went into the kitchen to make the coffee.

~

WHEN QUINN REALIZED Delilah had no idea why he was here, he had two choices. He could either politely excuse himself, maybe making up some bullshit reason for why he had to leave, or he could just roll with it and see what happened.

He decided to roll with it.

For one thing, the kids were cute as hell, and if they'd liked Quinn so much they'd concocted a scheme to get him here, well, that was pretty flattering. He'd always liked kids, and in his opinion, children had a kind of sixth sense about people that adults didn't. If a kid liked you, and you weren't one of his parents, it probably meant you were doing something right.

Then there was Delilah, who was more than a little appealing. On paper, she wasn't his usual type. He tended toward tall, willowy, leggy blondes, and she was none of those things. But looking at her, he started to think his usual type was wrong.

He liked her dark, glossy hair, her abundant curves, that face that might not be classically beautiful but that was nonetheless intriguing. He even liked her height—or the lack of it. The fact that she was so small made him feel bigger and stronger than he was.

He wasn't going to ask her out—hell no. He wasn't about to get himself entangled with an entire family. But that didn't mean he couldn't pass a pleasurable hour having coffee with her.

While Delilah made the coffee, the kids stood on either side of Quinn, bouncing and fidgeting the way kids did and asking him question after question.

"Do you have any kids?"

"We saw your van. Do you live in there?"

"How did you learn to hike and camp and stuff?"

"Did you ever see a bear? Like, in person?"

"Boys, take it easy on Quinn," Delilah said from the kitchen, where she was pouring coffee into two ceramic mugs. "He just got here. Let him catch his breath."

From the sound of her voice and the smile in her eyes as she said it, he could feel her love for the kids radiating all the way over to where he was sitting. Something about that caught in his chest and squeezed.

"It's okay," he told her. "I don't mind." And he took the questions one by one. "No, I don't have any kids. No, I don't live in the van. I do take it camping, though. It's much more comfortable than a tent when I'm going somewhere that has parking. I taught myself to hike and camp—and you could, too. It's not hard once you get the hang of it. And yes, I've seen a bear. In person."

"You did?" Gavin's eyes widened, and he bounced on his toes.

"Yep. I rounded a corner on a trail, and there she was. I think she was as surprised to see me as I was to see her. We both looked at each other for a minute, then she walked away."

"Were you scared?" This was from Jesse.

"You're damned … ah … darned right I was scared. Don't ever let anybody tell you it makes you less of a man to be scared of something that could rip your chest open with one swipe."

"Gross." Gavin said it with such gusto Quinn suspected he was more delighted than repulsed.

"Okay, here we go." Delilah put Quinn's mug in front of him, along with a sugar bowl, a spoon, and a small pitcher of milk. Quinn was a black coffee guy—he'd become that way because it was easier to make black coffee over a camp stove than to fuss around with sugar and milk—so he sipped his coffee without adding anything.

"Thanks," he told her. "It's nice of you to have me, especially since you weren't expecting company."

"Well, we really do owe you a big thank you." She was a milk and sugar girl, he noticed as she put both into her coffee and stirred.

They chatted about superficial things: his work, her vacation in Cambria with the boys, the weather, how long he'd lived here in town.

He tried to get down to what he suspected was the important stuff —"So, it's just you and the boys?"—but she kept it light, kept it firmly on the surface.

"Yep, just us."

And then she changed the subject.

The fascinating thing to Quinn was the contrast of emotions he could see in Delilah. Love, when she spoke to her boys or when she casually touched their shoulders or their hair. Joy, when she talked about something funny one or the other of them had done. And beneath that, a sadness that peeked out through the edges even as she tried to hide it.

He suspected the sadness had something to do with the guy who was conspicuously absent from the picture. What was the story there? The boys were obviously starved for male attention, so, yeah. The absent guy wasn't so absent—he was present in the room like a ghost, or like a lingering odor.

He read Delilah's body language, and when she was ready for him to go, he saw it.

He got up from his seat, took his mug into the kitchen, and made some noises about having somewhere to be. When he said it, she sagged a little with relief.

Gun-shy with men, maybe?

I'll see what I can do about that, he thought. Then: *Oh, fuck off. No you won't.*

There were more alarms going off in Quinn's head than at a school fire drill. She'd been hurt by somebody. She was going through something. And she was a mother.

Best to thank her, get out, and run like hell.

He managed the first part just fine. He thanked Delilah for the coffee, said some pleasant, polite things, and went to the door. Then he made the mistake of crouching down to the kids' level to say goodbye to them.

Gavin, his thumb in his mouth, ran up to Quinn and threw his arms around him, tucking his little head against Quinn's chest.

What could Quinn do but hug back? The kid smelled like baby shampoo and Cheerios.

And there was that sensation again, like something warm squeezing his heart.

He disentangled himself from the boy, stood up straight, cleared his throat, and waved down at him and his brother. "I'll see you, Gavin. Jesse."

"When?" Gavin said.

"When what?"

"When will you see us?"

Quinn blinked once, thrown by the question.

"Ah … I don't know. Maybe your mom will call me about taking a hike."

Then he got the hell out of there before he could get any more captivated by this little family than he already was.

CHAPTER 6

"And then Gavin ran up and hugged him. God. Those boys need a man in their lives so badly, and they don't even care who it is. I could strangle Mitch. I could light him on fire and spit on his ashes."

"Let me know if you need to borrow some lighter fluid," Roxanne said.

Delilah was sitting at a picnic table at Shamel Park, talking on her cell phone while the boys ran and tumbled and climbed on the play equipment. In the background, Delilah could hear the crash of the waves on the beach behind her.

"I don't know what to do," she told Roxanne.

"About Mitch, or about the guy?"

"About the boys. There's nothing I *can* do about Mitch, and there's nothing I *want* to do about the guy."

"Really? You've got the phone number of a super hot guy who your kids love and who's willing to show up at your house at the drop of a text, and you don't want to do anything with that?"

Delilah sighed and rubbed her forehead wearily. "In case you hadn't noticed, Roxanne, I've got my hands full right now. I'm raising two children alone, and in less than two months I need to find a new place to live. I don't have time for a relationship."

"Who said anything about a relationship? There's no law that says you can't have a little fun on your vacation. God knows you need it. And you deserve it. Plus, it might help you put Mitch in your rearview mirror. Emotionally. And that would be a bonus, wouldn't it?"

She supposed it might be. On the other hand, any benefit she might get would be outweighed by the damage she could do to her own heart—and her children's hearts—if she got involved with anyone at this stage in her life.

Besides, Quinn Monroe was so far out of her league he might as well be playing in the majors while she was in T-ball.

"No," she told Roxanne.

"No?"

"No."

"Well, maybe just keep your options open."

"No."

Shutting out the possibility of anything happening with Quinn—or with any other man—was so much easier than leaving that door open and then having it slammed in her face.

OVER THE NEXT FEW DAYS, Delilah tried to keep busy.

She took the boys to the beach; she took them to see the elephant seals; they visited Hearst Castle. Delilah did the grocery shopping and cooked nourishing meals, she kept Otter Bluff clean, and she tried not to think about what was going to happen when their time in Cambria was over.

She told herself she would not have thought about Quinn Monroe at all if the boys hadn't kept bringing him up.

"I want to go hiking again," Gavin said one morning over his bowl of cereal.

"Me too," Jesse said.

"You guys know what happened last time," Delilah told them. She sat down at the table with them, a mug of coffee in her hands.

"Yeah, but that's why we need to go with Quinn," Jesse said.

"He keeps people safe while they're hiking," Gavin put in. "That's his job. He said."

"I know that, honey." Delilah smiled at her youngest son. "But I'm sure he's got more important things to do than leading us around on some trail."

"But we'd be paying him," Jesse said. "And that's his job. He doesn't have more important things to do than his *job*."

"Oh, but he's probably expensive. And—"

"We have a lot of money. You said so." Jesse's expression was all stubbornness and persistence. "You said after our house got sold we don't have to worry about money anymore."

"I said we don't have to worry about it *for now*," Delilah corrected him. The truth was, they wouldn't have to worry about it for a long time, given the proceeds from the house and the spousal and child support Mitch had finally been ordered to pay. But Jesse didn't necessarily need to know that. "That doesn't mean we can just throw money around on—"

"It's not throwing money around if it keeps us safe!" Jesse insisted. "The last time we went hiking, I could have died! What are we supposed to do? Just *die*?"

"You weren't even hurt," Delilah reminded him. "Except for a few scrapes."

"What if that had been a cliff? What if I'd fallen into the ocean and a shark ate me?" Jesse, like all boys of his age, liked to spin scenarios out to their most outrageous conclusions.

"And then what if a whale ate the shark?" Gavin asked, giggling. "And then something bigger than the whale came along and ate the whale?"

"There's nothing bigger than a whale, dummy," Jesse said.

"Don't call your brother dumb," Delilah said.

"I could pay him," Gavin said.

The suggestion was so surprising Delilah thought she'd heard it wrong. "What, sweetie?"

"I could pay Quinn. To take us hiking. I've been saving my allowance. I have a hundred dollars in my bank account."

Jesse perked up. "I have money, too. If Gavin doesn't have enough, I could help."

"No. Boys … no."

"But that money is ours to do whatever we want with it," Jesse insisted. "You said."

Had she said that? She thought she probably had. She was running out of reasons to say no. The kids had backed her into a corner efficiently and effectively. But she couldn't let them spend their allowance on something like this, when the very fact that they wanted it so desperately threatened to break her heart.

With few options, she pulled out the answer every mother used when she was unwilling to relent but was out of other answers.

"We'll see."

"*We'll see* always means no," Jesse said.

"It doesn't mean no. It just means … we'll see."

"It means no," Gavin said.

And he looked so damned sad, so defeated, that Delilah almost wept. She couldn't do that, though—not in front of the boys.

"We'll see," she said, ruffling Gavin's hair.

~

QUINN DIDN'T EXPECT Delilah to call. Hell, he didn't even *want* her to call. And yet he seemed to be checking his phone more than usual even as he went about his life over the next few days—leading tourists on trail hikes, working on the furniture website, and researching an article about salmon fishing.

Thanksgiving was drawing closer, and he tried not to think about that. Maybe he would take a road trip over the long weekend. Yosemite, just him and his van. That ought to keep his mind off uncomfortable topics like family and the proper way to prepare cranberry sauce.

He was at home thinking about all of that, working on the dinette set section of the furniture website on a cool Tuesday morning, when his mother called.

He'd told himself to screen his calls—especially those from his family—but, God help him, he forgot. He picked up before he even thought about it, then mentally kicked himself when he heard his mother's voice.

"Quinn. Hello."

Before the blowup over his uncle's will, she'd have said, *Hi, honey.* But now it was so much more formal. So much more distant.

"Hi, Mom. What's up?"

Barbara sighed, as though the very act of talking to her son was more effort than she was capable of expending. "Well. I just wanted to ask you about your plans for Thanksgiving, and whether you're going to come."

"I already told you my plans. I'm not coming."

"You're being immature." He could imagine her expression: the tight lips, the little lines that formed around her eyes when she was upset with someone—usually him.

"I don't think I am. Jared and Alex made it clear they don't want to see me. I'm just doing what's best to keep the peace."

The sigh again. "Your brothers are hurt. That's all."

"Yeah? I'm hurt, too. The way they've been treating me? The things they said?"

"Quinn, you can still fix this. Come to Thanksgiving, and we can all talk."

He was an idiot. He was an absolute fool. The proof was that he was just about to agree, just about to let himself believe it. Then she said, "I'm sure if you were to offer them each a share of the money—"

It always came back to the money.

"The money's gone. It's gone, Mom. You know that. I used it to buy the house. If they want a share of what's left in my bank account, they can maybe use it to buy a latte at Starbucks. If they leave out the extra shot."

"You're just being difficult."

Ah, yes. The *you're being difficult* card, his mother's favorite one to play whenever Quinn failed to do whatever it was she wanted him to do. The line that magically made everything his fault.

"I don't think I am," he said.

"Your brothers are Nathan's nephews just as much as you are."

"Yeah. And they disowned him when he came out. I'm pretty sure that had something to do with Nate's decision about his will."

"You can't blame them if they—"

He didn't wait around to see what he could or couldn't blame them for. Instead, he hung up on her.

The familiar burning sensation jabbed him in his gut, and he grabbed the bottle of antacids he kept on his desk for just such occasions. He popped four of them in his mouth and chewed.

Goddamn it.

He'd let himself hope, just for a second, that she'd called him because she wanted to see him, that she'd invited him again out of love.

No such luck.

He tried to go back to work, but he couldn't focus.

Maybe a long walk would clear his head.

CHAPTER 7

Delilah tried to get the boys some kind of physical exercise every day—the more strenuous, the better. She'd found through hard-won experience that whenever they started to act up—talking back to her or just acting squirrelly, unable to sit still—it helped to wear them out.

She'd tried taking them walking on the bluff trails at Fiscalini Ranch, with its stunning views just steps from the rocky shoreline. But the narrow bluff trail was popular with the locals, some of whom didn't seem to appreciate the boys' roughhousing and general shenanigans.

So today, she took them to upper Fiscalini with its wider and less traveled network of trails. Up there, on the grassy hillside overlooking the ocean in the distance, the boys could get up to whatever they wanted without bothering anyone—and without the risk that one of them might tumble into the ocean.

The morning was foggy and cool, and Delilah pulled her sweater around her as she walked, the boys looking for squirrels up ahead.

These walks weren't just for the sake of the boys' fitness and behavior. When they went well—when the boys became absorbed in looking for rocks or chasing lizards or playing whatever game they'd concocted for themselves—it gave Delilah a chance to turn off her mind and just be.

And these days, she really needed time to just be.

Once the holidays were over and they vacated Otter Bluff, Delilah would have to do no less than invent a new life for herself and her children. Sometimes, the prospect of that threatened to drown her in anxiety and doubt. A stretch of time in which she didn't think of anything except the sounds of the birds and the feel of the wind was precious to her. She closed her eyes and tipped up her head to breathe in the ocean air.

"Looks like this walk is going a lot smoother than the last one." The deep voice interrupted her reverie, and her eyes flew open to see Quinn Monroe grinning at her.

~

WHEN QUINN HAD SEEN the woman and her two kids ahead of him on the trail, something about her silhouette had told him it was Delilah and her boys. He'd dismissed the thought at first. He was too far back to see her, really, and it had seemed like wishful thinking.

As he got closer, he saw that he was right—it was her. And those were her boys gamboling around on the trail, letting out the occasional hoot of joy.

He wondered for a moment whether he should turn around before she saw him. After all, he was undeniably attracted to her, and getting involved with a single mother was worse than opening a can of worms—it was more like diving into a swimming pool of worms. Carnivorous ones. With fangs.

But he couldn't seem to help himself, especially when she tipped her head back and closed her eyes, making him feel like he was privy to a secret, intimate moment that the two of them were sharing. Even if she wasn't aware they were sharing it.

So he spoke to her, and now she was looking at him as though she was returning to reality from wherever it was she'd been.

"Oh. Quinn." She blinked a few times, like she was just waking up after a restful sleep.

"I love the fog," he said, apropos of nothing. "The sun is too easy. Everybody loves sunshine. It's a cliché. Fog is so much more mysterious. So much more complex." And why was he doing a soliloquy on fog? No wonder she was looking at him like he was crazy. He'd have looked at himself the same way.

"Me too," she said after a while. "The fog. It's soft. It's gentle. Like all of the hard edges have been smoothed off of everything." Now she was doing a soliloquy on fog, too, so he guessed his own didn't seem so awkward.

Now what? Should he wish her a good day and walk on ahead? Go back where he'd come from and leave her to it?

He didn't want to do either of those things. What he wanted was to walk with her, to talk about her day and his, to get to know her a little.

The thing with Quinn and women was that he rarely denied himself what he wanted—no matter how many problems that had caused over the course of his lifetime.

He was probably too set in his ways to change, though, so he put it out there.

"Mind if I walk with you?"

"Oh." She looked surprised at first, then a slow grin spread across her face. "I suppose that'll be handy if Jesse hurls himself into a ravine."

"See?" he said. "It's just a matter of safety."

They might have exchanged more flirtatious repartee, but the boys chose that moment to look back toward their mother and notice that Quinn was there.

At first, the tilt of Jesse's head, the hesitation in his movements, suggested that he hadn't recognized the man talking to his mother. Then, he jerked to attention and yelled, "Quinn!"

Jesse, with Gavin at his heels, ran to where Quinn was standing, and the two of them began peppering him with questions.

"What are you doing here?"

"Did you come to see my mom?"

"Are you walking here, too?"

"Do you ever bring people here? Like, for your job?"

"Have you ever seen a snake?"

Quinn laughed and patted the air in front of him with his hands, willing them to slow down.

"Lemme take those one at a time. I just ran into your mom on accident, because yes, I'm taking a walk, just like you are. No, I don't bring clients here because it's an easy trail and people don't get lost or in trouble here. Not usually, although you might be able to manage it, Jesse. And yes, I've seen tons of snakes. Billions."

"Billions?" Gavin's eyes widened.

"Well, not really billions. But a lot. Most of them are harmless, and they'll leave you alone if you don't bother them."

"Boys, that's enough with the questions," Delilah told them.

"We just started our walk," Jesse said. "Mom says we have to get our ya-yas out, but I told her a ya-ya isn't even a thing."

"I know it's not a thing," Delilah said gently. "It's just an expression."

"So are they out yet?" Quinn asked.

"I don't think so," Gavin said solemnly.

"Well, then I guess we'd better keep walking," he said.

The look on Jesse's face—the joy and excitement at the thought that Quinn would be proceeding on the trail with them—embarrassed Quinn because he knew he couldn't possibly be worthy of that kind of admiration.

As they began walking together, Quinn wanted to reach out and take Delilah's hand.

That would have felt so natural, so right. But that was crazy, since they hardly knew each other. Since they'd barely talked.

His hand needed to get its damned impulses under control.

DELILAH HADN'T REALIZED how starved she was for adult conversation until Quinn showed up and suddenly she was having one.

Talking to Jesse and Gavin was fine—it was better than fine, in fact; it was one of her favorite things to do—but she always had to filter with them. She always had to act calm and in control so they wouldn't be scared about whatever their future held.

Sometimes, Delilah longed to admit to someone that her life had been run through a wood chipper and she now had to make something decent out of the resulting chips.

Why the hell shouldn't she admit all of that to Quinn? It wasn't like she was going to see him again after today.

"So, does their dad ever take them hiking or camping?" Quinn asked.

Delilah saw that for what it was—a fishing expedition regarding her marital status. She knew she should keep her private business to herself, but she was so tired of filtering, so tired of struggling to stay strong, that she couldn't do it for even one more minute.

The boys had run up ahead on the trail again, so they were out of earshot. Why not just come clean with it?

"No, he doesn't. Their father moved to Paris with his mistress, and we haven't seen him in months. Except when I took him to court for spousal and child support."

"Holy shit." His voice was tinged with awe. "How did the settlement work out?"

"Well enough. I can take care of the boys without having to work three jobs. Or any, for now. But no amount of money would be worth what we've gone through."

"I guess not. What does he do?"

Delilah glanced at Quinn as they walked. "He's an attorney. Corporate. Formerly of Wall Street, now of the firm's Paris office."

"He's an attorney and he didn't know he had to pay alimony and child support?"

"Oh, he knew. That's just it. He knew everything. He knew exactly how long he could put it off without having to pay, and he knew exactly how to do it. Meanwhile, I got a job bagging groceries for minimum wage so I could buy food for his children. It wasn't enough. I had to borrow money from my parents to pay the utility bills." She shook her head, the bitterness still fresh. "And he had zero remorse about it, even though he was the one who left me. He was the one who cheated." She could hear the anger and spite in her voice, and she willed herself to tone it down. Quinn didn't need to hear all of this. He didn't need to be saddled with the job of soothing her emotional wounds.

"I'm sorry," he said.

"Yeah. Thanks." They crested a hill and stood to look at the ocean spreading out far below them."You know what the worst part of it is?" she asked, continuing to talk about it even as she told herself to stop it.

"What?"

"Not bad-mouthing him to the boys. Keeping positive in front of them. Reassuring them that their father loves them and wants the best for them, contrary to all appearances."

"God. I can't imagine."

She glanced at him. "Are you married?"

"No."

"Ever been?"

He shook his head. "No."

"Well, don't." She couldn't seem to keep the venom out of her voice. "Because those vows? They didn't mean anything. He promised in front of God to devote his life to me, and that didn't stop him from walking away the minute things stopped being fun. The minute our marriage stopped meeting his own selfish needs ..."

Damn it. Now she was crying. Not loud boo-hooing, thank God, but a tear slipped down her cheek entirely against her will. She wiped it away and folded her arms across her chest. She let out a bitter laugh. "Clearly, I'm a ray of sunshine."

QUINN WONDERED WHAT, exactly, he'd stumbled onto.

He'd been interested in talking to Delilah, in walking with her a little, because she was attractive and appealing. But he hadn't anticipated the emotional landmines that had been set for him to step on.

He had conflicting emotions: Part of him wanted to excuse himself, make up some errand he'd forgotten to do or some appointment he was late for, and get the hell out of there. But another part of him wanted to fly to Paris, track down Delilah's ex, and kick the crap out of him.

What kind of man abandoned his wife and children? And what kind of man would want to leave Delilah in the first place?

Oh, there were two sides to every story—he knew that. But right now, damned if he could think of what her ex's side of it might be.

"So you're here, what? Taking a break from your problems?" he asked.

"Something like that. Our house was sold in the settlement, so we're between places." She smiled, just a little. "We came here so I could think. So I could take some time to contemplate what comes next. And, I might be running away from my family until the holidays are over. I'd have to admit that's a factor."

"Don't tell me they're taking his side."

"Not exactly. But they do think the split is just temporary—something we'll both get over. And they treat me like I'm damaged. As if I'm going to break into a thousand pieces like some delicate crystal figurine."

"Or like a bomb that's set to go off," he suggested.

"Yes, also that."

They walked a little more while the boys chased a rabbit that had found its way onto the trail.

"So, that's my story," she said. "What's yours?"

"I don't have a story."

She guffawed. "That's not true. Everybody has a story."

Okay, she was right. He had a story. But damned if he was going to tell it to her.

What was this, a competition for whose life was more fucked up? She'd probably win, all things considered, but not by much.

"Come on," she said. "I'm a stranger. You're probably never going to see me again. Why not tell me?"

He shrugged, then lied to her. "There's nothing to tell."

He could see on her face that she didn't believe him—not for a second. He gave her a half grin—tacit admission that she was right and he was holding out on her—then ran ahead to look at the lizard the boys had found.

CHAPTER 8

The accidental meetup with Delilah was nothing. Obviously. He'd been walking, and she'd been walking, and they'd run into each other. It happened. In a small town like Cambria, Quinn ran into people he knew all the time. You stopped, you chatted, and then you went on your way.

Except now that he was back home, he couldn't seem to stop thinking about her.

He wasn't mooning over her or anything. She wasn't the kind of woman he would moon over, even if he were inclined toward that sort of thing.

His usual woman was a solid nine on the one-to-ten scale, and Delilah was … well. She was too normal to even be on the scale in the first place. Too much like your next-door neighbor. Too much like somebody's mom.

Hell, she *was* somebody's mom.

And yet, right now if he had a chance to be with one of those nines or with Delilah, he would choose Delilah, hands down. She had those curves, for one thing. And that expressive face that told you whatever she was thinking. And that glossy hair. He loved her glossy hair.

And, damn it, none of this was useful. None of it was productive.

Because there was no way he was going to date her, or sleep with her, or do anything with her except casual chat should he run into her again sometime.

Maybe what he needed was to spend some time with a nine to get his mind off of mom-next-door Delilah.

The more he thought about it, the more it seemed like a fine idea.

~

THE PLUS SIDE of running into Quinn at Fiscalini Ranch was that Delilah had enjoyed a lovely time talking to an adult—and an attractive one, at that.

The negative side was that the chance encounter had started the boys back on their obsession with Quinn.

"Can we have him take us on a hike? Or camping? Please?" Jesse begged. "Mom? Can we?"

"Please?" Gavin asked, talking around the thumb that was plugged into his mouth.

This was lunchtime on the day after their meetup at Fiscalini, and the boys were still going on about it. Even though Delilah had already said no. Repeatedly.

"Guys, eat your lunch." She'd put out grilled cheese sandwiches and bowls of tomato soup, but both of the boys were too focused on badgering her to pay any attention to their food.

Jesse obediently took a bite of his sandwich, probably hoping she'd be more amenable to his demands if he were compliant. He still had a mouthful of grilled cheese when he started in again.

"It would be safer. I wouldn't get hurt. You wouldn't have to worry."

"Jesse, honey, don't talk with your mouth full."

"But Mom—"

"Chew, swallow, then talk." She'd repeated that refrain so many times she thought she should have it printed on a T-shirt.

He chewed, swallowed, and then, unfortunately for Delilah, began to talk again.

"We'd be doing him a favor," Jesse said. "Because it's his job, and he probably needs people to hire him, and he did us a favor, so it just makes sense."

Gavin nodded his agreement.

"Guys …"

"Why not?" Jesse demanded. "Why can't we?"

Delilah tried not to talk to her boys like they were kids. She tried to talk to them like they were people. Maybe it was time for some person-to-person straight talk.

She sat down across from them at the table and folded her hands on the tabletop.

"Do you know what I think?" she began. "I think you like Quinn so much because you both really miss your dad, and you want Quinn to be kind of like a substitute. Just for a little while, to make you feel better. And I'm not sure that helps anything. I'm not sure that's going to solve anything for either of you."

Gavin's wide eyes pooled with tears. "When is Dad coming back?"

Delilah's heart felt the tight squeeze of sympathy, and she blinked a few times to keep from crying herself. "Oh, honey. I don't know. Maybe you can talk to him about it the next time he calls."

Mitch hadn't called for weeks, and that was yet another thing that made Delilah blind with fury. She pushed the anger down to someplace inside her where her children wouldn't see it.

"He barely even calls," Jesse said, as though reading her mind. "And when he does, it's all, 'How's school going? How are your grades?' And then he says he has to go."

The anger in Jesse's eyes mirrored her own rage at her ex. If she didn't handle things right with Jesse, the anger in him might win. She couldn't let that happen.

"Honey?" She waited until Jesse looked at her, and she reached out and took both of his hands in hers. "None of this is your fault, okay? Yours either, Gavin. I mean that. What happened between me and your dad was his fault and mine. None of it was yours."

Taking part of the blame herself—the *and mine* of her statement—stung her, but she had to say it to avoid demonizing Mitch to the children who loved him. And it was probably true on some level, wasn't it? Surely part of the failure of her marriage was her fault. Mitch certainly thought so. And sometimes, in her darker moments, Delilah thought so, too. She'd done something wrong, and she didn't know what it was, so she hadn't been able to fix it.

Which just might mean she was now and would always be unworthy of love.

She got up, went around to their side of the table, kissed both of her boys on their sweet, fragrant heads, and went into the bedroom so they wouldn't see her lose her composure.

~

WITH ALL OF that going on, Roxanne chose exactly the wrong time to call Delilah to nag her about Thanksgiving.

"Are you sure you don't want to come? Mom and Dad really want to see you. And Grandma Joan's been asking. You know she doesn't have that many Thanksgivings left in her."

"That's low." Delilah propped one fist on her hip, her cell phone to her ear. "Using Grandma Joan to manipulate me, that's just ..."

"Did it work?"

"No!"

Why couldn't Roxanne understand that Delilah needed to be away from everything—including her family—for a while? Why couldn't she get it?

"But I just don't see why you wouldn't want to be around your family right now," Roxanne said. "I would think you'd want to surround yourself with people who love you and want the best for you."

Delilah, who was standing on the back patio so the kids wouldn't hear her conversation, tipped her head back and closed her eyes, willing herself to be patient with her sister. The waves crashing against the rocks below the house provided a soothing backdrop to the noise in her head. The day was clear, and the sky was a piercing blue.

"Look," Delilah tried again. "I know everyone means well. But they pity me."

"Oh, Delilah. That's not—"

"They do. And that would be bad enough, but they're also pushing an agenda. Mom wants me and the boys to move back home, and she's got Dad on her side, and probably you and Grandma Joan, too. And I can't. I can't move into my old bedroom and pretend that isn't a huge step backward. I can't make decisions based on what my mom and dad want me to do. I have to decide what's best for me and my kids. On my own. And I can't do that if—"

"Okay. Okay. I get it."

"Do you?"

"Yes."

The fact that she had to keep having this conversation with various members of her family was putting Delilah under stress she didn't need on top of everything else going on in her life. She was tempted to turn off her phone, screen all of her calls, and pretend she'd fallen off the earth.

She didn't mean to take it all out on her sister, but she did.

"I don't think you do get it!" she went on. "I think you pity me, too. I think you're smug and superior because, hey, your life isn't the one that's been run through a shredder. Your life isn't the one that's turned out to be a lie. You're not the one who's homeless and directionless, and ... and ... and you're not the one who doesn't know who you even *are* anymore! And I just don't need you or anyone else looking at me over the sweet potato casserole thinking, 'Poor Delilah. She's a total wreck.' Because I *know* I'm a wreck! I already know! And I don't need to hear it from you or Grandma Joan or anyone else! I won't have it!"

At first, Roxanne was silent. Then she said, "Are you done?"

"Yes."

"Do you feel better now that you've gotten that out?"

"I ... yes. I actually do."

"Good. Then my work here is done."

All at once, Delilah was flooded with guilt for the things she'd said. Roxanne wasn't smug and superior. She was just trying to help.

"Rox?"

"*Hmm?*"

"I didn't mean …"

"I know."

"I just needed to vent, and I—"

"I know. But, Delilah?"

"What?"

"It's really good sweet potato casserole, and you'll be missing it."

Delilah let out a laugh, and it felt good. It felt cleansing. "I love you, you know," she told her sister.

"*Pffft*. Of course I know that. Call me soon." And then Roxanne hung up.

CHAPTER 9

The boys were still nagging about Quinn two days later, and Delilah couldn't take it anymore. Her resolve broke and she called him.

"Quinn Monroe."

His voice was deep and resonant, and Delilah felt it down to her toes. But she couldn't get distracted by things like deep, resonant voices. She'd called for a reason.

"Uh … hi. This is Delilah. Ballard. Delilah Ballard." She was babbling like an idiot, which she hadn't done the last time she'd talked to him. There was something about calling a man on the phone that made her feel like she was back in high school asking Tony Martin to the Sadie Hawkins Dance. He'd said no, so there were scars.

"Oh. Hey."

"I was just … I was wondering if you had some time to take us on a hike. Me and the boys. They've really … They've been asking. Nagging, honestly. Pestering. Driving me to near insanity, if you must know."

He laughed, and that was deep and resonant, too.

"Any particular route in mind?" he asked.

"No. I'll leave that up to you. Just something we can do in a couple of hours that's not likely to result in one or more of my sons falling off a cliff."

The laugh again. It made her stomach do odd things she absolutely did not need it doing right now.

"I'm sure I can come up with something that'll work."

"Great."

They talked about his schedule and put something on the books for later that week.

"The kids are going to be really excited," Delilah told him. It was an understatement.

"You know what?" he said. "I kind of am, too."

~

QUINN GOT a kick out of the Ballard kids. Jesse had a bright and fiery personality, and Gavin seemed like a gentle soul—the kind of person you wanted to protect from the realities of the world.

The idea of hanging out with them wasn't the worst thing he could think of. And, hell, he was man enough to admit that their hero worship fed his ego in a way that wasn't at all unpleasant.

He found himself looking forward to Thursday, when he would lead them on an easy two-hour hike. He got on his computer and started researching routes. He knew most of the trails around here, but it paid to double-check for any hazards the boys might get into, given what had happened last time.

As he Googled and scrolled, he thought about Delilah.

She was funny—so there was that. She had a way of talking that wasn't inclined toward comedy, exactly, but her wry delivery made him smile or even chuckle all the same.

He found himself wishing he'd met her under different circumstances. Before she'd gotten married and had kids, to be specific.

It wasn't that he found mothers less attractive. Hell, a woman could have six kids and still be hot as hell, in his mind. But to him, the best kind of relationship was a casual one. No expectations, no responsibilities, just fun. Just two people enjoying each other's company—and each other's bodies.

But the whole no expectations, no responsibilities thing got shot to shit when you brought kids into the mix. When it was just two adults, you could put people's feelings at risk. Adults knew what they were getting into and knew what was at stake. But kids? Breaking a kid's heart just wasn't okay.

And the only way you could be sure not to break children's hearts was to avoid getting involved with their mothers.

If he'd met her when she was single? That could have been a hell of a lot of fun.

The other night, he'd told himself that spending time with an uncomplicated nine might be just the thing to get his head straight. So he'd called Jasmine, a woman from Morro Bay he'd dated a few times, and they were set to meet at Ted's—Cambria's dive bar—tonight.

Now, there was an uncomplicated woman.

If Jasmine couldn't get his mind off Delilah, no one could.

~

OF COURSE, it wasn't enough for Roxanne to call Delilah and beg her to come home for Thanksgiving. When that didn't work, their mother called, too.

Delilah was at the beach with the kids, sitting on a blanket and watching Jesse and Gavin chase each other with pieces of driftwood, when the call came in.

Earlier in the day when she'd talked to Quinn, the sky had been a clear blue. But now, a light fog had rolled in, shrouding the world in soft gray. Delilah was bundled up in sweatpants and a hooded sweatshirt, but the boys were shirtless, romping around in shorts and bare feet, oblivious to the chill in a way only children could be.

Delilah held the cell phone to her ear and shaded her eyes with her hand as she watched her children play.

"No, Mom. I'm not coming home for Thanksgiving. I thought Roxanne would have told you that."

"Well, she did. But I thought, that can't be right. Surely you want to be with family right now. Delilah, honey, don't you want—"

"What I want ... what I *need* ... is some time to myself to sort things out. Just me and the boys."

"But, Delilah, we love you. We only want to support you. We only want what's best for you."

Delilah felt the swell of love and guilt—two things inextricably linked when related to her family—and let out a sigh. "I know that, Mom. I really do. But this *is* what's best for me. And for the boys."

"Oh, but the boys need their grandfather right now, especially. They need a man in their lives, sweetheart. They need a role model now that their father—"

"Can we maybe not talk about Mitch?" Delilah said.

Her mother was silent, but of course, that couldn't last.

"Delilah, I'm worried about you."

"Well, I'm worried about me, too."

"That's why you need to come home. Not only for Thanksgiving. If you and the boys could just stay here for a while, until you get back on your feet ..."

"I'm on my feet, Mom. I'm standing. And I need to keep right on standing, for the kids' sake and my own. Don't you think I want to just be taken care of for a change? Don't you think I'd love that? But ..."

But if I let myself go, if I let myself just give in and fall apart, I'll never be able to put myself back together again.

"You have your pride," her mother said knowingly. "That's what this is about."

"Partly," she admitted. "And partly it's about the fact that I'm not broken, and I don't need to be fixed."

"Well." Jeanette Ballard was hurt—Delilah could hear it in the single syllable. "I would think you would want to see us just because you love us, not because of whether you are or are not broken and in need of fixing."

Delilah felt a surge of guilt for what she'd said and how she'd said it. "I do love you, Mom. I love all of you. So much. But I need some time to work things out on my own. You can see that, right?"

When Jeanette didn't say anything for a while, Delilah was sure she was gearing up for further argument. Instead, she relented. "Of course I can, honey."

Delilah felt so relieved she nearly collapsed onto the blanket as the pent-up tension within her eased. "Thank you."

"We'll miss you."

Damn it, she was starting to get teary-eyed, and she hated when that happened. "I'll miss you, too."

"Call me. Not just when you feel obligated. I want to know what's happening with you."

"I will." That was partly a lie. Delilah would call her mother when she had good things to report, but not when she was struggling. Not only didn't she need her mother's pity, she also didn't want to lay the burden of her problems on her mother's shoulders.

And the truth was, she was managing. She and the boys had enough money, finally; they had their health; they had this beautiful place to renew themselves and wait out the holidays.

Delilah took in a deep breath of ocean air and tried to be grateful.

Sometimes, it took a lot of trying.

~

WHEN QUINN SHOWED up at Ted's that night, Jasmine was already there, seated at the bar and sipping something from a highball glass.

He took a moment to admire her before she noticed him. Tall with long, shiny blond hair in a cascade down her back. An athletic body encased in a dress as tight as an Ace bandage. Muscular calves leading down to feet nestled in four-inch heels. As he looked at her, she turned, saw him, and let a slow, predatory grin spread across her face.

At the sight of him, she plucked the cherry out of her drink by the stem, put it in her mouth, and bit down in a way that, somehow, seemed obscene.

"Quinn. Have a seat." She pulled out the barstool next to her and patted it with her manicured hand.

Jasmine. God. He hadn't seen her in a while, and she looked just as good as he remembered. Had he thought she was a nine? Right now, for the life of him, he couldn't remember why he'd deducted the point.

As he sat down beside her, he reflected that she smelled exactly like her name.

"Hey, Jazz. How've you been?"

"Lonely. You?"

"Pretty much the same." He gestured to Ted, the bar's owner, for one of whatever she was having. Ted brought it over and smacked it down on the bar with a very Ted-like grunt.

Quinn took a sip. An old fashioned. He tried not to wince at the sweetness of the cocktail. He'd have preferred his whiskey straight up, but ordering the same as what she was having had seemed more smooth and flirtatious, somehow.

They made small talk—she asked about his work, and he asked about her brother, who was an acquaintance of Quinn's. Somewhere during the conversation, he felt her hand on his thigh, which caused an immediate physical response higher up.

When she slid her hand along his leg and squeezed, giving him a grin that suggested far more interesting things to come, he reflected that the evening was working out very well, indeed.

He swallowed the rest of what was in his glass, put the glass down on the bar, laid some money next to it, and said, "So. You want to get out of here?"

~

THEY WERE BARELY in the door of his place before Jasmine started taking off his shirt. He pulled off her dress, and before they'd even gotten to the bedroom they were tangled up in one another, a jumble of arms and legs and hands and naked skin.

It was around then that he realized it was all going to hell.

Which was a puzzle, really. How could a situation like this, with Jasmine looking the way she did, possibly go wrong?

Delilah, that was how.

Her face kept popping into Quinn's head at inopportune moments. Like the one when Jasmine put her hand down his pants.

It wasn't that he imagined he was with Delilah instead of Jasmine. It wasn't as if he thought Delilah would somehow disapprove or judge him—and it certainly wasn't as if she had any right to do either of those things even if she were here, and even if she wanted to.

Instead, he kept thinking of her—that was all. Her face, her voice, the sound of her laugh kept popping into his mind like a snippet of music you couldn't get out of your head.

Goddamn it.

"What's wrong?" Jasmine paused and withdrew her hand, and it was only then that Quinn realized he'd uttered the curse out loud and hadn't just thought it.

"Ah ... nothing. Nothing. I just ... I've got something on my mind that happened earlier, that's all. Nothing to be concerned about."

"Oh. Do you want to talk about it?"

"No, no. Just keep doing what you were doing, and I'm sure it'll go away."

She slid her hand inside the open fly of his pants again, an event that, under normal circumstances, would have caused his brain to shut off entirely. But now, it wasn't working that way.

He just couldn't get his head in the game.

Jasmine reclaimed her hand, stood back, and put her fists on her hips. She was standing there in just her bra, her panties, and the four-inch heels. God help him.

"Something's really bothering you," she said. "You know, Quinn, we could just talk. We could just discuss whatever it is that's upsetting you. It doesn't have to just be sex."

But for him, it did just have to be sex. With Jasmine, that was all it could be or ever would be. They had zero in common except for their attraction to each other. But that didn't mean she deserved to be treated like an object rather than a person. It didn't mean she deserved to be with him while he was thinking about someone else.

"I'm sorry." He raked a hand through his hair. "I guess I'm not in the right head space for this."

"You think?" She raised one sculpted eyebrow.

She plucked her dress up off the floor and pulled it over her head, wiggling her hips a little as she slid it down into place.

"Look, it's not you," he said.

"Clearly."

She picked up her purse, fished her car keys out of it, and went to the front door. As she let herself out, he said, "I'll call you."

She turned back and looked at him. "No, you won't."

CHAPTER 10

None of it was Delilah's fault. Hell, she wasn't even there. She didn't know Jasmine, and she barely knew Quinn.

But none of that stopped him from being pissed off at her.

When the day of the hike came, he showed up at the parking lot at the trailhead feeling grumpy and out of sorts. Delilah had ruined his chance for no-strings sex, and a man couldn't let that stand.

"Hi, Quinn." Delilah waved to him as she got out of her car, which was parked next to his day-to-day car—he hadn't brought the van this time. The boys piled out of the back seat, jumping around with the enthusiasm of puppies.

"Hey," he said. Grunted, really.

"The boys are excited," she said. "I guess you can see that, though." Delilah looked excited, too—she was bright-eyed and cheerful, her face lightly flushed in a way that made her even prettier than usual.

For some reason, that annoyed the hell out of him.

"Quinn! Quinn! Mom says I have to stay on the trail this time, and I will, I promise," Jesse said. "We have sunscreen and bug spray and bottles of water and some energy bars, because your website said to bring them."

"We brought some for you, too." Gavin pulled an energy bar out of his little backpack and waved it.

Ah, shit. His impulse was to snap at them that he could bring his own damned energy bars—which he would hardly need for a hike of this length—but how could you snap at a little kid who brought you food? It was impossible. Which meant he couldn't even keep a good grump going, as much as he wanted to.

"Thanks, Gavin. Jesse. That was really nice of you." He accepted the energy bar Gavin had offered him. "I'll just tuck this away for later." He slid the bar into his own pack.

"The weather is perfect, isn't it?" Delilah tipped her head back to face the sky. "Look at those clouds."

"I've seen clouds," Quinn said.

"Oh."

Delilah looked puzzled, and why wouldn't she be? It had been a dick thing to say.

"Is everything all right?" she asked.

"I just want to get started so we can be back on schedule. I've got other appointments."

"All right." But he could see that he'd dimmed her glow, and he felt like shit about it. Nobody should ever dim Delilah Ballard's glow. Her asshole ex had done that, and Quinn didn't want to do it, too.

"Sorry," he told her. "I'm just in a bad mood. Hey, guys." He turned to the boys. "Who's ready for a hike?"

~

DELILAH HAD STARTED the outing feeling pretty good—the outdoors, some exercise, happy kids—but Quinn was obviously in a pissy mood, and that was making her start to question the whole thing.

"Are you sure everything's all right?" she asked him.

"Yeah, why wouldn't it be?"

The words themselves were okay, but the tone behind them wasn't. Definitely pissy.

They started the hike heading east into the hills south of Big Sur.

The trail was narrow, with brush and wild growing things on either side of them.

"Watch out for poison oak," Delilah called to the boys, who'd gone up ahead of her.

"That's not poison oak," Quinn said. His tone suggested a schoolmarm who'd had enough of someone's misbehavior.

"I didn't say it was," Delilah responded. "I said they should watch out for it."

Quinn grunted something back at her.

"Look." She stopped where she was, planting her feet and glaring up at him. "Should we just cut our losses and go back to the car? Because I'm paying you for a delightful hike, and your attitude is decidedly … undelightful."

He stopped and turned to look at her. "I don't have a dictionary handy, but I don't think *undelightful* is a word."

"Whatever. You know what I mean."

"Yeah." He rubbed at the stubble on his chin—stubble that made him even more insanely sexy than he was without it—and raised his eyebrows in something that might have been conciliation.

"So. Do we quit, or not?" Delilah asked.

"No. I'm sorry. I'll snap out of it."

The fact that there was something for him to snap out of made her worry about him, just a little.

"Is everything okay?"

"Yeah. Sure. Yes."

"Okay …"

"I'm putting on my professional guide persona now. It's fine. It'll all be fine. Hey, boys!" He called ahead to the kids, who were quite a distance up the trail now. "Wait for me, okay? And, ah … that's poison oak right there to your left. Stand back from that, would you?"

QUINN KNEW he was being an ass, and he didn't want to be. Hell, he was working right now, and he usually avoided being an ass to even the worst of his clients. And the Ballards weren't that. They'd followed the instructions on his website to the letter, and they deserved better from him than what he was giving them.

Since the source of his angst was his unwanted attraction to Delilah, he decided to focus on the boys instead.

He trotted up the trail to where the kids were standing. Then he knelt down at their level and pointed at the poison oak he'd warned them about.

"See that? See how it's got the three leaves together, and it's kind of red? That's something you don't want to touch. It'll make you itchy and give you blisters."

"I know. Mom told us," Jesse said. "She showed us pictures and everything."

Gavin nodded solemnly.

Good clients, Quinn reflected. They'd done their homework.

"Okay. Let's keep walking and see what other interesting things we can find," he suggested.

BY THE TIME they were twenty minutes into the walk, Quinn had needed to bring Jesse back onto the trail twice when he'd wandered into the brush to look at something, and Gavin was already complaining that he was tired.

So, thinking of creative solutions, Quinn picked Gavin up, raised him over his head, and settled the boy on his shoulders. That would solve the tiredness problem. He still wasn't sure what he was going to do about Jesse's wandering.

Then a solution presented itself.

"I want to ride up there," Jesse said.

"Tell you what," Quinn said. "If you stay on the trail for the next fifteen minutes—no stepping off—I'll give you a turn."

"Really?" The kid perked up, his eyes going wide.

"Sure. Let's see if you can do it."

After that, the kid stayed on the trail like he was glued to it, and

Quinn congratulated himself on his ingenuity.

DELILAH OBSERVED ALL of this from a few paces behind Quinn and the boys.

A few thoughts hit her, more or less at the same time: one, Quinn was a natural with kids, and two, Jesse and Gavin should have been doing all of this with Mitch instead of with a man they'd just met.

Instead, Mitch was probably at some Paris cafe right now eating fancy French food with his girlfriend. Unless it was the middle of the night in Paris. Who knew? Delilah was in no mood to figure out time zones.

Why had it been so easy for Mitch to walk away from his family? If he didn't love Delilah anymore, that was fine. She was an adult—she could take it. But how had he walked away from his sons?

Quinn was so easy with the kids, joking with them, talking to them like he was truly interested in everything they had to say. And the boys looked so happy they were glowing.

The fact that they were so starved for positive male attention made her want to fly to Paris and throw her ex off the Eiffel Tower.

"You okay?" Quinn glanced back at Delilah and asked her the same thing she'd asked him not long ago. Maybe his bad mood had rubbed off on her.

"I'm fine." She was walking with her arms crossed over her chest, the anger toward her ex building like steam in the center of her body.

"You don't seem fine."

"So now you're an expert on who is or isn't fine?"

"No. Nope. I'm just going to walk for a while."

THEY CONTINUED ON THE TRAIL, Quinn pointing out plants and animals to the kids, Jesse and Gavin changing places at the agreed-upon interval. Gavin was on foot now, which could have been a hazard since he was smaller than Jesse, but Gavin was also more compliant. When Quinn told him to stay on the trail, he got the sense that Gavin had never considered doing otherwise.

About an hour into the walk, they came to a clearing with a couple of boulders that were good for sitting, so Quinn pulled Jesse off his shoulders and they all sat to take a break.

"This is a good time for that water and those energy bars," Quinn told the boys, and they obediently rooted around in their packs for their snacks.

"It's going well with the kids," Quinn remarked as Delilah sat down on the trunk of a fallen tree.

"Yeah. It is." She couldn't seem to keep the bitterness out of her voice.

"I'd have thought that's a good thing," Quinn said.

"Oh ... it is." Delilah scrubbed her face with her hands.

"So, is there a problem?"

He'd been the one showing unnecessary attitude at the start of this outing, now she was doing it. She told herself to stop.

"No. There's no problem. The boys are having a wonderful time."

"But you're not?"

She couldn't talk about it now, not with the kids within earshot. She couldn't tell him how distressing it was to see a virtual stranger bonding with her children in a way their father never had and probably never would.

None of that was his fault—he was just showing her children a good time, the way she'd paid him to do.

Delilah took a deep breath, let it out, and told herself to grow up. She could put on a smiling face for the sake of her kids. She'd promised herself she would give her boys a happy holiday season. And right now, they were happy.

So she would be, too.

"You know how earlier, you had a mood?" she asked him.

"Yeah."

"Well, now I'm having one. Ignore it. It'll go away."

"Okay. You all right?"

"Yes. I am. Or, I will be." Time to change the subject. "You know, those energy bars don't look half bad."

~

BY THE TIME they got back to the car, Jesse and Gavin were tired, filthy, and content—just the way kids were supposed to be when they were on vacation and had just enjoyed some time outdoors.

Delilah got them into the back seat of her car and made sure they were buckled up, then closed them in and turned to Quinn.

"Thank you. They had a great time." She'd paid him for the outing beforehand, and she had to admit it had been worth the price. He'd been an engaging guide, not only keeping her children entertained and under control, but also pointing out landmarks, wildlife species, and interesting plants and sharing anecdotes about the history of the region.

"I'm glad." He put his hands into his pockets and stood there looking down at her in a way that didn't feel professional. It felt decidedly personal.

"People probably tip you, right? Is that a thing?"

"It is, yeah. But you don't need to do that."

"Really, I could …"

"I don't want you to. I had fun, just as much as the boys did."

"Well."

"You know what you could do instead?" he asked. "To show your appreciation for a job well done?"

"What?"

"You could let me take you to dinner."

~

THE WORDS CAME out of Quinn's mouth before he'd known he was going to say them. He absolutely did not want to date a single mother. Christ, hadn't he established that in his dialogue with himself since he'd met her? Somehow, his mouth hadn't gotten the memo.

He could see her hesitating, and he wished he could take it back. But part of him didn't want to take anything back. He wanted to take her out to dinner and talk to her and be with her, and maybe kiss her. The part of him that wanted all of those things was winning.

"I can't," she said.

"Why not?"

"The boys. I can't leave them alone, and we don't know anyone here, so …"

"There's a reputable babysitting service in town that I sometimes refer clients to. A lot of the hotels on Moonstone Beach use them. I could give you the number."

"Oh, but—"

"Look. You showed them a great time today. When was the last time someone showed you a great time? And when was the last time you got to take some time to just be you and not somebody's mom?"

That last part got her. He could see her starting to sway.

"I'll think about it."

"I'll text you the babysitting service's number. While you're thinking."

~

DELILAH GOT in the car and drove back toward Cambria, thinking about Quinn's offer.

That had been unexpected. What would a guy like him want with a woman like her? She was a mother. She was notably lacking in glamor. She hadn't waxed her legs in months. And her makeup had sat unused for so long in her cosmetics bag that it had probably turned to dust by now.

She hadn't been out on a date in years, not since she and Mitch had started seeing each other. She didn't even know how to do it anymore.

Except, she kind of wanted to try.

"Hey. Guys?" she asked as she drove south on Highway 1. "What would you think if I … well, if I wanted to go someplace sometime, just by myself, and you guys stayed with a babysitter? How would you feel about that?"

Gavin was the one who answered. "Dolly's nice. We could stay with her."

Huh. Delilah hadn't thought of Dolly. It was an interesting idea.

"Jesse? What do you think?" In the rearview mirror, Delilah saw Jesse shrug, indicating a lack of strong feelings one way or the other.

She hadn't decided whether she wanted to go out with Quinn, but she had to admit it was probably feasible.

She just didn't know if it would be smart.

CHAPTER 11

"You remember the mythical god who rescued Jesse?" Delilah asked Roxanne on the phone later, after the boys had showered and changed their clothes and were playing with Legos in Jesse's room.

"Yeah, what about him?"

"He asked me out."

"*Shut. Up.*"

Roxanne reacted with such astonishment that Delilah couldn't help thinking that her initial thought had been right—nobody as hot as Quinn Monroe could ever take an interest in her.

"You don't have to be quite that surprised," Delilah said.

"Well, I'm not," Roxanne lied. "But … it's just … you said he was really, super hot. Smoking. And I just …"

"You just thought that a guy that super smoking hot could never want me. That's what you meant."

"Oh, Delilah. No, I didn't."

Delilah felt the sting of tears in her eyes, and she chided herself for it. She hadn't meant for the conversation to go this way. She'd called her sister for advice, not so she could dissect her own worst, most painful insecurities.

"You're amazing," Roxanne went on. "You're beautiful, and smart, and caring, and—"

"Stop."

"Look." Roxanne assumed a stern tone, as though she were scolding a child. "I didn't mean anything by it, and you know it. Don't you think that when Lisa Bonet told her friends she was dating Jason Momoa, they might have been a little excited?"

Delilah smiled a little, despite herself. "I suppose."

"Just because Mitch told you that you were worthless, doesn't mean you are."

Delilah felt the tension build in her chest at the mention of her ex's name. "Can we please not talk about Mitch?"

"Okay. I'd much rather talk about you. What did you say when he asked you?"

"I said I'd think about it."

"What's to think about?! He's hot and he saved your son's life. You owe it to him to go out with him. And you sure as hell owe it to yourself."

Roxanne had reached peak outrage at the idea that Delilah might not accept the date, and her tone combined both shock and disappointment.

"He didn't save Jesse's life. Jesse wasn't even hurt. And even if he had, does that mean I owe him sex?"

"We're not talking about sex," Roxanne said. "At least, I wasn't."

But Delilah was, which meant she'd been thinking about it.

She'd have to be an idiot not to think about it.

Lacking any other argument, she fell back on the one she'd used with Quinn. "I don't have anyone to watch the boys."

"Oh, come on. Surely they have babysitting services out there, with all the hotels and everything. Somebody bonded and with references."

"That's exactly what Quinn said."

"Well, there you go."

"You make it seem simple," Delilah said.

"It is simple. You don't have to get into a relationship with this guy. You don't have to fall in love. You don't have to sleep with him. Just go out with him as a way of ripping off the Band-Aid. Just ... you know. Dip your toe. You have to start somewhere, so you might as well start with a super hot guy who saved your kid."

"Just dip my toe," Delilah repeated. "Or rip off the Band-Aid. You really need to pick a metaphor."

"Don't try to distract me. You need to do this, Delilah. I mean, why not?"

Because it might not be as simple as dipping her toe. If she got involved with Quinn—if she just dipped her toe—she worried that the rest of her would get pulled in until she was over her head.

QUINN TRIED NOT to think about the invitation he'd left standing between himself and Delilah.

Usually when he asked a woman out, he got an answer in the affirmative. It wasn't that he'd never been turned down or put off—of course he had—but it happened rarely enough that he was out of practice.

Either she would say yes or she wouldn't. And if she didn't, it wasn't the end of the world. She was just another woman. Just another attractive female who'd caught his eye, like many before her and like many more would in the future.

Except that was bullshit, and he knew it.

His thoughts regarding Delilah—he couldn't even call them feelings yet—weren't the same as his thoughts about other women.

Usually, when he was attracted to someone, he thought about her in terms of sex. What they would do together and how much fun they both would have doing it. But with Delilah, it was different. Yes, he thought about having sex with her—he thought about touching her and tasting her, God yes—but he also thought about talking to her. Spending time with her. Getting to know her.

Even worse, he wanted to get to know her kids.

When you were interested in getting to know someone's kids, you were thinking about things like being a family. And that was something he'd carefully and successfully avoided up until this point.

He didn't want to change that now.

Except, he did want to know her kids. They seemed like great kids.

You'd better hope she says no, he thought. *You'd better hope she takes her massive load of baggage and goes somewhere else.*

In the days following his offer, he put it aside and focused on other things. He worked on his salmon fishing article, which was starting to take shape. He moved on to the Bedrooms section of the furniture website. He took a group on an overnight hike to Vicente Flat campground in Big Sur.

And he tried not to think about Delilah.

~

BY THE TIME a week had passed, Quinn was so tired of not thinking about Delilah that he decided to try thinking about her instead.

He'd just finished the first draft of the fishing article and was taking a break on his front deck, drinking a soda from the can and watching the midmorning dog-walkers go by, when he decided to text her.

Are you done thinking yet?

He sent the text, wondering if it was flirty enough or amusing enough or casual enough. And since when had Quinn ever worried about his game with women?

The response came back a moment later.

Not quite yet.

Oh, for God's sake. He needed to push for an answer, if only so she could put him out of his misery.

While you're thinking, why not have a meal with me? Thinking goes better on a full stomach. So I'm told.

He sent the text and waited, a half grin playing on his features.

A white-haired woman walked by with a sheltie on a leash, and Quinn gave her a friendly wave.

You're pressuring me, she wrote back.

Just a little. And it doesn't have to be a big thing. It's just dinner. Or lunch, if you'd rather.

He waited while another dog-walker came by, then a jogger. He waited as a bank of clouds rolled in and brought the temperature down a few degrees. He waited as the mail truck stopped at his house, then passed. He waited until he was certain she had no intention of responding.

Then his phone pinged.

I'll see if I can find a sitter.

~

ONCE DELILAH HAD SAID YES, she began second-guessing herself immediately.

But that was just stupid. Roxanne was right—she needed to dip her toe into the water. Her recovery from the collapse of her marriage wasn't going to happen quickly or easily, God knew, but if it was going to happen at all, she needed to take the first steps.

Delilah's goals for the date were simple: She wanted to get the whole first-date-after-the-divorce thing over with so she could begin to get used to the idea of putting herself out there again. She wanted to make one tiny bit of progress toward being a person instead of a divorcée.

What she *didn't* want was more complex: She didn't want a new relationship—not right now. She didn't want a fling, because she wasn't ready for that. She didn't want to complicate her life even further, and she didn't want to involve her boys in something that wouldn't last and that would inevitably leave them disappointed—again.

It was probably important to lay all of that out to Quinn in the interest of openness and fair play.

But for now, she just needed to find a babysitter.

~

SHE STARTED WITH DOLLY, reasoning that if it didn't work out, she could try the babysitting service Quinn had mentioned to her.

As it happened, that wasn't necessary. Dolly was thrilled with the idea when Delilah and the kids brought it up at her house the next day.

"Oh, it's going to be so much fun!" She clasped her hands together, looking at the boys as though she couldn't wait to pinch their cheeks and kiss the tops of their heads. "We'll bake brownies. Or would you boys prefer cookies?"

"I like brownies," Jesse said.

Gavin nodded vigorously, his thumb plugged into his mouth.

"Stop sucking your thumb, Gavin." Jesse scowled at his brother. "Only babies do that."

"Oh, now, Jesse, it's his thumb, and I imagine he's got a right to do what he wants with it," Dolly said.

To Delilah, that was a good sign. She herself had decided that if thumb-sucking was the worst way Gavin acted out in response to the divorce, then he was welcome to it.

The fact that Dolly had taken a stand in Gavin's favor boded well.

"I still don't know which night it'll be, exactly. I have to work it out with my... friend."

"Well, that's fine," Dolly said. "What else have I got to do? Just tell your *friend* to pick any evening he chooses." The way Dolly said the word *friend* indicated she knew exactly what kind of friend they were talking about.

When they left Dolly's place, Delilah sent the boys across the street to Otter Bluff and hung back a moment to talk to the older woman.

"I really can't thank you enough," she said.

"Honey, is this your first date after the divorce?" Dolly asked gently.

Delilah hesitated. "I didn't say it was a date."

"I know you didn't. But you're not answering my question."

Delilah figured that if Dolly was going to put herself out to do this favor, she at least was entitled to the truth.

"Yes. It is."

Dolly smiled encouragingly, then took Delilah's hand and gave it a squeeze. "I figure you deserve a little fun after all you've been through."

Delilah thought so, too. So far, though, this wasn't fun. It was an anxiety fest that felt more like gearing up for a root canal.

She hoped the actual date would be less painful.

CHAPTER 12

They decided to have dinner on a Thursday night. Thursday, because the tourists made the local restaurants too crowded from Friday through Monday. On a Thursday, it would be easier to get a reservation, and the atmosphere wherever they went would be more casual and less hectic.

Quinn made a reservation at Madeline's, a little place on Main Street in the West Village.

He picked her up at Otter Bluff at seven, and when she opened the door, he couldn't help grinning at the way she looked. He was used to seeing her in jeans and a T-shirt, with no makeup and her hair in a ponytail. But tonight, she looked ... well, girly. In the best possible way.

The ponytail was gone, and she'd done something to her hair that made it full and wavy. Her makeup was understated, but it was there, and it had the effect of making her look just a little more vibrant, a little brighter, than usual. The jeans and T-shirt had been replaced by a dress with a kind of loose, swingy skirt and a neckline that was just low enough to be intriguing.

"You look nice," he told her.

He ran the pad of his thumb along his lower lip in an unconscious gesture that, had he noticed he was doing it, he would have admitted was sexual in nature.

"You too."

"So, what did you end up doing with the kids?" he asked.

"The neighbor across the street is babysitting. She's a very nice older woman, and the kids love her. So that worked out."

"I'm glad."

He'd thought she was attractive in her usual mom mode. But he was delighted by how well she cleaned up.

He raised his eyebrows in question. "Are you ready to go?"

~

DELILAH HAD THOUGHT tonight would be fine. It would be friendly. But the way Quinn looked at her when she answered the door wasn't friendly.

It was predatory.

Normally, having a man like him look at her like that would be a positive development. But tonight, it just made her nervous.

For one thing, what was his game? A man who looked like Quinn Monroe didn't feel raw sexual hunger for someone who looked like Delilah, so why was he pretending he did?

For another, he was just too damned good-looking for her to think. It was ridiculous. Bad enough when she'd seen him in his regular life, but now, with his fresh shave and his pressed slacks and his combed hair—not to mention the light, spicy smell of his cologne—she could barely remember where she was or why. For God's sake, how was she supposed to function in the presence of all that?

She hadn't realized how well the children had served as chaperones, making everything between Quinn and Delilah sunny and innocent, until they weren't there. Being alone with him was unsettling.

Didn't Quinn notice she was carrying twenty extra pounds? Didn't he notice she wasn't especially glamorous even under the best of circumstances?

She felt like she was in some teen rom-com where the captain of the football team asked the nerdy girl out as a prank.

Those movies usually involved a lot of crying.

"You're quiet," he said from the driver's seat of his car as he parked in front of Madeline's. "Is everything okay?"

"What? Sure. Yes." She'd been so lost in her thoughts that she'd barely heard him.

"You worried about the kids?"

"I ... no."

"Well, whatever it is, maybe a nice meal will get your mind off it," he suggested. "Let's go in."

~

QUINN COULDN'T HELP THINKING that maybe he'd screwed this up, even though the date had barely started and there wasn't much he *could* have screwed up, even if he'd wanted to.

Delilah had barely spoken two words to him since they'd left the house, and he didn't know whether that had anything to do with him. Usually, though, when he was with a woman who had a pissy attitude about something, it was a safe bet that he'd somehow caused it.

Was it something he'd said? Or something he hadn't said? The choice of restaurant, maybe? Or was she just worried about her kids and trying to pretend she wasn't?

Why did everything have to be so complicated? Why were women such a puzzle?

They went inside and the host showed them to their table.

Madeline's had a small dining room with white tablecloths and dim lighting. The place was about half-full, and their table was halfway back, along the wall. A glass partition separated them from the couple at the next table.

Quinn picked up the wine menu and perused it. "Would you like some wine?"

"Hmm?"

She hadn't been listening to him. Either that, or she was annoyed.

Maybe it was the whole man-taking-the-menu thing. He offered the menu to her in case that was it. "Wine menu," he said.

"Oh." She took the menu and looked at it for such a brief moment that she couldn't possibly have read anything. Then she put it down. "Just water for me."

Okay, it wasn't his imagination, then. In his experience, when a woman who had no objection to drinking alcohol refused a drink on a first date, it was because she thought she might need to flee before the appetizer.

Goddamn it. He was on his best behavior. What was going wrong?

"Look, Delilah. Obviously, something's bothering you. Do you want to reschedule?"

"Is that what *you* want?" She sent the question back over the net in his direction.

"No, I want to have dinner. But if you've got something going on …"

"I don't. There's nothing. Let's just order."

DELILAH WAS FLUBBING THIS, and she knew it. She was failing miserably at trying to hide her doubts and insecurities. And now Quinn wanted to abort the whole thing, and really, who could blame him?

This is an exercise, she reminded herself. *It's a step toward living happily without Mitch. So try, damn it.*

"I think I will have some wine after all."

QUINN DIDN'T KNOW what was going wrong, but he knew for sure that something was. Delilah seemed tense and uncomfortable, and he had no idea what he'd done to cause it.

Maybe he hadn't done anything. Maybe this was about her ex. He was pretty sure this was her first date since the divorce, so maybe that was all this was—the pain and difficulty of trying to move on.

They ordered their wine and their food without saying much, while Quinn tried to figure out the best approach for breaking through this wall she'd erected between them.

When his steak and her pasta had been set on the table and the server had left, he gave it his best shot.

"Are you thinking about your ex-husband?" he asked gently. "Because if he's on your mind, I can certainly understand why this might be hard."

She looked at him, her fork in her hand. Then she put the fork down, and her eyes got shiny and red.

"I'm making a mess of this." She blinked a few times, and one tear squeezed out. "I'm sorry."

"Don't be." He refolded the napkin in his lap. "I get it. First time out with someone since the divorce, right?"

She nodded.

"Which, what? Makes it seem real? Makes it clear that the marriage is really over?"

"It's not so much that," she said. "It's more a complete lack of optimism. You know? Why try, if that's how things end up?"

It struck him that if she was worried about how things would end up, in a larger, where-is-my-life-going sense, then she probably had entirely different expectations for this date than he did. Quinn had hoped things would end up in someone's bed, and he really hadn't thought much beyond that. But Delilah apparently was seeing a future of emotional devastation and inevitable heartbreak.

"They don't always end up that way," he offered. "And anyway, sometimes things are just fun. Sometimes they're just … light."

"Light," she repeated.

"Yeah. Sure." He shrugged. "Why not?"

~

In other circumstances, it might have offended Delilah if a man she was out with implied that all he was looking for was fun. This time, though, it wasn't an offense so much as a relief.

She was putting too much pressure on herself, that was all. She was so conditioned to thinking of dating in terms of a long-term relationship that she'd forgotten what it was like to spend time with a man just for the pleasure of it.

If a good time was all Quinn wanted and they both knew that up front, then surely she wasn't in any danger. A serious long-term relationship with any man might have been an unattainable goal for Delilah, but fun? That was something she could do.

"I'm out of practice with keeping things light," she admitted. "But I'm willing to try."

~

And I'm out of practice being sensitive to women's emotional needs, Quinn thought. *But I'm willing to try, too.*

In the interest of keeping things low-key, they kept the conversation off of things like exes and relationships and people's futures for the rest of the meal. Instead, they talked about his work, her kids, what kinds of books they both enjoyed, and what she planned to see and do in Cambria for the rest of her stay.

To Quinn's mind, things were going better. They shared a bottle of wine, and Delilah even smiled and laughed a few times.

The laugh—that was something he wouldn't mind seeing and hearing more of. When she laughed, the happiness reached every part of her face until she was aglow with it. When Delilah laughed, Quinn felt some warm thing in his chest squeeze his heart.

It wasn't an unpleasant sensation, but it was alarming, nonetheless.

~

After they left the restaurant, Quinn wasn't ready to take Delilah home yet, so he considered other things they might do—a movie in San Luis Obispo, maybe? Or listening to some music at the Cambria Pines Lodge? He'd have been happy just to take a walk on the beach with her, but it was already dark and the moon was obscured by an overcast sky.

Next time, he thought, which made him note that he was already thinking about a next time.

"It's still early," he told her. "There's not a whole lot of nightlife in Cambria, but there's some. Or we could go to Morro Bay. There's a club there that—"

"I'd better get back to the boys," she said.

"Right." He nodded. "Of course."

Either she really was just worried about her kids or she was fleeing at the first opportunity because the date had sucked just that much for her.

"I had a good time," she told him as they stood next to his car.

"Really?"

"Yes. After a rough start, I did."

He hesitated, then took a chance. He lay his hand on the side of her face, leaned in, and kissed her.

She let out a little noise at the touch of his lips—a little whimper—and it was maybe the sexiest sound he'd ever heard. His body reacted as the blood rushed to one of his favorite body parts.

He wanted to ask her to come home with him—God, he wanted that so much—but he knew she'd never go for it. Not now. Not yet. So instead, he pulled away, took a ragged breath, and opened the car door for her.

"You ready?" he said.

~

DELILAH HADN'T KISSED any man besides Mitch for more than twelve years. She'd met Mitch during her freshman year in college, when she was only eighteen, so there hadn't been many kisses before that, either. All in all, she could count the number of people she'd kissed on one hand and still have one finger left over.

So, maybe her reaction had something to do with her lack of experience. All she knew was that her entire body had felt like it was melting at the touch of his lips.

How could one man's lips on hers make her thighs weak and her toes hot? For God's sake.

She got into the car feeling grateful that it was dark inside so he wouldn't see how his kiss had affected her.

He drove her back to Otter Bluff, and she thanked him for dinner and got out of the car before he could try kissing her again.

If he did, she didn't know how she could summon up the will to stop him. Or herself.

CHAPTER 13

Well, she'd done it, Delilah reflected the next morning as she made coffee and got breakfast ready for herself and the boys. She'd gone out on her first date since the divorce. She'd ripped off the Band-Aid. It had stung some, but it hadn't killed her.

She felt like she deserved some kind of ribbon or certificate of accomplishment—something that showed she'd survived her divorce and emerged on the other side in one piece.

Delilah felt grateful that Quinn had done that for her, grateful, too, that he'd shown her she could still be attractive to a man who wasn't Mitch.

Now, with all of that achieved and behind her, it was time to forget about frivolous things like dating and get down to fixing what was left of her life.

She put cereal, milk, and a plate of cut fruit in front of the boys at the dining room table, ate some toast, then poured herself a cup of coffee and went onto the back patio to enjoy the view while she drank it.

She'd just settled into the Adirondack chair when she heard someone calling her.

"Delilah? Yoo hoo!"

She looked up and over the waist-high fence to find Dolly walking across the street and waving at her.

"Oh. Dolly. Hi." Delilah indicated the chair next to her. "Have a seat. You want some coffee?"

"No thank you, honey. My doctor says I have to lay off the caffeine. Blood pressure." She let herself in through the gate and settled into the chair next to Delilah.

"Oh. Well. Thanks again for watching the boys last night," Delilah said. "I really appreciate it."

"Think nothing of it." Dolly waved a hand dismissively. "Those boys of yours are dolls. Just dolls. They had a lot of fun, and I think I enjoyed it more than they did."

"Still, it was a big favor, so thank you."

Dolly stole a glance at Delilah out of the corner of her eye. "I heard you had a pretty nice time, yourself."

She'd heard about Delilah's date? How? From whom? Delilah was thrown off, and she sat up straighter in her chair and turned to gape at Dolly.

"What did you hear? How?"

"I heard that you were out with Mr. Gorgeous, that Quinn Monroe. As for how I heard it? Well, this is a small town, honey. Everybody hears everything."

"But …"

"My friend Lola is the general manager over at Madeline's."

"But how does Lola even know who I am? How would she even know to tell you? I—"

"She was over at my place the other day having coffee—well, decaf for me, like I told you, my blood pressure—and you were getting Jesse and Gavin loaded into the car for some outing or another. Lola wanted to know if I had a new neighbor, so I told her about you."

"Oh, Dolly. I don't—"

"Now, you'd better get used to that sort of thing if you're going to be spending time here." Dolly let out a cackle. "Nobody means any harm in it, but we do like to mind other people's business."

Once Delilah got over the surprise of knowing her activities had been monitored and reported, the other part of what Dolly said hit her.

"So … you know Quinn?"

Dolly waved a hand airily. "Like I said, everyone—"

"Knows everyone," Delilah finished for her.

"That's right. Another friend of mine—Deb Foster—lives next door to him. I have to say, you couldn't have done better in the looks department. That man could be a movie star or a model or something. If my Melissa wasn't already married …"

Of course, Delilah already knew Quinn was hot. What she didn't know was pretty much everything else.

"Quinn and I just met," she told Dolly. "What kind of person is he?"

Dolly readjusted her butt in the chair and seemed to consider it. "Well, I don't know him personally, I just know who he is when I see him at the Cookie Crock or out on Main Street. But Deb says he's a nice boy."

Well, that was something. "That's good to know."

"He checks on her, you know. Deb's in her seventies, and she doesn't walk so well anymore—her doctor says she should start using a cane, but she's so stubborn she keeps refusing to do it—and he makes it a point to stop in and make sure she's okay."

Oh, God. It wasn't bad enough that he was irresistibly gorgeous. Did he also have to be helpful to old ladies? Delilah needed reasons *not* to like Quinn, not additional reasons to like him.

She was in enough trouble as it was.

Except I'm not, because I'm not going to get involved with him, she reminded herself. *We had a date, that's all. And that's all it's ever going to be.*

But that *wasn't* all it was. There had also been the kiss, and Delilah suspected she'd reacted to it in a way that would embarrass her if she were viewing it as an outsider. She'd reacted as though she'd been drowning and he'd saved her.

The only one who was going to save Delilah was herself.

"You've gotten quiet," Dolly observed.

"I'm just tired, that's all."

Dolly glanced at her with a mischievous grin. "You're tired after a date with a handsome man? Well, honey, good for you. Whatever happened last night to tire you out, I hope it was worth it."

Delilah felt herself blush, but she didn't correct Dolly. All that had happened was a kiss—that was true. But she'd wanted it to be so much more.

Dolly's smirk was at least somewhat justified.

TO QUINN'S MIND, the fact of the kiss, and the chemistry behind it, meant he and Delilah were going to see each other again.

Why wouldn't they? The kiss held so much promise. You kissed somebody as a test of whether you'd be good together physically, and they'd passed the test with spectacular success.

He still held firm on his idea that he was never going to get seriously involved with a single mother. But that was the beauty of the situation. She was only in town until the first of the year. The thing had a built-in expiration date. So, there could be no misunderstandings, no unrealistic expectations. They could have fun until January first and then part on happy terms.

It was perfect.

That was why he found it so puzzling when she ghosted him.

He texted her the afternoon after their date and got no reply. He waited a while, then called her. The call went straight to voice mail, so he left a message. He waited for her to call him back or text him, but again ... nothing.

Really?

Surely there had to be something wrong with her phone or some crisis she was dealing with. She couldn't just be ignoring him.

His conviction on this issue came from years of experience with women. He was the ghoster, not the ghosted. To have it go the other way was just ... surprising.

He told himself to forget about it as he went about his day. He finished the salmon article and submitted it to his editor at the fishing magazine. The furniture website was mostly complete, with just some fine-tuning left to do, so he sent an e-mail to the client with a link to what he'd done so far so he could get approval to finish up.

He played his music loud, because Mrs. Foster was out at her book club meeting. Aerosmith this time.

Should he go over to Delilah's place? Make some excuse, show up on some pretense, like bringing something for Gavin and Jesse?

That would be both pathetic and transparent, and you know it.

So he didn't do that. He just worked and tried to get lost in the music, and when that didn't get his mind off things, he took a walk.

Women. There was absolutely no making sense of them.

It was foolish to even try.

WHEN DELILAH GOT Quinn's text that afternoon, she was at the Cookie Crock, pushing a cart down the cereal aisle with Jesse and Gavin beside her. She looked at her phone, saw that the message was from him, and felt a jolt of what could only be described as pure electricity.

She stared at the screen, unsure what to do.

"Mom! Can we get this?" Jesse held up a box of sugary cereal, something with a cartoon character on the front.

"Honey, no. It's nothing but sugar."

"That's not fair."

"I want it," Gavin added.

She shoved the phone into her pocket and negotiated a cereal purchase until they'd found something kid-friendly that also resembled actual food. The boys weren't entirely happy, but they weren't complaining too loudly, either. To Delilah, that represented a win.

They proceeded down the aisle toward the granola bars, and Delilah took her phone out and looked at the message again.

I had a good time. When can we do it again?

He wasn't talking about the date itself—she was sure of it. He was talking about one specific part of it: the kiss.

Part of her really wanted to do it again—and soon—but another, wiser part of her knew that would be foolish.

She couldn't have flings with hot men who just wanted to toy with her. She was too mature for that. She had too many responsibilities.

"Mommy?" Gavin held up a box of granola bars in question.

"Okay, honey." She gave her consent, and Gavin put the box into the basket.

"Why are you on your phone?" Jesse demanded. "You always say it's not polite for people to be on their phone while they're supposed to be doing something else. You say that. And you're just on your phone when we're supposed to be buying groceries." His face held the indignation of the righteous.

Delilah let out a sigh. "Okay. You're right. I'll put it away." She slid the phone back into her pocket, but that didn't mean she'd stopped thinking about the text.

When can we do it again?

The problem was, if they did it again, she wouldn't want to stop at a kiss. She wouldn't want to stop at having sex—even great sex. She'd want to bury herself in him and forget everything in her life that was worrying her, everything that was weighing on her.

And she simply couldn't afford to do that.

The adult thing would be to tell him so, in clear, unambiguous terms. But he was so persuasive, she wasn't sure she'd be able to resist him.

Instead, she didn't respond, and she didn't respond later, at Otter Bluff, when he called and left a voice mail.

I'm being smart, she told herself. *I'm doing what's necessary.*

What was necessary really sucked sometimes.

CHAPTER 14

In the days leading up to Thanksgiving, Delilah's family was still nagging her to come home for the holiday, and the boys were still nagging her to see Quinn again.

She'd have been hard-pressed to say who was more persistent—her mother and her sister, or Jesse and Gavin.

When she started preparing for the Thanksgiving meal, it turned out that the persistence award went to her sons.

"We should invite Quinn for Thanksgiving," Jesse suggested as Delilah made her shopping list for the holiday meal.

"No, Jesse. We're not going to do that."

"Why not?" Gavin asked.

"Because he's probably got his own family and his own plans."

"You said probably!" Jesse pointed out in triumph. "That means you don't know. And that means he might not have any plans. So you should invite him."

It was early morning on the Tuesday before Thanksgiving, and Jesse's tawny hair was still mussed from sleep. He was wearing a pair of pajama pants and a Star Wars T-shirt, his feet bare and his eyes alight.

Next to him, Gavin was like a smaller version of his brother, his personality so different but his physical appearance—his hair, his eyes, and the shape of his nose—all nearly identical to his brother.

"Thanksgiving is for family," Delilah said. "Our family."

"That's not what you said before," Gavin put in. "You said it's for friends, too."

Had she said that? She probably had. Damn it.

"Quinn's our friend," Jesse insisted.

"I know he is, but we're not inviting him for Thanksgiving," Delilah said. "And the discussion is over."

Jesse's eyes narrowed. "No it's not, because I'm still talking about it. So that means the discussion is still happening."

"Well, I'm not still talking about it, so I guess you'll just have to talk to yourself."

Delilah picked up her note pad and pen and went into her bedroom, because she'd learned that walking away was sometimes the only way to end an argument with Jesse.

He pressed the issue a few more times later that day, but when Delilah threatened to take away his screen time if he didn't stop, he finally let it go.

In the relative peace that ensued, she was able to shop for ingredients for the meal, bake a pie, and enjoy the feel of the fall weather. She even bought a pumpkin spice coffee drink from Cambria Coffee Roasting Company on Main Street and sipped it as she sat at the beach while Jesse and Gavin romped on the sand.

Things were going to turn out okay.

And then the oven at Otter Bluff broke.

~

ON THE MORNING of Thanksgiving Day, Delilah set the oven to preheat, got the turkey out of the refrigerator, stuffed it, then opened the oven door to slide the pan onto the rack.

The only problem was, the oven wasn't hot.

She checked the digital readout and confirmed that she'd set it to

375 degrees. Maybe it actually was hot—maybe she just didn't feel it from where she was standing.

Carefully, she stuck a hand into the air inside the oven.

Nothing.

Tentatively, she touched a rack. Then, feeling no warmth whatsoever, she pressed her hand to the side wall of the interior.

Damn it.

She wrapped up the turkey, put it back in the refrigerator, then called Central Coast Escapes, the rental company that managed Otter Bluff. She got a recording that said the office was closed for the holiday. Just when she was about to lose hope, the recording offered a number to call in case of a house-related emergency.

Delilah called the number.

"Yes?" The voice on the other end was brusque.

"Is this the emergency number for Central Coast Escapes?"

"It is, yes. This is Elliot, the owner."

"Oh! Great. That's great. This is Delilah Ballard at Otter Bluff. My oven is broken."

"Oh, my," he said. "Well, I'm sorry to hear that, but I'm afraid it doesn't constitute an emergency."

"What? How can it not be an emergency? It's Thanksgiving, and I've got a stuffed, raw turkey in my kitchen." Delilah's voice rose with indignation.

"Well, I'll admit that's unfortunate. Be that as it may, when we say 'emergency,' we mean something dire. A gas leak, that sort of thing."

"A raw turkey on Thanksgiving isn't dire?"

"I'm afraid not, no. I can send someone out there to look at it on Monday, but with the holiday, I'm afraid I can't get it seen to before then."

Delilah forced herself to sound calm, even if what she really wanted was to yell at this asshole until he cried. "When I signed the contract to rent Otter Bluff, I was promised a working oven."

"Yes, I realize that. But if you check the contract, you were also promised that broken appliances would be attended to in a reasonable time frame. Immediate service on a national holiday isn't reasonable."

She hung up feeling defeated.

All she'd wanted was a nice, simple holiday meal with her sons. They didn't have their father, but at least she'd wanted to give them the things they were used to on Thanksgiving—and that included a damned turkey.

She put the phone on the counter and tried not to cry.

"What's wrong, Mommy?" Gavin wrapped one arm around her leg. The other one was occupied with thumb-sucking.

"Oh … nothing, sweetie. I'm fine." But then a fat tear slid down her cheek, and she knew she wasn't fooling anyone. "It's just … the oven broke, so I can't make the turkey."

Jesse had been listening in from where he'd just emerged from his room. "Remember that sign we saw yesterday that said Free Turkey Dinner? We could go there. It's free."

Delilah ruffled Gavin's hair. "Oh, sweetie, that's probably for people who can't afford to eat."

"No, it's not. It said everybody. That's what the sign said."

Delilah hadn't noticed the sign, and she figured Jesse had to be mistaken. But when she looked it up online, she saw that he was right. There was going to be a free community Thanksgiving dinner at the veterans' hall—apparently, it was an annual tradition. The needy were welcome, but so was everyone else.

It seemed wrong to show up for something like that, given the fact that the Ballards were just visitors. She didn't want to impose. So she started calling restaurants to find somewhere that was offering a traditional Thanksgiving meal.

It turned out that several restaurants were offering such a thing, but all of them were booked up.

Of course they were.

Desperate, she called the local supermarkets—not just the one in Cambria, but those in Morro Bay as well—to see if it was too late to get a cooked turkey.

It was.

"Why can't we go to the free one?" Jesse asked after Delilah had experienced one failure after another. She was sitting at the dining room table with her cell phone and her laptop, having failed to find any reasonable avenue for her family to eat a turkey.

"Well ... I guess that's what we're going to do," she said.

~

DELILAH HAD IMAGINED a soup-kitchen type of situation, with dry turkey, gummy gravy, and mashed potatoes out of a box with a slice of white bread on the side.

But when she and the boys arrived at the veterans' hall, she was impressed with the operation they had going. The food smelled wonderful, and the greeters at the door were warm and friendly. An older woman offered them name tags shaped like fall leaves and chatted with Jesse and Gavin about where they were from and how they were enjoying Cambria.

They proceeded into a buffet line that took them past hot trays of turkey, mashed potatoes, stuffing, rolls, salad, and cranberry sauce that looked as good as anything Delilah could have made herself. Smiling volunteers filled their plates. Against one wall was a table groaning with the weight of dozens of pies.

"This looks really good," Delilah said, looking down at her plate.

"See? I told you," Jesse said.

"You did," she agreed. "Gavin, did you get a roll? Come on, let's find a seat."

~

THEY GOT SETTLED in at a long table—one of dozens—in the big hall. Across from them was a local family with two teenagers, and next to Delilah on her left was an older man who struck up a conversation about how he'd come to live in Cambria more than thirty years before.

To her right, the boys were already wolfing down their food in the hopes of getting to their pie that much sooner.

The hall was decorated in turkeys, gourds, and fall leaves made of colorful paper, and the place was abuzz with the sounds of clinking silverware and conversation.

Delilah was starting to feel better about things when she saw Quinn Monroe come into the hall holding a plate of turkey and stuffing.

Her heart sped up and her palms started to sweat. She put down her fork and wiped her hands on her napkin.

Maybe he won't see me. There are a lot of people here. I can just get lost in the crowd.

It would be so much easier if they didn't talk, if she didn't feel that soft, gooey feeling she got when she was with him. If they didn't decide to go out again, and, please God, if they didn't kiss.

He sat down a couple of tables away with his back to her and started chatting with the gray-haired woman sitting beside him.

Okay. He wasn't facing her, so that was good. Maybe he would just eat his turkey, have his pie, and get the hell out of there without ever noticing her.

It might have worked that way if Jesse hadn't looked up just as Quinn turned his profile toward them.

"That's Quinn!" he said, loudly enough for half of the room to hear him.

Quinn certainly heard him. He stopped in the middle of whatever he'd been saying and looked back at them.

"Quinn!" Jesse waved excitedly.

Gavin joined in. "Hi! It's us! We're here having Thanksgiving dinner!"

A few people within range chuckled, remarking on how cute Gavin was, saying it that way as though all of them weren't there for the same reason.

Quinn waved at the boys, said something to the woman he'd been talking to, then got up and came toward them.

Oh, God.

"Jesse. Gavin." He nodded at the boys, his hands shoved into his jeans pockets. Then, almost reluctantly: "Delilah."

"Hi, Quinn. Happy Thanksgiving." Delilah tried to put some

enthusiasm into it, but it didn't come out the way she'd intended. It sounded more like she was a checker at Walmart who was repeating the greeting to conform with company policy.

"You too." He met her eyes in a way she found distinctly uncomfortable—as though those two words, *you too,* were actually an indictment of how she'd treated him.

She hadn't done anything wrong though, surely. Sometimes people only had a first date. Sometimes they tried it out and it didn't work. It happened all the time. She had a right to step away, damn it.

Even if she really, really hadn't wanted to step away.

Instead of getting into any of that, Quinn turned his attention to the boys. He squatted so he'd be at eye level with them as they sat at the table.

"So, how have you guys been?" he asked.

They told him what seemed like every single thing that had happened to them since he'd last seen them. Jesse told him about their beach outing and how he'd gotten a new video game at Target and how the oven had broken that morning. Gavin told him about his day-to-day activities in Cambria and then branched out into a story about his best friend at home—a friend Gavin was likely to never see again, Delilah thought with despair.

"Well, that's a lot of stuff going on," Quinn said, rubbing the stubble on his chin. "Sounds like you've been busy."

Delilah thought maybe that would be it—maybe he'd say goodbye and excuse himself and go back to his seat.

But at that moment, the couple sitting across the table from Delilah gathered their empty plates and their silverware and napkins and got up, vacating the spot.

"Sit here!" Jesse said. "Sit here with us! There's a space now! You can eat with us!"

"Please?" Gavin said.

Nobody except the most hard-hearted monster could resist Gavin when he said please.

Quinn hesitated, glanced at Delilah, then said, "Sure. Just let me get my plate."

DELILAH HAD SUDDENLY LOST her appetite.

It was hard to think about food when every molecule of your body was occupied with lusting after someone who was sitting less than three feet away from you. Even harder still when part of your conscious mind was busy fighting those urges.

Quinn got settled in, chatted a bit more with the boys, ate some turkey and mashed potatoes, then looked at Delilah in a way that, she was sure, was supposed to be casual.

"So. How are you?"

"Good." She nodded. "I'm good."

"Except for the oven at your place," he said.

"Right. Except that. I've got a raw, stuffed turkey in the refrigerator at Otter Bluff that's going to waste. Well, I suppose it won't go to waste. I can cook it when they fix the oven. Or, if that takes too long, I can probably ask Dolly—that's our neighbor—if I can borrow her oven. Still, it'll be too late for Thanksgiving, so."

She was rambling hopelessly, and she urged herself to shut the hell up.

"You can never have too much turkey," Quinn put in helpfully.

Privately, Delilah disagreed, but it seemed foolish to dig her feet in on the issue.

They made small talk about what they'd both been doing until Jesse and Gavin showed Delilah their empty plates and asked if they could go to the dessert table to get pie.

"Oh. Sure." Delilah put her fork aside and started to get up to take them.

Then one of the volunteers, a woman in her sixties who was wearing a fall-themed apron and who had been patrolling the hall, clearing plates, and refilling beverages, offered to do it. "I can take them," she said. "You enjoy your meal. I'll have them back in a jiffy." She took Jesse and Gavin by the hands and walked them across the hall to where an array of pies—pumpkin, pecan, chocolate, apple, and more—awaited.

Quinn hadn't mentioned anything about their date in front of the boys, and Delilah was thankful for that. But now the boys were out of earshot, and she had no more cover.

He put his elbows on the table, interlaced his fingers beneath his chin, and regarded her.

Here it comes, she thought.

~

QUINN HAD GONE through an entire turkey dinner without asking Delilah the one question that was on his mind. But now that the boys were occupied, there was nothing to keep him from asking it.

His pride—that might prevent him from asking. But, screw it. He needed to know.

"So, what happened? Why didn't you return my text messages or my phone calls?" He kept his voice neutral, as though it were merely idle curiosity.

"Quinn …"

He interrupted her. "I'm not mad about it. I'm not going to be one of those guys who turns creepy as shit when you reject them. I just want to know, that's all."

She avoided his eyes, looking down at her plate instead. "Maybe I'm just not ready."

He nodded. "Okay."

"I just … It was a big step for me, Quinn. Going out with someone. And that's what it was—one step. I'm not ready for more. I'm not ready to run a marathon."

He didn't say anything for a moment. His eyes narrowed a little as he regarded her and tried to decide how much of what she was saying was true and how much was bullshit.

Mostly true, he thought, and that was fine.

But it wasn't going to get him where he wanted to go—if he even knew where the hell that was.

"I get it," he said at last. "But I'd just like to point out that a first step is usually followed by a second one, and then one after that.

Otherwise, that marathon might as well be in outer space for all the chance you have of finishing it."

He stood up from his seat, picked up his plate, silverware, and glass, and nodded once. "See you later, Delilah. Or maybe I won't. Either way, happy Thanksgiving."

The boys ran up just as he was making his escape, Jesse holding a plate of pumpkin pie piled high with whipped cream, Gavin with apple. The volunteer who'd taken them to get the pie was leading them back to Delilah.

"Quinn! Where are you going?" Jesse wanted to know.

Gavin had his free thumb plugged into his mouth, his eyes wide, so he didn't say anything.

"I've gotta go, buddy. I've got somewhere to be," he lied.

"Are you going to see your family for Thanksgiving?" Jesse asked.

"Something like that."

"But you didn't get any pie," Jesse said.

"Ah ... I'll grab some on the way out."

Gavin pulled his thumb out of his mouth and held out his pie plate to Quinn. "You can have mine." He said it so earnestly that the sweetness of it—the kindness—nearly broke his heart.

"That's okay, Gavin." He knelt down at the boy's eye level. "That's really nice of you, but you have it. I'll get some from over there." He gestured toward the pie table.

"Are we going to see you again soon?" Jesse said.

"I hope so." His voice sounded a little rough, and he cleared his throat. "Listen, you guys go back to your mom, all right? Enjoy that pie."

Then he got the hell out of there before he could do something stupid, like hug them.

DELILAH COULDN'T HELP WATCHING Quinn go. He hadn't said anything to indicate he was hurt, but something in the set of his back, the fluidity of his movements, told her he was.

Damn it, she'd never wanted that. She'd never wanted to hurt him.

But she hadn't wanted to hurt herself, either, and that would be inevitable if she'd let this thing go any further.

She waited while the boys finished their pie, then she mopped up their messy faces the best she could with napkins.

Finally, she put on the most cheerful voice she could manage.

"Okay, guys. Are you ready? Let's go back to Otter Bluff, and we can watch a movie."

CHAPTER 15

Later that day, Delilah called her mother to say happy Thanksgiving, because she could get away with not being there—just barely—but there was no way she could neglect her family entirely on the holiday.

On the phone, she could hear the clamor of people and activity in the background—the murmur of football on the TV, and the sounds of her father, her uncle, and a couple of cousins yelling at the screen.

"How'd dinner go, Mom?" She raised her voice above the ruckus.

"Delilah? Honey, let me get somewhere quieter. I can barely hear you." A moment later, the noise died down. "There, I'm in the bedroom. Men and football. I swear."

Delilah tried again. "I was just asking how dinner went."

"Oh, you know. It was fine. Three days of cooking just so everyone can devour it in twenty minutes and leave me with all the cleanup." She chuckled in a way that let Delilah know she wouldn't have it any other way.

"You should tell Dad to help."

"Oh, he's enjoying his game. And Roxanne's helping. I just like to complain."

In truth, Delilah's mother rarely complained, even when she had a right to it.

"We missed you," Jeanette said.

"I miss you, too."

"Well, there was nothing stopping you from being here." Her mother's tone was firm, and she sounded a little put out.

Delilah closed her eyes and willed herself not to get into it. To change the subject, she told her mother about how the oven at Otter Bluff had broken, and how that had led her and the boys to the Cambria community Thanksgiving dinner.

"It was really nice," she went on. "And the food—my God. An entire team of people must have been cooking for a week."

"You ate your holiday dinner with strangers instead of your own family?"

Delilah felt the pressure of stress building in her chest. "Hey, Mom? Is Roxanne there? I'd like to talk to her."

"Delilah, I wasn't finished. I'd like to know why you—"

"Just give Roxanne the phone, Mom. Please."

Jeanette was quiet for a moment. Finally, she relented. "Fine. Hang on a minute."

~

"HEY." Roxanne sounded cheerful. "How's it going out there on the West Coast? See any movie stars lately?"

"That's in Los Angeles. I'm hours north of there."

"Well, that's a shame. I hope you at least had some good turkey."

Delilah told her the story of the oven and the dinner—and about how she'd run into Quinn.

"Ooh, the plot thickens," Roxanne said. "I guess that's the trouble with ghosting somebody in a small town. They have a way of turning up when you least expect it."

"I didn't ghost him."

"You didn't return his texts or his calls. I'm pretty sure that's what *ghosting* means."

Delilah wasn't about to get into a debate over the definition of a term that hadn't even existed five years ago. And that wasn't the point, anyway.

"He asked me what happened. What he did wrong." It hurt Delilah even to think of it—to remember the conversation and all of its nuances.

"So what did you tell him?"

"I ... Well. I basically admitted that I'd used him as training wheels to ... you know. Get back on the bike. Not in those words. It was a lot more polite than that, but that was the gist."

"And he objected to being your training wheels?"

"Not exactly."

"Well, what then?"

"He suggested that maybe, once I've gotten my balance, I might want to actually ride somewhere."

"Or some*one*," Roxanne put in.

"Charming," Delilah said.

"Well, I think he's got a point." Roxanne jumped to Quinn's defense. "Why bother with the training wheels if you're not, at some point, going to go for a really great ride? A really great, exciting, high-speed, satisfying ride."

She was clearly enjoying herself more than Delilah was.

"I think we've taken that metaphor as far as it needs to go," Delilah said.

"I'm not sure we have. I haven't even touched on the possible handlebar references yet."

"You're hilarious."

"I really am." Roxanne's voice turned serious. "Delilah, I mean it, though. If you're not ready to get into something, I understand that. I really do. But if you like this guy, it seems a shame to let him go just because Mitch is an asshole."

This last bit took Delilah by surprise. "That's not the reason. This isn't ... I'm not letting Mitch make my life decisions for me."

"Aren't you, though? He's out of your life, at least on a day-to-day basis, and if you ask me, that's great. That's a big step forward. But you're still living based on how he makes you feel. And in a way, that's worse than you still being married to him."

~

OVER THE NEXT couple of days, Delilah couldn't get what Roxanne had said out of her head.

Was she still letting Mitch control her? Were her feelings about him and her divorce determining what she did with her life? Was she still emotionally tethered to him in a way that would allow him to continue hurting her, over and over, until she was so used to the abuse that she considered it normal?

She couldn't allow it. She wouldn't.

She stewed over it as she took the boys to the natural history museum in Morro Bay; as she dealt with the repair guy Central Coast Escapes had sent over to fix the oven; and as she scanned real estate listings in Connecticut—not in Greenwich, where she'd lived with Mitch, but in Danbury, where she'd grown up and where her parents still lived.

The more she thought about it, the more indignant she became about the idea of Roxanne—or anyone—thinking she was still being controlled by Mitch.

And the more indignant she was about Roxanne thinking it, the more outraged she became at the idea of Quinn thinking it, too.

Of course, Quinn had never said outright that he thought that, but it seemed likely that he did. What, was the whole world convinced that Delilah had no backbone, no spine? And why? Because she didn't leave Mitch when she first suspected he was cheating on her? Because she hung in there, hoping the problem would go away? She was being a wife, damn it. She was upholding her vows.

And now here she was with no husband, no home, no dignity, and no earthly idea how to move forward.

The least—the very least—she could do was tell Quinn Monroe where he could shove his ideas about her and her goddamned bicycle.

It was Tuesday before she'd worked up a full head of steam. Once she did, she called Dolly, pried to find out where Quinn lived—Dolly had said his next-door neighbor was her friend, so of course she knew—and arranged to leave the boys with Dolly for an hour while Delilah went over there to hand him his ass.

She could have called him, but a good ass-handing needed to be done in person, in her view.

Delilah drove to Lodge Hill, followed Google Maps to find the house where Dolly's friend lived, then used her powers of deduction—and the fact that Quinn's van was parked at the house next door—to find him.

She parked her car, marched up the front walkway, her feet slapping determinedly against the paving stones, and banged on his door.

He didn't respond to the banging at first, probably because of the music that was blasting so loud it seemed to make the windows rattle. She banged louder, pounding the side of her fist against the door.

"Quinn! Open the door!"

She must have gotten through, because the music turned off, and a few seconds later, the door swung open. Quinn was standing there in nothing but a pair of jeans, his hair mussed, a two-day growth of beard shadowing his jaw.

His lack of a shirt threatened to throw her off of her mission, but she refused to be deterred.

"What's wrong? What happened? Is everything okay? Are Gavin and Jesse all right?"

That threw her off a little. "What? Yes. Why wouldn't they be?"

"It's just, the way you were hammering on the door and yelling, I thought—"

"I was hammering and yelling because you couldn't hear me over the music. I think I suffered partial hearing loss. Good God, are you sixteen? What the hell?"

His expression hardened. "I like it loud."

"Apparently."

"So if there's no emergency, why are you here?"

Right. Back to the point.

"I'm here because you apparently think I don't want to go out with you again because I'm so emotionally stunted after my divorce that I can't function. And that's just offensive! It's just wrong! And I won't have it, Quinn. I won't have it."

He rubbed the stubble on his chin. "Is that what I believe?"

"It's what everyone believes! It's what my sister believes, and it's just ... it's demeaning! And cruel. And wrong. So you can take your assumptions about my emotional state and ... and ..."

"And what?" He raised his eyebrows in question.

"And go to hell!"

Delilah was so fired up that she was glaring at him, her fists balled up at her sides.

"Is that right?" His own manner was calm, reasoned.

"Yes. It is."

He seemed to consider her. "Well, if I'm already going to hell, I guess this won't make it any worse." He reached out, grabbed her around the waist, pulled her to him, and devoured her mouth with his.

~

QUINN HADN'T MEANT to kiss her. He'd meant to tell her she didn't know what the hell she was talking about in regard to him and what he thought about her. But what he meant to do and what he actually did got mixed up somewhere between the thinking and the doing.

Now that he was kissing her, thinking was no longer part of the equation.

God, she felt good. And she smelled good—like the lavender in Mrs. Foster's garden. And the way she tasted made him want to lick and kiss and run his tongue down every part of her.

They'd get to that later, God willing. For now, there was this gorgeous, delicious kiss, and there might as well have been nothing else in the world.

If she'd pushed him away, he'd have accepted it gracefully. He'd have apologized and taken his hands off her and let her go on her way.

But this—the way she was clinging to him and melting against him and grasping at him—that was less expected but entirely more welcome.

His senses were alive and thrumming even as his brain shut off, making it impossible to think. Which was why he didn't consider, even for a second, his resolution not to get involved with a woman who had more baggage than the carousels at LAX.

He pulled her into the house and shoved the door closed with his foot without breaking the kiss and without taking his hands off her.

Delilah was much shorter than he was, which was hampering him somewhat, so he lifted her and pressed her back against the closed door, his hands under her ass for support. She wrapped her legs around his waist, and that made him wish she were doing it naked.

Well, they could make that happen.

He broke the kiss just long enough to grunt, "Bedroom." Apparently, he'd reverted to some primitive version of himself. Otherwise, he'd have been speaking in full sentences to ask her how she felt about taking things to the next level.

As it was, there were no full sentences. There was only her body and her mouth and the way they were making him feel.

Until she put her hands on his shoulders and started shoving him away.

"Quinn. Wait. Quinn." Delilah pushed at him, and his eyes, which had been half-closed, opened and blinked as though he were slowly coming back to full consciousness.

He lowered her to her feet, stepped back to put the barest space between them, then took in a ragged breath and ran his hands through his hair. "Don't try to tell me you don't want me. Not after that. Because I won't believe you."

"I do. I do want you. It's just ..."

"It's just what?"

She laid her hands flat on his chest, not pushing him away anymore, just feeling the solid warmth of him. "If we do this, it'll be for the wrong reasons. I'd be using you to get back at my ex. Or, maybe not to get back at him, but to get over him. I'd be treating you like a ... like a *thing*, Quinn."

He looked at her with something inscrutable in his eyes. A muscle in his jaw tightened.

"Works for me," he said.

She stared at him, then nodded. "Me too."

Delilah let out a yelp of surprise as he picked her up and carried her into the bedroom.

CHAPTER 16

"Oh, my God! You did it! You finally did it!" Roxanne practically squealed with glee that evening when Delilah called to tell her what happened. "They say the best way to get over someone is to get under someone else, right? Oh, my God. This is so great."

Delilah got the feeling her sister didn't fully understand the situation. "But ... you don't get it. I'm not ready for a relationship! I was just ... just relieving stress!"

Privately, she worried that she was lying, both to herself and to Roxanne. It hadn't felt like she was just relieving stress. It had felt like a hell of a lot more than that.

But it couldn't be more. She wasn't ready for more, and she didn't know if she ever would be.

"Well, did it work?" Roxanne asked. "Did it relieve your stress?"

"God ... did it ever."

Roxanne whooped in joy. "Well, good for you!"

"But what about Quinn?" Delilah protested. "I mean ... I slept with him knowing it's not going to go anywhere! When men do that to women, we think they're awful. We think they're the worst kind of lowlife scum. I don't want to be scum, Roxanne!"

Roxanne's voice changed as though she were speaking to a particularly dense toddler. "Delilah. Did you at any point suggest to Quinn that you might want to marry him and have his children?"

"No! Of course not."

"Did you persuade him to give you sexual favors by hinting that you might want to be his long-term sweetie?"

"Roxanne—"

"I'll assume you didn't. Did you tell him you wanted to go steady even though you secretly know you're not ever going to wear his letterman's jacket?"

"You're a scream." Delilah's delivery dripped with sarcasm.

"Since you didn't tell him any of those things," Roxanne went on, "nor did you even *suggest* any of those things, I'm going to assume he went into it with his eyes open. He can make his own decisions. He's a grown man."

"You can say that again."

"Oh ho! Now we're getting into it. Give me the details, Delilah. I need to live vicariously through you. It's been years since Joey and I got it on."

"Years? Oh, my God. I had no idea."

"Well, it's been a week. But it feels like years. Don't change the subject. Come on. Details."

Delilah told her sister what happened: how she'd worked up a head of steam over the things she imagined Quinn thought of her, how she'd gone over there prepared to tell him off, and how he'd grabbed her and kissed her senseless. And then had done things to her she'd previously only read about in the sex articles in *Cosmo*.

"He picked you up? He literally picked you up?" That, for some reason, was the detail Roxanne had chosen to fixate on.

"He just lifted me up like I weighed nothing. He was like a … a caveman or something."

"But better smelling, I hope," Roxanne said.

The thought of Quinn's smell sent Delilah into a reverie so deep and engaging that she momentarily forgot she was in the middle of a conversation.

"Delilah? Are you still there? Hey, focus!"

"I ... I'm here."

"Look," Roxanne said. "I know you're worried about all of this and what it means, but you don't need to be. Just have fun. Just see where it goes."

Where it might go—that's what was worrying Delilah. She hadn't thought much about where things might go when she'd started dating Mitch, and look how that had worked out. Marrying him had been like sticking her leg in a bear trap.

If she let things with Quinn get out of control, next thing she knew she might be pondering the option of gnawing off her own foot just to get free.

~

IN THE WAKE of his encounter with Delilah, Quinn didn't feel the way he was supposed to feel.

In his experience, hooking up with a woman left him relaxed, happy, and carefree. But this particular hookup had him thinking about what came next, and that was decidedly unsettling.

He wasn't used to thinking about what came next. And he wasn't used to worrying about what that would be.

Quinn wasn't the kind of guy who rejected a woman after he slept with her just because the thrill of the conquest was over. He hated those guys.

But usually, after he'd been with someone, he didn't think about whether to call her, or when, or what to say when he did. If he wanted to call, he called. If he didn't want to, he didn't. He never gave anyone any false impressions about where things might lead, so it was okay.

It was simple, mostly because he didn't play games, and he didn't lie to anyone.

Except he'd lied to Delilah, hadn't he? When he'd said he was okay with being used—with being treated like an object—that wasn't true. It had *felt* true at the time, but now? Now he wanted her to see him as a person.

And not just any person, come to that. He wanted to be *the* person.

When the hell had that happened? When had he gone from casually flirting and thinking about an attractive woman to wanting a prominent place in her life?

It was stupid, that's what it was.

After spending the night tossing and turning, thinking about Delilah, Quinn decided he needed to get away—mostly so he wouldn't go over to her place and make a fool of himself.

So the day after they'd been together, he packed up the van with some winter clothes and snow boots, tire chains, and a cooler full of drinks and snacks, and he headed out to Kings Canyon National Park.

The park was a three-hour drive from Cambria, but he figured the time on the road would do him some good and help him clear his head. Plus, something about being among the giant redwoods made him feel small and vulnerable, but in a good way—as though his own problems were insignificant and therefore not worthy of his own anxious worry.

He got on the road a little after nine a.m., grabbed some lunch in Visalia, then rolled into the park by early afternoon.

He'd prepared for snow, because you never knew, but there wasn't much this early in the season. He opted for his hiking boots instead of the snow boots, put on a warm jacket against the late fall chill, slipped a bottle of water and a protein bar into his pocket, and set out to do a brisk five miles on the Cedar Grove Overlook Trail.

For a while, out there among the trees and the boulders, with the crunch of the earth underneath his feet and the bright blue sky spread out above him, he felt great. He stopped feeling the cold as a light sweat formed on his skin from good, solid exertion. His muscles were loose and his movements easy as he made his way along the trail, accompanied only by the occasional wildlife scampering around at the edge of his vision.

But then, something horrifying happened.

He realized he had no cell coverage out here and wouldn't know if Delilah tried to call him.

What was he, in high school? Since when had he obsessed over whether a girl was going to call him? Hell, he hadn't done that even when he *was* in high school.

Traditionally, the man was the one to call the woman. But that didn't really apply here, since Delilah had made it clear she was using him for his body. If he called, he would seem like some needy asshole who couldn't handle that kind of arrangement—even though he'd assured her he could.

If anyone called, it should be her. In a perfect world, she would call him and tell him she'd realized she wanted more than what she'd said. That their time together had meant more than she'd said it did.

Of course, this was far from a perfect world.

In *this* world, this real world, he might have to make it happen, if that was what he wanted. He might have to convince her to let him into her life. Which would mean he had to call her instead of waiting around for her to decide she wanted him.

Only he *couldn't* call her, because he was out here in the goddamned wilderness.

If she did call and he didn't answer, would that solidify her thought that he wasn't worth the effort? Or would it work for him in a playing-hard-to-get kind of way?

Okay, it was official: he was losing his mind.

People always said women could do that to you, but somehow, he'd gotten this far in life without it happening.

Until now.

Shut it down, Quinn. Just shut it down.

He needed to be in the moment, enjoy his hike, and stop thinking. And that's what he did for another mile or so, until he saw a man and a couple of kids on the trail up ahead of him. The kids were two boys, maybe ten and twelve years old, and from back here, they looked a lot like how Gavin and Jesse would look when they got to that age.

Gavin and Jesse. If they were here, he'd show them all of the great stuff in the park—the General Sherman tree, Crystal Cave, and the tunnel log you could drive through.

They'd love that.

It occurred to him that thinking wistfully about Delilah's kids was an even bigger warning sign than thinking about Delilah herself.

He finished the hike, got checked into an RV parking spot with power and water hookups, lay back on his bed for a nap—and then thought, *fuck it.*

Whether she called him or he called her, somebody was calling somebody, by God.

He unhooked the van, drove out of the park, and headed back toward civilization where he could get some damned cell phone service.

CHAPTER 17

Delilah got a call from Quinn the afternoon following the unintended sex. And that was how she thought of it: *the unintended sex.* That way, it seemed more like an accident—as though she'd tripped, maybe, and fell on him—instead of a calculated thing she'd done to screw up her life.

She hadn't expected him to call, and she certainly hadn't intended to call him. After all, they'd made it clear that it was just physical release, nothing more. You didn't expect follow-up calls for something like that.

That was why she was surprised when her cell phone rang and the readout on the screen said his name.

She was in Jesse's room picking up dirty clothes from the floor and piling them into a laundry hamper when it happened.

She clicked on the button to accept the call, took a moment to collect herself, and answered.

"Hi, Quinn."

"Hi? That's all you have to say to me? Just, *hi?*"

She blinked once in surprise. "Was there something else I should have said?"

"No. Of course not. You shouldn't have said anything, because we shouldn't even be talking, because you were never going to call me, were you?" He sounded angry. Behind him, she heard voices and the clatter of plates.

"Where are you?"

"Does that matter?"

"I guess not."

"I'm at a Denny's in Visalia. Not that you care."

She shifted the laundry hamper onto her hip. "Why are you at a Denny's in Visalia?"

"Because I was camping, and there's no cell service at the park, so I came here to check my phone. Because I thought, foolishly, that maybe you'd called me. But you didn't, so."

Confused, Delilah put down the hamper, rubbed her eyes with her free hand, then waved at the air as though her confusion were a cloud of smoke in front of her.

"Back up, Quinn. Walk me through what's happening, because I don't know what you're talking about."

She heard him take a deep breath and let it out. "Ah, shit. I'm losing my mind, that's what's happening. I'm acting like a girl."

"You're acting like something."

In the background, she heard a waitress offer him coffee, and Quinn declined. Then he turned his attention back to her.

"We had a … a moment," he said. "A very good moment. And after two people have that kind of moment, it's customary for them to talk to each other. Often, on the phone. But I didn't want to be the one to call, because you told me you were using me for my body, and I told you I was okay with that, and then I didn't want to suddenly not be okay with that."

Delilah sat down on the edge of Jesse's bed. "All right …"

"But it turns out, I'm not okay with it. The sex part, yes. But the part where that's all you want from me? Not so much."

Delilah's heart began to hammer in her chest. "Quinn, what are you saying?"

"I'm saying I want us to be more than that. More than somebody using somebody. More than sex. I want us to give this thing a chance and see where it goes."

"Oh." Something fluttered inside her belly—something that threatened her security, her sense of safety, her very way of life. Something that might be irresistible. "But, tell me again why you're in a Denny's in Visalia?"

He sighed. "I wanted to call you, but I then I *didn't* want to because of what you'd said about using me. But I also didn't want to be some needy asshole waiting around for a woman to pay attention to him. So I went camping to get my mind off the whole thing. But it didn't work, so here I am at a Denny's in Visalia. I'm here because I couldn't stop thinking about you."

~

QUINN HELD HIS BREATH, waiting for Delilah's response. Then he realized he was holding his breath and forced himself to let it out.

He hadn't meant to tell her all of that, but then again, he hadn't meant to do any of this—he hadn't meant to call her, and he hadn't meant to want her like this in the first place.

He hadn't meant to need her.

None of this was going the way he'd planned.

But now that he'd said what he'd said, he found himself hanging on her answer.

"I can't stop thinking about you, either," she said. "But …"

Ah, God. Of course there was a *but*.

"But what?"

"But it's complicated." Her voice was small, as though if she couldn't hear herself saying these things, then maybe none of it was really happening.

"Of course it's complicated. Relationships are always complicated. At least, the best ones are."

Hadn't he, just days before, promised himself that he would not get involved with a single mother? Hadn't he assured himself that it was far too much baggage for him to carry? And now here he was, arguing in favor of complications. Funny how much things could change in a day.

"The boys need stability," she said. "They've been through too much for me to bring another man into their lives, just for it to—"

"To what?"

"Just for it to *end,* Quinn! Because it's going to end! I have a life in Connecticut, and you have a life here, and even if that weren't the case, even if I weren't going to leave in a month, things end! And when they do, it hurts like hell, and I can't do that again—not to myself, and not to the boys."

"Who says it's going to end? Sometimes it doesn't. Sometimes it just keeps going."

He hadn't planned to say that, and now that it was out of his mouth, he was a little bit appalled. He'd gone from wanting to sleep with her to wanting to date her to suggesting that this might, in fact, be permanent.

All in a span of twenty-four hours.

He was right when he'd told her he was losing his mind.

"Look, why not give it a chance?" he said, summing up his argument. "If it doesn't work for you, you've got an out already built in. You're going home in a month. If we give it a try and you decide I'm not for you, then you just stick with the plan and flee as soon as your rental period at Otter Bluff is up. But if it does work, if you decide it's worth more time ..." He left it hanging, just left it out there for her to mentally fill in the blanks.

"Quinn ..."

"I'm just asking you to leave your options open. That's all."

With his free hand, he repeatedly crumpled a paper napkin and then smoothed it atop the booth's table. Crumple, smooth, crumple, smooth.

Kind of the way his heart felt these days.

"I'll think about it," she said finally.

He sat up straighter in his seat. "You will?"

"Yes."

"Does that mean you'll see me again?"

"That's what I'll be thinking about."

He grinned. "Well, think fast, because I already miss you."

~

It wasn't supposed to be like this, Delilah thought as she sat on Jesse's bed, holding her cell phone in her lap and thinking about Quinn's call. She wasn't supposed to jump into another relationship. She was supposed to take time to get herself together and decide what she wanted in the wake of her divorce.

Was that too much to ask?

She wasn't the kind of woman things like this happened to. She'd never been someone who had handsome men falling all over her. She'd barely dated before she'd met Mitch, and then, once she was married, she must have given off housewife vibes, because men had barely looked at her after that.

Until Quinn.

So, what was she supposed to do? Was she supposed to just put herself out there—put her kids out there—and pray that they didn't get hurt?

That's how it works, idiot. You put yourself out there and pray you don't get hurt. That's how relationships have always worked since the beginning of time. There's no other way.

The fact was, he made her feel good. Scared, but good. She hadn't felt good in so long that she'd forgotten what it was like. She'd given up on the idea of feeling good—at least when it came to men.

If it doesn't work, I've got an out.

That's what he'd said, and he was right. She could walk away in a month if she had to. Or even if she just wanted to.

God, she was so tired of being alone. Of being lonely. She'd been alone and lonely since long before Mitch left—she just hadn't realized it.

She wanted to let herself be happy, but the risks were substantial.

Delilah pulled up her text message app and typed in a message: *The boys can't know we're dating. Not until we know how it's going to go. They have to think we're just friends.*

She sent the message, cursing herself for being weak and stupid enough to put herself at risk again.

In a moment, his response came.

Are we dating, then?

She closed her eyes, took in a deep breath, and let it out. Then she answered him.

God help me, yes. I think we are.

Life was nothing without risk.

CHAPTER 18

Now that he and Delilah were officially a thing, Quinn wanted to show her a good time—not only so she'd want to keep seeing him, but also, if all went well, to get her hooked on Cambria itself. He figured he had a better chance of getting her to stay around past January first if he could sell her on the town's charms as well as his own.

Fortunately, Hospitality Night was coming up, and that seemed to him like just what he needed.

"What's Hospitality Night?" she asked when he called to invite her to go with him.

"Well, I'm sure you've noticed that everything tends to close up early around here," he said. It was an understatement. Most of the restaurants were only open for breakfast and lunch, and the boutiques tended to shut down at five p.m.—earlier if business was slow.

"Yes. I have noticed."

"Every year for one night in December, everybody stays open late and puts out drinks, snacks. There's music, everybody's out on the sidewalks. It's like a party," he told her.

"That does sound fun. I'll see if I can get a babysitter."

"No, don't." He said this last part on impulse. "The whole thing's kid friendly. Santa's gonna be there. The boys will love it. Bring them."

"Really? Are you sure you don't mind?"

He thought he detected a hint of excitement in her voice.

"You bet. I can take you all out to eat first. Let's make a night of it."

Delilah hesitated. "Oh, but ... the boys ..."

He knew what she was getting at, and he jumped on it before it could become an issue. "I remember what you said—they can't know we're dating. So we won't kiss or hold hands or declare our undying love for each other in front of them. We'll just be friends hanging out."

"Just friends hanging out," she repeated.

"Sure. Except that I'll be imagining you naked."

She giggled, and he knew he was in—at least for the date, if not for the naked part.

THEY STARTED at the Main Street Grill for burgers, because burgers seemed kid-friendly. They sat out on the patio, because the evening was mild, and they shared a basket of fries as big as a hubcap.

As they ate, the boys excitedly told Quinn about everything that was going on in their lives—how Jesse had enjoyed a phone call with his best friend from home, how Gavin had done a video call with his grandmother, and how both of them were missing school to be in Cambria.

"Yours doesn't matter, though," Jesse told Gavin. "It's only preschool. It's not even school. I'm missing kindergarten."

"Preschool is school," Gavin said around a mouthful of burger. "It's in the name, even."

"Honey, don't talk with your mouth full," Delilah admonished him gently. "And yes, Jesse, preschool is school."

"That's kind of a shame, missing kindergarten," Quinn remarked.

"Yeah, well," Delilah said. "Jesse was going to have to change schools anyway. Now that the house is sold, and with the divorce, we're not going to be staying in the same school district. In Connecticut they let you skip kindergarten with a waiver, so ..."

"So you're going to go straight into first grade?" Quinn asked Jesse. "Dude, that's cool. Kindergarten's kid stuff anyway, right?"

"I can already read," Jesse said. "And I know my numbers and I can add and stuff. So I don't need kindergarten."

"He misses his friends, though. And his teacher." Delilah's eyes started to well up, and she blinked quickly so the boys wouldn't see. Quinn saw, though. "And," she went on, more brightly, "he won't miss the whole rest of the school year. Once we get settled somewhere, he can do the last semester."

"I don't need to," Jesse insisted. "I don't. Mom—"

"You *do* need to." Delilah rested her hand on Jesse's head for a moment, then changed the subject. "Quinn, tell us more about Hospitality Night."

~

DELILAH HADN'T WANTED to get into it about Jesse and Gavin's schooling or how unsettled they were as a family, but it was hard to avoid the topic once the kids started talking about friends and family and school.

And now that Delilah and Quinn were dating—however covertly—it seemed like a delicate subject to talk about what the Ballard family might be doing next.

The topic of Hospitality Night was a handy diversion. The more Quinn talked about the Christmas cookies and cider, the carolers, and the events that were planned, the more excited the boys got.

"And, of course, we'll have to swing by and see Santa," Quinn said.

Gavin's eyes widened. "Santa?"

Quinn waved a hand dismissively. "Are you kidding? Of course Santa's going to be there. It wouldn't be much of a celebration without him, would it?"

"Santa's not real, dummy," Jesse told Gavin.

"Of course he is," Delilah said.

"If you don't believe, you don't receive," Quinn said. "We'll see who's the dummy come Christmas morning."

Jesse looked doubtful. "You mean I won't get any presents if I don't believe in Santa?" he asked Delilah.

"Well, you'll get gifts from me, of course. And your grandparents and Aunt Roxanne have sent some things, so you'll get those. But Santa ..." She gave him a rueful look. "I'm afraid I can't guarantee anything."

Jesse spent the rest of the meal looking worried.

~

AFTER DINNER, they started walking along Main Street and visiting boutiques, most of which had tables of cookies and cupcakes along with carafes of coffee, cocoa, and hot apple cider.

The boys wanted to grab the first cookies they saw, but Delilah cautioned them. "You're going to have to choose two cookies each, because I don't want you two making yourselves sick. So, you'd better take your time and choose carefully."

"Your mom's right, guys," Quinn added. "Plus, last year, one of the shops did s'mores. You wouldn't want to miss that because you're already filled up on substandard grocery store cookies."

Jesse and Gavin both perked up at the mention of s'mores, and they contented themselves with paper cups of hot cocoa for the time being as they walked from store to store looking at locally made crafts, Cambria souvenirs, paintings of the local coastline, and even a selection of plush sea creatures like sea lions and the occasional narwhal.

The mood was festive as Quinn called out to people he knew, making small talk and introducing them to the Ballards.

"This is Delilah, and this is Jesse and Gavin," Quinn told one of the shopkeepers who'd greeted Quinn enthusiastically.

The shopkeeper was wearing a Santa hat, its tip flopping down around the man's left shoulder. "You boys having a good time?" he asked.

"Yeah. This is really cool," Jesse said, and Gavin nodded, his thumb in his mouth.

They listened to carolers, watched a group of people perform a choreographed dance in the street to the tune of "Jingle Bell Rock," and had their pictures taken with Santa at the Cambria Historical Museum on Center Street. Then they found the s'mores station, and Delilah finally gave the okay for the boys to indulge.

A guy manning an outdoor gas grill browned two marshmallows, assembled the s'mores, and handed them to Jesse and Gavin. Within minutes, both of the boys were a mess of chocolate and marshmallow fluff.

Delilah wanted to maintain her emotional distance, wanted to keep the reality of her situation firmly in her mind. But before she knew it, she was caught up in the festivity of the event. She found herself smiling, and for a while, it was possible to think she was actually happy.

When Quinn stole a kiss while the boys were looking the other way, she didn't try to stop him. She just savored it, not knowing when she might have something that simple and perfect again.

~

QUINN HAD NEVER REALLY UNDERSTOOD why people had kids. Someone to take care of you in your old age? Sure, that made sense. Someone to carry on the genetic line? Okay, if you were into that sort of thing.

But hanging out with Jesse and Gavin made him see the point of it. The two of them were kind of a kick. Their excitement over Hospitality Night—and over Christmas itself—made the whole thing seem a lot more fun.

Hell, if he could have kids like these two, he wouldn't mind a bit. It might even be pretty cool to be a father. One day. Eventually. If he met the right woman.

The thing was, he was starting to think he'd already met the right woman.

He told himself to slow his roll as they walked amid the crowd on Main Street, enjoying the holiday decorations and the overall sense of community fun.

Delilah had barely agreed to date him, and she was planning to move to the other side of the country after New Year's. The thing to do was to have fun. Spend some enjoyable time with an intriguing woman, and not make more of it than it was.

That was all.

Hell, he didn't want anyone messing up his lifestyle, anyway. He liked his lifestyle. He'd tailored it specifically to his own preferences. If you got serious about someone, you had to start considering their preferences, too. You had to compromise. And if there were kids involved? Well, he could only imagine that the kids' needs crowded out everything else.

Who wanted that?

He thought about all of it as they went through their evening together. But all of his best intentions—all of the ways in which he cautioned himself—were overwhelmed by one simple fact.

Here, with Delilah and her boys, he felt happier than he had in some time. Maybe ever. He felt so happy that he could imagine, for one fleeting moment, that all of his problems had simply vanished in the wake of this perfect sense of contentment.

That was an illusion, of course.

But it was a pretty damned powerful one.

CHAPTER 19

Delilah found herself humming the next morning as she bustled around the kitchen making pancakes for the boys.

"Can we have chocolate chips in them?" Jesse wanted to know. He'd just come out of his room wearing pajama bottoms, his chest bare. His hair stuck up in all directions.

"We don't have any chocolate chips," she said. "But I can slice some bananas to go on top."

"Okay." His tone indicated that it was anything but okay, but that he would somehow try to muddle through the travails of breakfast.

She used a spatula to turn a batch of pancakes on the griddle. "Did you have fun last night?" she asked.

"Yeah!" Jesse perked up, the lack of chocolate chips forgotten. "The s'mores were really good. And it was cool going with Quinn. I didn't think we would do that kind of stuff with him. I thought you didn't even like him."

Delilah looked at her son, surprised. "Of course I like him. Why did you think I didn't?"

Jesse shrugged. "You always said we couldn't call him or invite him anyplace. And whenever we did see him, it was like you didn't want to."

He was right. She had acted that way. But she couldn't tell her son that she'd pretended not to like Quinn because she liked him too much—so much that she worried he would hurt her, hurt her boys, and tear open the old wounds that were barely starting to heal.

"Well, we didn't know him very well," she said. "That's all. But now he's getting to be a friend, isn't he?"

Gavin came into the room, rubbing his eyes as he yawned and struggled to fully wake up. "Who's our friend?"

"Quinn," Jesse said, catching him up on the conversation.

"Oh. Yeah." Gavin nodded his agreement.

Delilah slid some pancakes onto a plate, sliced some banana on top of them, then drizzled on a modest amount of maple syrup. She put the plate in front of Jesse, who scrambled up onto a barstool at the kitchen island to eat.

"What would you guys think if we spent more time with him?" Delilah asked, already knowing the answer.

"That would be so cool!" Jesse said, his mouth full of pancake.

Gavin nodded vigorously.

"We're going back to Connecticut in less than a month," she reminded them. "But that doesn't mean we can't have some fun with Quinn while we're here."

"We could go camping maybe," Jesse said. "Or fishing. Quinn said he likes fishing."

"Maybe," Delilah agreed. She poured more batter onto the griddle to form Gavin's pancakes. "I just don't want you to be sad when we go home and we have to say goodbye to him."

"We won't be going home," Jesse reminded her. "We don't even have our house anymore. We'll be going to Grandma's."

"Just until we can get our own place," she said.

Gavin climbed up onto the barstool next to Jesse's and waited for his pancakes, his thumb in his mouth.

"We could just stay here," Jesse said.

Delilah froze. She didn't want Jesse thinking that way—not when it meant reality was going to leave him disappointed.

"This house isn't ours," she said. "We just have it until the end of the month."

"There are other houses in Cambria, Mom," he said.

Time to change the subject—and fast. "So, what do you guys think you want to do today? Here, Gavin. Your pancakes are ready."

"I JUST FEEL bad about the kids, that's all," Delilah's mother said on the phone later that day as Delilah sat in an Adirondack chair on her back patio, watching the kids explore the tide pools just below the house. It was low tide, and the waves slapping into the rocks were small. After some argument, Jesse had convinced Delilah that if they were allowed to go down there alone, neither he nor Gavin was likely to be swept into the ocean.

"Why do you feel bad? The kids are fine."

"Well, they're all alone at Christmas."

Delilah stifled a sigh. "They're not alone. They have each other, and they have me."

"You know what I mean. Why, you probably don't even have a Christmas tree."

It was true—she didn't. That hadn't seemed like something you could do in a vacation rental house. But why not? Of course they should have a Christmas tree.

"We're getting one this weekend," she said, deciding it on the fly.

"But what are you going to decorate it with, Delilah? All of your ornaments are in storage. And the kids' stockings …"

"We'll buy more ornaments. We'll buy more stockings, Mom. I can do that, you know. I got a whopping settlement in the divorce."

Jeanette made a scornful sound. "You say that like it's a good thing."

"The settlement? It *is* a good thing. Especially because Mitch didn't leave me enough money to buy food before the court made him do it. He didn't leave me enough to take care of his own children."

She heard the bitterness in her voice and told herself to suppress it. The kids might hear, even over the sound of the surf. And she'd vowed never to trash Mitch in front of his sons. And anyway, she didn't need her mother to hear her anger, her hurt.

"Well, divorces hurt everyone, Delilah. Especially the kids. That's why I keep thinking that if you and Mitch could just get counseling—"

"He lives in Paris. With his new girlfriend. That's going to make the logistics of counseling kind of complicated, Mother."

"Oh, honey ..."

Delilah didn't want to talk about the divorce. She didn't want to talk about Mitch or her financial settlement, and she absolutely did not want to talk about any scenario involving her getting back together with her ex. Instead, she shifted to the original topic —Christmas.

"You know, the boys are having a good time in Cambria. There's this local event called Hospitality Night...." She told her mother about it—about Santa and the s'mores and all of the fun the kids had. The one thing she didn't mention was Quinn. Her mother definitely didn't need to know she was seeing someone.

"That does sound like fun," Jeanette admitted. "Are the boys handy? I'd love for them to tell me about it."

So Delilah called out to the boys, and they scrambled up from the rocks below and onto the patio via the small stairway that led to the beach.

She handed her phone to Jesse, then listened with growing horror as he told his grandmother all about Quinn.

Delilah made frantic hand gestures, trying to communicate with her son that this topic was off-limits. Either he didn't notice or didn't catch the gist of what she was trying to tell him, because he went on and on about their new friend and how he'd escorted them through town on Hospitality Night.

After Jesse, Gavin talked to his grandmother a bit, mostly responding to her inquiries in single syllables. Then he handed the phone to Delilah.

"Well, Mom, I'd better get going," Delilah tried as the boys ran back down the stairs to the tide pools. "I promised the boys we'd—"

"Who exactly is this Quinn person?" Jeanette asked in frosty tones.

Delilah tried to make her voice casual. "Oh … he's just a friend. Someone we met here." She waved a hand airily as though her mother might hear the gesture and conclude there was nothing to dissect.

"A man."

"Well, yes, he is a man, Mom."

"Delilah! You're seeing someone so soon? And you're bringing him into those boys' lives? I never imagined you'd—"

"It's nothing, Mom."

"It certainly isn't nothing, Delilah, if you're bringing a new boyfriend around your sons so soon after what they've been through. And how are you supposed to work on things with Mitch if you're—"

"I'm not! I'm not going to work on things with Mitch!" She said it in the kind of whisper-yell you used when you wanted to be emphatic but you didn't want the whole world to hear your business. "Mitch left me for another woman and moved to Paris! He was with her since long before that. Why shouldn't I have someone? Why shouldn't I have a little fun? A little pleasure?"

"Your *pleasure* has to come second to your children's well-being." Delilah could practically see her mother's expression, pained and stern.

"I know that. I've always known that. It's Mitch who didn't." She took a breath and composed herself. "Now, I really do have to go. Bye, Mom. I love you." And she hung up before her mother could say another word.

~

IT DIDN'T TAKE LONG for Jeanette to report the news to Roxanne, who called Delilah to follow up.

"It sounds like you and the hottie are having fun," Roxanne said.

By now, Delilah and the boys were back in the house, the kids in front of a TV show and Delilah in the kitchen putting together their afternoon snack.

"Mom told you."

"Of course she did. She's outraged. She wanted me to call and talk you down."

"Is that what you're doing?" Delilah asked. "Calling to talk me down?"

"Oh, hell no. I'm calling to say good for you. Seriously, Dee. I hope you milk this fling for all it's worth. You deserve it."

"Well … thanks."

Except, something about that made Delilah uneasy. Not *something* —one specific thing. The word *fling*.

Was that what this was? Was it just a fling?

The word didn't seem to fit, somehow. But then again, neither did the word *relationship*.

But why did she have to define it, especially when it was so new? So fresh?

"Delilah? Are you there?"

"Yeah. I'm here."

"Enjoy, is all I'm saying," Roxanne went on. "And see if you can send me a picture. If he's as hot as you say, I've got to see him."

~

QUINN TEXTED Delilah the afternoon following their Hospitality Night date.

What are you doing tomorrow?

He was busy today—he'd led a hike in the morning and had another one in an hour—but tomorrow was all clear, and the only thing he wanted to do with that free time was spend it with Delilah.

When she didn't answer immediately, he tried to focus on other things. He'd finished the furniture website and was waiting for the client's comments and change requests, so he worked a little on his own websites, both the one that advertised his wilderness adventures and the one offering his web design services.

He was just updating the price list for his hiking trips—time to bring his rate up a little—when his phone pinged with Delilah's response.

I have to put up a Christmas tree.

Three dots bounced around, indicating that she was typing.

My mother thinks I'm giving my sons a crappy Christmas, so I have to get a tree and lights and ornaments.

Quinn sensed some angst there, so he abandoned the texting and called her.

"Hey," she said when she picked up.

"Hey yourself."

He'd been right about the angst. She started unloading it right away.

"Do you know that I actually hadn't thought about getting a tree until my mother mentioned it? I'm a horrible mother. Of course the boys need a tree. It's just, with the divorce, and selling the house, and everything we're going through, it seemed like the last thing in the world I wanted to worry about. But it's Christmas! And we're here, and I have to make it as nice for them as I can. God. I don't have anything. A stand, a tree skirt. I need everything."

"What's a tree skirt?"

"It's the cloth you put over the tree stand so it's not visible."

"Ah. We always used a bedsheet for that."

"Right. Okay. That would work."

He'd clearly caught her when she was already worked up about it. This seemed like a good opportunity to make himself indispensable.

"Tell you what—I'll help."

She was silent for a second, either in hope or dismay. "You don't have to do that."

"I want to." He leaned back in his desk chair and switched the phone to his other ear. "I don't have anything going tomorrow, and besides, have you ever tried to put a tree in a tree stand by yourself? It can't be done."

"That's—"

"It'll be fun," he said, interrupting her before she could say no.

"We'll play Christmas carols and make hot chocolate. The boys will love it."

So will I, he thought but didn't say.

"Okay. That's really nice of you. I could use the help."

He grinned, feeling satisfied with himself.

"No problem. Is ten a.m. too early?"

CHAPTER 20

The boys had been happy when Delilah told them they would be getting a Christmas tree. But that was nothing compared to their reaction when she told them Quinn would be helping them.

"Quinn's coming?" Jesse's eyes widened, and his face held an expression of hopeful expectation, as though what he'd just heard might actually be a miracle.

"Yes, he is. He's going to help us pick out a tree and ornaments and all the things we need, and then he's going to help us put it up."

Gavin, usually less verbal than his brother, jumped up and down on his toes and started listing the things they'd need.

"We have to get a tree, and lights, and a star for the top like the one at Gramma's house. And that shiny stringy stuff."

"Tinsel?" Delilah tried.

Gavin nodded vigorously.

"I want a really tall one!" Jesse said. "Like, really tall. Tyler's dad had to cut a piece off the top of their tree last year because it touched the ceiling."

Apparently it was important for him to best Tyler, his closest friend from home.

"We'll see," Delilah said, beginning to feel the infectiousness of her sons' enthusiasm. "You know what else? Quinn thinks we need hot cocoa."

"Yeah! With marshmallows!" Jesse said.

Gavin nodded. Then his face fell, his expression filled with concern.

"Gavin? Honey, what is it?"

"How is Santa going to know we're here instead of at home?"

Delilah crouched down to his eye level. "Remember when you talked to Santa last night?"

Gavin nodded.

"Well, I gave a note to one of his elves with our temporary address on it. He knows we're here, honey. And Otter Bluff has a nice, big chimney for him to use, so I think we're all set."

DELILAH HAD EXPECTED to buy a pre-cut tree, probably at one of those roadside stands that popped up every year right after Thanksgiving. But Quinn showed up at Otter Bluff in full man-in-charge mode, insisting that the only proper way to obtain a Christmas tree was to choose a living pine and cut it down like Paul Bunyan.

"You want us to cut down a tree," Delilah said, giving him a significant amount of side-eye.

"Not *us*, per se. All you and the boys have to do is choose one. I'll cut it down."

"Because my womanly arms are too weak to hold a saw?" She awaited his response with her arms crossed over her chest and her eyebrows high.

"Yeah, now that you mention it." He made a show of inspecting Delilah's biceps, poking first one and then the other with his finger. "Maybe when it's time to trim some of the scrawny little branches."

Jesse and Gavin giggled.

"Yeah, Mom," Jesse said. "Cutting down trees isn't for girls."

"Plus, I might ruin my manicure," Delilah put in. She didn't, currently, have a manicure, but it seemed like the right thing to say to play her part in this little bit of theater.

"I'm glad that's settled. There's a tree farm in Atascadero," Quinn said. "Once you've cut your own, you'll never go back to those sad, pre-cut, poor excuses for trees that drop their needles two weeks before Christmas. But first, we have to stop by the hardware store."

"For an ax?" Jesse asked.

"For a proper tree stand. The ones they sell at the tree farm are complete crap."

AS THEY VISITED FIRST the hardware store and then a variety of local shops looking for lights, ornaments, and other tree essentials, Delilah found herself amused at how seriously Quinn was taking the whole endeavor.

Not only had he insisted on a particular kind of tree stand, he'd also frowned in concentration looking at extension cords and strings of lights, enumerating the relative pros and cons of each type.

"You don't want this one." Quinn examined a set of tiny white lights that Gavin had handed him at the True Value in Cambria. "These are incandescent. You want LED."

"We do?" Gavin asked.

"Sure. They save energy, plus they don't get hot, so they're less of a safety hazard." He examined the boxes of lights on the shelf, then plucked one from the display. "See? This one costs a little more, but you'll save it in energy costs." He handed the box to Gavin, who peered at it intently as though he could read the information on the package.

"You're really putting a lot of thought into this," Delilah said.

"If something's worth doing, it's worth doing right. Don't you think so, Jesse?"

"Yeah! Can we get colored lights instead of white, though?"

QUINN, reasonably enough, had insisted that they buy all of the ornaments, lights, and other supplies first, before getting the tree. It would be awkward driving all over town with a tree tied to the roof, for one thing, and besides, you wanted to get the tree into some water as soon as possible, he'd explained to the Ballards.

So, it was midafternoon before they got to the tree farm. The boys had been dragging a little from all of the stops, but they both perked up as they walked amid rows of trees, inspecting each of them to find the best one.

"How about this one?" Gavin pointed to a nicely shaped Douglas Fir.

Quinn examined the tree thoughtfully. "It's a good one, all right. Nice and symmetrical, with good needle coverage. But it's only five feet tall. Otter Bluff has, what, eight-foot ceilings?" He looked to Delilah for confirmation.

"That seems right," she said.

"Then we're gonna need a seven-foot tree."

"Yeah, Gavin," Jesse said, as though he'd known that all along.

Under most circumstances, Delilah would have been irritated by the way Quinn had asserted himself as leader of the expedition. She should have been irked after his remarks about her weak biceps. Somehow, though, she found it cute as hell.

All those years she'd been married to Mitch, she would have welcomed the occasional moment when he took it upon himself to handle things so she wouldn't have to. But that rarely happened, because he was always too busy with work. Or, as it turned out, with other women.

How do you think we're going to pay for all of the things you and the boys want? He'd asked that question more times than she could count. As though she was the one who'd wanted an oversized house in a rich neighborhood. As though she was the one who'd wanted the designer clothes he'd insisted she wear. As though she'd wanted anything other than a happy, well-adjusted family—the one thing he'd never managed to provide.

She'd never had this: a man taking charge of her family's good time. And now that she did, if only for a day, she decided to just sit back and enjoy it.

"How about this one?" She pointed to a big Scotch pine.

QUINN WAS aware that he was being pushy. He was aware that he was maybe being a little sexist. But he couldn't seem to help himself—not because he actually was sexist, but because he'd thought he wouldn't be celebrating Christmas, and his enthusiasm was getting the better of him.

When they were driving back to Cambria with the tree tied to the roof of Delilah's car, he glanced at her, trying to gauge her mood.

"You know … the thing about you being weak with scrawny biceps …"

"What about it?"

"I was just kidding. I don't really think you're a pathetic weakling who can't cut down a tree." As he said it, he reflected that it hadn't come out right and he was probably making things worse.

"Well, that's good to know." The whisper of a smile on her face either meant she was amused or she was feigning amusement to hide her inner rage.

After the excitement of the day, the boys had both fallen asleep in the back of the car, so they both kept their voices low to avoid being overheard.

"I was playing up my manly prowess for the boys."

"Right."

"You get it."

"Sure." She gave him that hint of a grin again. "Of course, one could say that modeling sexism for the boys isn't optimal. Especially when they have a woman as the head of the family."

Shit, she was right. Now he felt like an idiot. He rubbed his forehead with his hand. "Ah, man. You've got a point. A good one. I'm sorry."

"Don't worry about it."

He glanced at her from his place in the passenger seat. "Are you saying don't worry about it because I really shouldn't worry about it? Or because you're pissed and you've written me off entirely, so there's no point in worrying about it since we'll never see each other after today?"

She let out a laugh. "You've got a whole drama playing out in your head, don't you?"

"Yeah, I guess I do." He shifted in his seat to face her. "I just … Christmas hasn't been a thing for me for a couple of years. I guess I got overly excited. Maybe a little bit carried away."

"Why hasn't Christmas been a thing?"

Of course she had to ask that. He'd left himself wide open.

He shrugged. "Family problems. You know."

She shot him a brief look as she drove. "I know family problems in general, sure. But I don't know yours specifically. What's going on there?"

He shrugged again, feeling uncomfortable and wishing he could rewind the conversation by a few minutes so they wouldn't have to go down this particular rabbit hole.

"I don't get along with my brothers, that's all. We had a falling-out. And my mom and stepdad took their side, so …" He left it at that, hoping like hell she would let it drop.

Instead of prying, she sympathized, which was almost worse.

"That must be really hard," she said, her voice soft.

The way she said it made him want to lay his head in her lap while she stroked his hair. Maybe later, after the kids were in bed.

"It is. It is hard," he said.

"And you don't want to talk about it."

"Not really, no. I'm having a nice time, and if I start talking about all of that, I won't be having a nice time anymore."

"I get that." She drove for a moment in silence. Then she said, "I do think we need to address an important topic, though, whether you want to or not."

"What's that?"

"Hot cocoa—marshmallows or whipped cream?"

He grinned, feeling the relief of it. "Whipped cream, obviously. It has so many other uses."

The way she blushed, he knew she was imagining exactly what some of those uses might be.

CHAPTER 21

The rest of the day was a flurry of holiday-related activities as they put up the tree, strung the lights, and hung the ornaments, all while Christmas music played on the Otter Bluff sound system.

When they were done, Delilah fulfilled her promise of hot cocoa, serving steaming mugs to the boys and to Quinn.

She plopped down onto the sofa with her own mug, feeling exhausted but happy.

"This living room is a train wreck," she said, looking over the piles of empty packaging from the lights and the ornaments. Fallen pine needles were scattered beneath the layer of debris. "A really bad one. With casualties."

With a sigh, she put her mug on the coffee table and started to get up to attack the mess. Quinn caught her arm. "Don't worry about it right now. We can deal with it later. The boys and I will help. Right, Jesse? Gavin?"

Gavin nodded gamely, but Jesse complained.

"Aww. Do we have to?"

"After everything your mom went through today to make you guys happy, I think it's the least we can do," Quinn said.

"Okay." Jesse said it as though he were agreeing to something he knew he'd regret.

"There," Quinn said. "We'll all do it together, but not yet. Enjoy your cocoa."

Grateful for the reprieve, Delilah sat back down on the sofa, took up her mug, and enjoyed a warm, chocolaty sip. The tree really did look good. Tiny colored lights sparkled amid the branches, and a wildly eclectic assortment of ornaments gave the tree a look of riotous festivity.

How the Grinch Stole Christmas was playing on the television, and Jesse and Gavin watched intently as Quinn and Delilah relaxed.

"You want to step out on the patio and enjoy the view?" Quinn asked. Something in his voice said he was interested in more than just watching the waves.

"Sure."

They took their empty mugs into the kitchen, left the boys in front of the movie, and stepped onto the back patio, closing the sliding glass door behind them.

It was getting late—dinner and the usual evening rituals were behind them—and the sky was dark, with just the moonlight reflecting on the water.

"Come here." Quinn took Delilah's hand and stepped over to a part of the patio where they couldn't be seen from the living room, drawing her along with him. When they had privacy, he pulled her into his arms and kissed her.

Delilah sank into him, molding herself against him as she savored the warmth of his body and the taste of his mouth.

"I've been wanting to do that all day," he said.

"Me too."

"Yeah?" He grinned, still holding her against him. "Maybe after the kids are in bed, we can slip into your room and—"

She put her palms flat against his chest and pushed against him playfully. "Quinn, we can't."

"Why not?"

"What if they hear us?"

"We'll be quiet."

"What if one of them comes in?"

"We'll lock the door."

Her eyebrows rose as she considered him. "What are we going to tell them when they see you in the morning?"

"I'll climb out the window at dawn. I'm not above that sort of thing. And it wouldn't be unprecedented."

"I'll bet."

Part of Delilah wanted to give in and let it happen. They'd had such a lovely day. Was it so wrong that she wanted to keep that loveliness going and take it to new levels?

But she couldn't let the boys know that she and Quinn were romantically involved. It was one thing to let them spend time with Quinn as a friend, with the understanding that they would go home in January, leaving him behind.

It was entirely another to get their hopes up that Quinn might be a permanent part of their lives, just to devastate them when it ended.

Because things always ended, even if you were promised they wouldn't. Even if you were promised a lifetime. Nothing was forever—she'd learned that the hard way.

Even though she couldn't risk that, she could risk another kiss. She raised onto her toes and pressed her mouth to his, and he held her and caressed her tongue with his.

"I had a good time. Thank you." She laid her cheek against his chest.

"Ah. I guess that means I'm going."

"I guess it does. But don't go without saying goodbye to the boys."

"I wouldn't think of it."

With a groan of regret, he tore himself away from her and went back inside to help clean up—as promised—and to say goodbye to Jesse and Gavin.

~

When Quinn was gone, the living room was tidied up, and the movie was over, Delilah told the boys it was time for bed.

They did the usual complaining combined with the customary pleas for water, books, and more time.

She finally got Gavin tucked in with Waffles beside him, then she went into Jesse's room to kiss him and wish him goodnight.

"Oh." Jesse perked up as he remembered something. "Dad called on your cell phone while you and Quinn were outside. I answered it, even though it's your phone, because I saw his name. I hope that's okay."

"Of course it is." She sat down on the edge of the bed and smoothed his hair back from his forehead. "Did you and he have a good talk?"

Jesse nodded vigorously, his eyes wide. "Yeah. I told him all about the stuff we did today. I told him about the tree and the ornaments and stuff, and the movie and the hot cocoa. And I told him all about Quinn."

Delilah tried not to wince at that. "That's great, sweetie."

"He said you should call him back because he has stuff he wants to talk about."

"Did he?"

I'll just bet he's got stuff he wants to talk about.

He was going to give her hell about Quinn. Well, that was fine. She didn't owe him anything—not anymore. Still, she didn't look forward to the conversation.

She kissed Jesse, then turned out the light on her way out of the room.

In the living room, she picked up her cell phone from a side table and found a text message from Mitch.

Call me ASAP.

She closed her eyes and said a silent curse.

No sense putting it off. She stepped onto the front porch so the boys wouldn't hear the conversation from their rooms and called her ex.

"Delilah." He already sounded pissed.

"Hi, Mitch. You called?"

"Yeah, I did. I talked to Jesse more than an hour ago—I've been waiting for you to call."

She shifted her weight from one foot to the other and leaned against the porch railing. "Why are you even up? It's, what, six a.m. in Paris?"

"Don't change the subject."

"What is the subject, Mitch?"

"The subject, Delilah, is the man you brought around my children. That's the subject. Who the hell is he, and what's going on?"

Delilah felt her body tense, and she reflected, just for a moment, on how much of her marriage she'd spent in that state of coiled discomfort. It was a feeling specifically linked to her ex-husband.

"None of that is your business," she told him.

"The hell it isn't. Those are my sons you've got hanging out with some random asshole."

"Well," Delilah said dryly, "they spent the first several years of their lives hanging out with you. I don't see how this could be any worse."

"Delilah, goddamn it ..."

"You left me for someone else, Mitch. You don't have the high ground, so don't you dare pretend you do."

"Who is he?" Mitch said again. "Are you fucking him?"

"I'm finished with this conversation."

"We'll see about that," Mitch growled at her. "We'll just see."

CHAPTER 22

Quinn could feel himself getting more and more deeply entangled in his relationship with Delilah, but he didn't feel much motivation to do anything about it.

Once you started doing things like decorating Christmas trees with someone, you were headed for serious relationship territory—there was no question about it. With most of the women he'd dated over the years, that would have been cause for panic and immediate evasive action.

With Delilah, though, he felt the strong urge to just let it happen. His only regret about his day of Christmas fun with the Ballard family was that he'd had to go home at the end of it.

The part where he'd offered to climb out the window in the morning hadn't been his proudest moment as a man, but, hell, it would have been worth it if she'd said yes.

Even if the neighbors spotted him falling into the azaleas.

This thing was more work than most of his previous girlfriends had been—any time you got together with someone who had kids, it was more work—but he had the feeling Delilah was worth the effort.

When he got home that night, he went into his empty house, turned on the lights, then turned on some music—quietly enough that it wouldn't disturb Mrs. Foster—but the place still felt sad and lonely without the noise and raucous activity of the Ballard family.

He went to the kitchen, got a beer out of the refrigerator, opened it, then sat on his sofa and drank a swallow.

He had to win her over, and he didn't have a lot of time to do it. She was planning to go all the way across the country in less than a month unless he could give her a reason not to.

Or unless he could give her a reason to invite him to go with her.

Had it really come to that? Was he really thinking of picking up his life and traveling from one coast to another for a woman he'd just met?

Yes. Yes, he was.

It wasn't like there was anything left for him here on the West Coast.

It wasn't like his own family wanted anything to do with him. Well, they did, but only if he made it profitable for them. He wasn't going to buy his family's love, so where did that leave him?

It left him longing to be a part of something greater than himself. It left him wanting to have people who cared for him and for whom he could care in turn.

Ah, shit.

He knew it wasn't healthy to be jumping into something so fast. Especially when there were kids involved—kids who'd already been hurt by their father and who didn't need to be disappointed by a man in their lives again.

Except, he was pretty sure he wouldn't disappoint them if they gave him a chance to show them the truth of who he was.

He pulled his cell phone out of his pocket and texted Delilah.

I had a really great time today.

He watched his screen as he saw the notification that she'd read his message.

A moment later, the phone pinged with her response.

I did, too. Thank you for showing the boys a good time.

He thought about what to say and carefully composed the text.

It was my pleasure. Speaking of pleasure, when do you think we could have some time for just the two of us? I'm not done showing people a good time.

There was still a chance she'd pull back—still a chance she would distance herself from him. She'd been hurt badly and recently, and though none of that had been his fault, she had to be skittish. She had to be tempted to protect herself from anything resembling love.

Love.

Now that he'd thought the word, there was no escaping it.

When her text came in, he half expected it to be a brush-off. Instead, she wrote, *I'll see if I can get Dolly across the street to watch the boys one night this week.*

I can't wait, he wrote.

He really couldn't—not if he wanted to win her over before January first. He didn't have any time to waste.

DELILAH KEPT TELLING herself to slow down. She couldn't let this thing with Quinn get out of hand.

Still, the idea of having an evening alone with him was undeniably appealing. She called Dolly the next day, reassuring her that she could find another sitter if Dolly wasn't up to watching the boys.

Dolly said she wouldn't hear of it and immediately began planning what she was going to cook and what activities she and the kids might do when they were together.

With that taken care of, Delilah texted Quinn to decide which evening they'd go out.

As soon as possible, he wrote. *It was hard to stay on my best behavior with the boys around.*

It had been hard for Delilah, too, though she'd tried to pretend it wasn't.

They set the time and day, and Delilah told Dolly and the boys about her plans. Well, she didn't tell them *all* of her plans.

Some parts were better kept private.

"THIS QUINN THING is getting out of control," Delilah told Roxanne on the phone the day before her date. "I mean, it was just supposed to be fun. But now he's buying Christmas trees and taking us for s'mores, and … and taking me out on dates."

"Horrors," Roxanne said.

"Be serious. This is serious!"

"If you're that worried about it, why did you agree to go out with him again?" Roxanne's point was a good one, and Delilah didn't have a good answer.

"It's just … I don't know. I'm having a good time, and I haven't had a good time in so long I've forgotten what it's like."

"Well, there you go."

Delilah was irritated that her sister didn't seem to realize how dire the situation was. Maybe if she brought Mitch into it, that would give things the sense of impending doom that they deserved.

"Jesse told Mitch about Quinn," she said.

"Oops."

"Yeah."

"So, what happened? How did he react?"

"He said he doesn't want his sons hanging out with, and I quote, 'some random asshole.'"

"So much better that they should hang out with him, the asshole we know," Roxanne said.

"That's pretty much what I said."

Then Roxanne asked the question that had been on Delilah's mind since Mitch had called.

"I mean, do you think he's going to *do* anything?"

"He said, 'We'll just see about that.' About Quinn being in the boys' lives. So, it really sounded like he plans to do something."

"Or he could just be trying to intimidate you," Roxanne said.

If he'd still been living near Delilah—hell, if he'd still been living on the same continent—she might have worried more about what Mitch might do regarding Quinn. But he couldn't make trouble for her all the way from Paris.

Could he?

"He's a lawyer," Delilah pointed out. "A really good one. The kind big corporations hire to help them screw the IRS. If he can screw the IRS, Roxanne, he can probably make trouble for me if he wants to."

"He doesn't really want to," Roxanne reassured her. "He just wants to bluster around and make noise so you'll do whatever he wants. He's a bully, that's all."

Delilah hoped she was right and that his veiled threat wouldn't come to anything. He didn't want Delilah anymore—he'd made that clear. And he didn't want his sons in his life, either, because if he did, he wouldn't have moved thousands of miles away from them.

What could he possibly hope to gain from fighting her on this?

"You see what I mean?" Delilah asked her sister. "This whole thing is a can of worms."

"Delilah. If you don't want to date this guy, then don't do it. But don't you dare let him go because a weasel like Mitch is trying to intimidate you. And, while I'm at it, don't you dare let him go because you're scared to take a chance. I raised you better than that."

"You're two years younger than me," Delilah pointed out.

"Whatever. I'm still right."

CHAPTER 23

Delilah already knew this would be a sex date. If she hadn't known it, the fact that Quinn cooked dinner for her at his place would have been an unmistakable signal.

At least, she thought he cooked—until she spotted some takeout containers from Indigo Moon in his kitchen trash can.

He'd made everything beautiful. His house was spotless and inviting, the table was set with cloth napkins and candles, he'd chilled a bottle of Chardonnay, and a vase of flowers—yellow calla lilies—was displayed on the countertop that separated the kitchen from the dining area.

She'd almost wanted to let his deception go, but once he'd plated the food with the care of a chef and placed it in front of her, she couldn't help herself.

"This looks wonderful," she said, admiring the seafood fettuccine on her plate.

"Ah, well." He waved her off. "It's just something I put together."

"This must have been a lot of work. And yet you managed to get the kitchen spotless before I came," she said.

"I just ... planned. I planned it out, is all." He was starting to blush a little.

She took a bite of her pasta and moaned with pleasure. "God, this is delicious. You know what it reminds me of? A dish I ate recently at ... what was it called? Indigo Moon?"

He scowled at her. "You saw the takeout boxes."

"Yes. Yes, I did."

He sighed. "Is this going to affect my chances of getting lucky? Because I put a lot of thought into this even if I didn't—"

She leaned over and interrupted him, pressing her lips to his. As she pulled away, his eyes were still closed, his lips still gently pursed.

"Okay then." He opened his eyes as though he were waking up after a long nap. "Okay."

"It's not that I didn't want to put in the effort," he said later as they lay in his bed in the glow of the candles they'd brought in from the dining room. "It's just that I can't cook. And I wanted this to be nice, so..."

"It's all right." She rolled onto her side to face him and gave him a long, lingering kiss. "It really was nice, so you achieved your goal."

"Well, good." He ran his hand up her arm to her shoulder and back down again. "But the dinner wasn't the nicest part."

He hadn't wanted to get Delilah into bed to satisfy his physical desires. Well, okay—yes, he had. But it wasn't only that. He'd just wanted to be close to her.

Something about Delilah made him feel comforted and warm and well-tended.

So, yes, he'd wanted to sleep with her, but more than that, he'd wanted to be *one* with her.

And, yeah, that sounded wussy as hell, but there it was.

He'd thought he wanted to keep his freedom and avoid complications. He'd thought he wanted to keep things simple and low-risk.

He hadn't known what he wanted, because it turned out he didn't want freedom or simplicity or to keep himself unburdened by someone else's baggage.

He just wanted her.

He didn't think she was in the same place as he was—not yet—but he'd get her there. The whole thing felt too right for him to believe otherwise.

Then again, maybe this wasn't about Delilah at all. Maybe he was just so damned lonely since his family had cut him loose that he was looking for a substitute family he could belong to.

If that were the case, it would mean he was using her—even if he didn't realize it or intend it.

Well, that was why you were supposed to date someone for a while before deciding on whether to commit to them. The problem was, he didn't have time. He only had until January first.

"So. How do you like Cambria?" he asked, feeling her out. If there was any chance she might stay …

"It's lovely. Really. The beaches and the forests … the boys and I saw a flock of turkeys yesterday."

He could hear the hesitation in her voice. "But?"

She shrugged. "But after this, we have nowhere to go. I have to decide what happens next. We can live at my parents' place until we figure it out, but after that …"

"What do you want to do?" He propped himself on one elbow to look at her.

"I want … I *need* … to find out who I am when Mitch isn't forcing me to be whatever it was he wanted. I just don't know who that will turn out to be."

Quinn wanted to be there with her when she became that person. He knew that, if he knew nothing else. He wanted to watch her as she transformed into someone new, someone who was more than what she'd been.

~

LATER THAT NIGHT, when Delilah came home, Dolly was sitting on the sofa at Otter Bluff watching a TV show on low volume.

"Are the boys asleep?" Delilah asked.

"Sleeping like angels. We had dinner at my house, then when it was time for bed, I brought them over here."

"I can't thank you enough." Delilah reached for her purse and took out her wallet.

"Oh, you can just put that away." Dolly reached for the remote and switched off the TV. "I had so much fun, it would hardly be fair for me to expect payment too."

"Are you sure? I'd like to give you something."

"Honey, I was just being neighborly." She patted the seat next to her. "Now, sit down and tell me how your date with Mr. Handsome went."

Delilah's first instinct was to say some vague thing or change the subject.

But somehow, she found herself talking to Dolly about it.

She sat down and let out a contented sigh. "It was wonderful. Really wonderful."

"Oh, Delilah, that's great. Tell me all about it, and don't leave anything out."

She did leave some things out, mainly because she wanted to keep the conversation G-rated. But she told Dolly about the dinner, and how Quinn had bought flowers and lit candles, and how it had made her feel special and wanted.

"It's been so long since a man has treated me this way, I almost didn't recognize it." Then, upon further thought: "Actually, no man has ever treated me this way. I met Mitch when we were both young, and I'd barely dated before that. And it seemed like he was always too busy to pay attention to me."

Dolly scowled. "I want to ask you why you put up with that, but you were young, and we all tend to undervalue ourselves when we're young."

"I guess we do. And it was always supposed to be temporary." Delilah sank back into the sofa cushions. "You know? All of the busyness, and the way he prioritized everything but me. First, it was just until he graduated college. Then, it was just until he got through law school. Then he had his first job with a big firm, and he worked sixteen-hour days, and it was just until he could make partner. And then? He left me for someone else before we could get to the end of the *just until*."

"My first husband was like that," Dolly said. "Always worrying about his career, always working long days that stretched into night. Finally, I'd just had it. 'Bob,' I said, 'you can have that damned job or you can have me, but you can't have both.'"

"What kind of work did he do?" Delilah wanted to know.

"Oh, he was a financial analyst. Still is. His second wife left him a few years after I did." She shook her head, frowning. "He had a stroke two years ago. The way he's going, it won't be his last." She perked up and patted her hands once on her thighs. "But, my Harold is a gem. If I hadn't gotten that divorce, I never would have met him. Things have a way of working out, honey."

Delilah was beginning to feel the first stirrings of hope that for her, they just might.

CHAPTER 24

Over the following weeks, Delilah spent a lot of time with Quinn, mostly in the company of Jesse and Gavin.

They drove to Solvang, where the faux-Danish village with its Delft figurines and its pastry shops was holding an array of Christmas-themed activities.

At a mall in Santa Barbara, they split up into various combinations of adult plus child so everyone could shop for everyone else without ruining the surprise.

The boys and Delilah baked festively decorated cookies, which Quinn pronounced delicious.

And Quinn perfected his technique of sneaking out the sliding glass door in Delilah's bedroom, then making his escape through the back gate, as they couldn't keep imposing on Dolly every time they wanted to be alone together.

On top of all of that, there was no way they could miss the biggest holiday event in town: the Cambria Christmas Market, hosted every year by the Cambria Pines Lodge.

They attended the market on a Wednesday evening—Quinn had warned Delilah that the event got far too crowded on the weekends for them to achieve optimal fun.

"You're going to love it," Quinn told the boys when he arrived that night to pick up the Ballard family. "Santa's going to be there, but you've already talked to him, so we can skip that part."

"I want to talk to Santa again," Gavin said earnestly, looking up at Quinn with wide eyes, Waffles tucked under his arm.

Quinn looked skeptical. "Well, he's busy, and he's already got your list. But I'll ask if he can squeeze you in a second time. You never know—he might have a cancellation."

Gavin nodded and bounced up and down a few times on his toes.

They drove along Main Street, up Santa Rosa Creek Road, and to the high school, where Quinn found a parking space in the student lot.

"This doesn't look like a Christmas thing." Jesse looked around in dismay as they got out of the car. "This just looks like a closed-up school."

"We're just here to catch the bus to the market," Quinn reassured him. "The parking lot at the lodge is too small, so people park other places and go there on the bus. You'll see."

They waited in a long line of people dressed in down jackets, hats, and gloves against the December chill. Jesse and Gavin had resisted letting their mother bundle them up, but she'd insisted, and now she was glad she had. The temperature had dipped into the forties, which was mild compared to what they were used to in Connecticut, but which still required proper outerwear.

The four of them piled onto the bus, rode across town to Lodge Hill—and emerged into a wonderland of so many tiny colored lights that they seemed to make the night sky vibrate in hues of red and green.

Lights covered wire-framed animals and elves. Lights covered the hedges that separated the lodge grounds from the road. Lights adorned the ground amid imitation snowdrifts and fairy-tale hills. Lights formed an archway over their heads. And even more lights formed the outlines of sleds, reindeer, angels, and gingerbread men.

Christmas carols played on the speaker system as they followed a path that wound through the lodge grounds, past the Grinch's hideout, past stands offering hot cocoa and Christmas crafts, and through the beer garden—which they avoided for the sake of the children.

They stopped at Santa's cottage, where a line of children waited with their parents to have their photos taken on St. Nick's lap.

Jesse had hedged his bets by visiting Santa once, but he'd decided that doing it twice would wound his dignity. So he and Delilah sat on a nearby bench while Quinn took Gavin through the line.

Delilah watched as Quinn bent down to murmur something in Gavin's ear and Gavin nodded solemnly in response.

After they visited Santa and came back, Delilah asked Quinn, "What did you say to him just before you went in?"

"I told him I had to pull some strings to get him in." Quinn grinned as they watched the boys, who were ten yards away looking at a display of carved wooden toys. "I said I took the head elf on a nature trek some years back, so I had an in."

Delilah laughed. "You did not tell him that."

Quinn's eyebrows shot up. "I did. I told him we had to use elf magic to scare away a bear."

Grinning, she linked her arm in his. "You're great with them. Really great."

So much better than their father ever was.

He shrugged. "I like them. I like the hell out of them. I didn't know kids could be so much fun."

"They can be, when they're not fighting with each other or refusing to pick up after themselves."

"Those two?" Quinn made a show of his surprise. "I can't imagine they're ever anything but perfect angels."

"Right. Let's see what you think when you've known them for a few years." As soon as she said it, she wanted to take it back. How could she assume that Quinn would stick around that long? Or that she would?

"I didn't mean ..." she began.

"How about some kettle corn?" he said, interrupting her. "There's a booth back over there, I think."

JESSE AND GAVIN were asleep in the back of the car by the time they got back to Otter Bluff. Carefully, Delilah unbuckled Gavin from his booster seat and Quinn unlatched Jesse's seatbelt, and they carried the boys inside and lay them down in their beds. The fact that they managed to do it without waking the kids was a minor Christmas miracle.

When the kids were down, Delilah and Quinn sneaked out of their rooms, closing their doors softly.

Quinn wanted to tell Delilah she was a lucky woman to have such smart, inquisitive, loving, and funny sons. But telling her that would have left his own wounds raw and exposed. So far, he'd managed to keep this thing with Delilah separate from his issues with his family, and he wanted it to stay that way.

When they were standing together in the living room, she turned to him. "That thing I said earlier, about how you'd feel differently when you've known the boys for years ..."

"Yeah. You looked like you swallowed your tongue right after you said that." He ran his hands up her arms and let them settle on her shoulders.

"I just ... It popped out, and I ... If you thought I was making any assumptions ..."

He kissed her once, briefly. "Don't worry about it."

"This thing between us is so new, and I shouldn't have expected that you—"

"Really. Don't worry about it."

But he knew they would have to worry about it at some point—and soon. The clock was ticking, time was running out, and they would have to decide whether to continue their relationship once Delilah's stay at Otter Bluff was up.

From his end of things, the answer was yes—he definitely wanted to continue seeing her. But if he said that now, he might be pushing it. He wasn't sure she was there yet.

So he played it casual, shrugging it off: d*on't worry about it, we don't have to talk about it, of course you didn't mean it.*

But he hoped she had meant it, even if she wasn't ready to admit it yet.

"Delilah?"

"*Mmm?*"

He ran one thumb gently along her cheek, and her eyes slipped closed as she tipped her face up toward his. Then he kissed her. It was a slow and leisurely kiss, soft and caressing, and he ended it by taking her lower lip gently between his teeth before letting her go.

"Am I staying or going?" His voice was a low murmur.

Her eyes fluttered open, as though she were waking from a particularly satisfactory dream.

Instead of answering him, she took his hand and led him toward her room.

~

DELILAH HAD SET her bedside alarm so Quinn could leave before Jesse and Gavin got up. They were both early risers, so it was barely past six a.m. when she nudged Quinn's shoulder and whispered for him to wake up.

Before he'd even opened his eyes, Quinn reached for her, but Delilah put her hands on his chest and held him at a respectable distance.

"Quinn, you've got to go. The boys will be up in half an hour. Maybe less."

Despite the gap between them, Quinn nuzzled his face against hers and nipped her earlobe with his teeth.

"Quinn!" Her tone was the same one she used when she needed to reprimand one of the boys in public: a kind of whisper-yell that communicated urgency without the volume.

"Maybe they'll sleep in," he said.

"They never sleep in."

"Maybe they will today. We had a big day yesterday."

"They *never* sleep in. Never. So get out of bed and put your pants on."

Quinn grumbled a little, but he did get out of bed and reach for his pants. "You know, it might not be a complete disaster if they knew I was here." He scratched at the stubble growing on his chin. "I mean, they like me. I like them. What's the harm?"

Delilah got out of bed and put on a robe. "The fact that they like you is the problem. If they get their hopes up that you and I are going to be a permanent thing ..."

"Well ... you've made it pretty clear you don't want that to happen." He pulled up his jeans and snapped them, then found his shirt and put it on over his head.

"Quinn, that's not—"

"I get it, okay?" He slipped his shoes onto his feet, realized he'd forgotten his socks, then found the socks and stuffed them in his pockets. He grabbed his jacket off the chair next to the bed and plucked his car keys from the dresser.

"Are you mad at me?" Delilah stood there with her hair mussed and her robe pulled around her, her feet bare and vulnerable-looking.

"Nope. Not mad. Just ... adjusting my expectations." He opened the sliding glass door and stepped out onto the patio.

Delilah followed him. She caught his arm as he headed toward the gate that separated the back yard from the road.

"Quinn, stop. I didn't mean—"

"I gotta go, like you said. Wouldn't want the boys to be crushed when you dump me."

He went through the gate, got into his car, and drove away.

CHAPTER 25

Quinn hadn't meant for his overnighter with Delilah to end so disastrously. The date with her and the kids had gone so well—and then he'd had to show her his hurt feelings.

Damn it, he knew better than that. When you showed a woman your hurt feelings, you lost your advantage. If he'd ever had an advantage in the first place.

He could blame it on the fact that he'd been groggy from sleep. He hadn't had coffee yet. Hell, he hadn't even peed yet.

But he'd only said what he was really feeling. He *had* been hurt by the implication that what he had with Delilah was some dirty secret that had to be hidden from her sons. He'd been hurt by her constant reminders that this thing wasn't going anywhere and was only a fling.

He drove home, let himself into his house, and went through his normal morning routine of coffee, shower, breakfast. While he did, he brooded about everything that had happened.

Quinn had told Delilah that he didn't mind climbing out the window and falling into the hedges. Metaphorically. But he did mind, it turned out. He wanted a clear, visible place in her life. He didn't want to be some kind of shameful secret.

When he was dressed and fed and ready to begin his day, he

responded to some e-mails from potential clients wanting to book day hikes; he began making corrections to the furniture website in response to the notes the client had sent him; and he made some notes for an article about largely overlooked hiking trails in the Big Sur area where you could go when you wanted to get away from the tourist crowds and be alone with nature.

It occurred to him that if he managed to sell the article to one of the larger outdoors magazines, the trails might not be so overlooked anymore. But that couldn't be helped.

Just as he was brainstorming ideas for the article, listing trails and some pros and cons for each, someone knocked on his door.

He got up, dressed in faded jeans and a sweatshirt that was fraying at the edges, and answered it.

"Oh. Mrs. Foster."

His first thought was that he'd been playing his music too loud, then he realized he hadn't been playing any music.

"Quinn, dear. I was just popping by to see if you're okay. I noticed you didn't come home last night."

He ran a hand through his hair. "I don't come home a lot of nights." She'd never come asking about him when he slept in the van after a long hike, so why was she here now?

"Well, I suppose that's true. But I'm a worrier, so—"

"You're not really a worrier, Mrs. Foster." Where was this going? What was she getting at?

"Oh, all right." She deflated a little at being caught out in her lie. "My friend Dolly told me your car was in front of that Delilah Ballard's place all night, and I came to find out if you're finally going to settle down with a nice girl. By the way, I'd love a cup of tea. Do you have some?"

~

"So, she basically told me to get out." Quinn wrapped up his story as Mrs. Foster finished her tea. "It's like she thinks I'm going to corrupt her kids or something."

"Oh, Quinn, she doesn't think that."

They were sitting at his dining table, a mug of tea in front of Mrs. Foster, Quinn with a cup of strong coffee. He'd scrounged around in his cupboard and found an unopened pack of cookies he'd forgotten about, and several of them sat on a plate between them.

"Really?" he said. "Because it sure seemed that way."

"She's protecting her children. You can't blame a mother for that."

"Protecting them from me? I've never been anything but nice to those boys."

"Oh." She waved a hand to dismiss what he'd said. "She's not protecting them because she thinks you're some kind of danger. She's protecting them because she doesn't want to break their hearts. Honey, those kids have lost their father. Yes, he's still there, but he's half a world away, and he didn't choose them. That hurts. Delilah doesn't want her boys to love you and then lose you if things don't work out."

He shifted in his chair to face her more fully. "Who says things won't work out?"

"Delilah's life experience, for one." She shook her head sadly. "A woman gives her life to a man—really gives it to him—and then gets thrown aside for someone else? You don't get over that right away, and for her, it probably feels like it happened yesterday."

He could see the sense in what she was saying, and he reluctantly had to admit she had a point.

Even though he felt like shit, he allowed Mrs. Foster a slight grin. "You know a lot about Delilah for someone who's never met her."

"I know a lot about people, that's all." She shrugged. "That, and the fact that Dolly and I do like to talk. What fun is it to live in a small town if you can't know everything about your neighbors?"

DELILAH WENT through her morning routine worrying about how she'd left things with Quinn.

Part of her was angry. She'd explained to him why she couldn't let

Jesse and Gavin know they were a couple. Hadn't she? And hadn't he said he understood?

If he couldn't live with the conditions she'd set on their relationship, then maybe he should find someone else and move on.

But the idea of him finding someone else made her sick with dread. What if he did? What if he really did decide that dating Delilah was too complicated? He could find another woman—someone single, someone fully available to him—in a heartbeat.

When Delilah thought of how he made her feel, when she thought of all of the fun they'd had together, the thought of never having that again felt like a death—like a tragedy.

And, okay, maybe she hadn't been fair to him.

As she made pancakes for Jesse and Gavin, she thought about how she would feel if she were seeing someone she cared about and that person treated their relationship like some kind of shameful secret.

She hadn't done that—not really. Quinn had spent lots of time with the boys. She wouldn't have allowed that if she hadn't thought he was good for them.

But she'd kept the nature of the relationship a secret from them, and to Quinn, that had to hurt. He might understand it better if he were a father, but he wasn't. There were some things you just couldn't explain to someone who hadn't lived them.

She flipped a batch of pancakes on the griddle, lost in thought. She didn't realize Jesse was talking to her until he'd raised his voice to repeat himself.

"Mom! I asked if we could have chocolate chips in our pancakes."

She blinked a few times as though she'd been startled awake. "Oh. No, sweetie, we still don't have any."

"Aww."

"But we do have some leftover whipped cream from our hot cocoa. You could put that on your pancakes."

Mollified, Jesse scrambled down from the barstool at the kitchen island and went to tell his brother about the whipped cream windfall.

It seemed to Delilah that she had to make a decision. Did she think things with Quinn were serious enough to let the boys in on the fact that they were dating? Or was this secrecy thing a hill she was willing to die on?

She called Jesse back into the kitchen, put a plate of pancakes with whipped cream in front of him, and went to work on making a batch for Gavin.

As she worked, she said casually, "Jesse?"

"*Hmmf?*" His mouth was too full of pancake for him to utter more than a vague sound.

"I was just wondering ... What would you think if I ... if I maybe started seeing someone? Like a boyfriend? Someone other than your father?"

Jesse chewed, swallowed, and without hesitation said, "Quinn should be your boyfriend."

She was so startled that her mouth fell open. Then she composed herself. "He should? Do you think so?"

Jesse nodded. "Yeah. He's fun. And you're different when he's around."

"I'm different?"

He nodded again and shoved a forkful of pancake into his mouth. When he'd eaten the mouthful, he said, "Yeah. You're like ... sparkly."

"I'm sparkly?" For some reason, she seemed to be repeating whatever he said.

"Kinda. It's neat."

Delilah finished making Gavin's pancakes, then called him in for breakfast.

When he was seated with his food in front of him, she posed the same question to him. "Hey, Gavin? What would you think if Quinn was my boyfriend?"

Gavin's reaction was even more enthusiastic than Jesse's. He bounced up and down in his seat, his eyes wide. "Is he? Is he really your boyfriend?"

"Well ... maybe."

"So are you going to get married? Is he going to come and live with us?"

"No, honey. No. We're just getting to know each other."

"But when you're done getting to know each other? Maybe then?" Jesse asked.

The boys were so excited, so enthusiastic, that Delilah knew she'd been right to worry that their hearts would be broken if things didn't work out.

But what if things did work out?

"Guys." Delilah leaned her elbows against the counter to face them. "It's way too soon to think about Quinn living with us. Way too soon. And I want you to know that if Quinn and I are a couple ... it might work out, or it might not. We could date and get to know each other and still decide we don't want to be together."

"Like you and Dad," Jesse said.

"Well ... sort of." She reached out and took Jesse's hand in one of hers and Gavin's in the other. "Guys ... people date to find out if they want to be together. And sometimes they do, and sometimes they don't. I'm just afraid that if Quinn and I do become a couple and it doesn't work out, all three of us will be really sad. Just like when Dad left."

"Or we could be happy," Gavin said.

She squeezed his hand. "You're right. That's possible, too. We could be really, really happy."

~

SHE CALLED Quinn later that day.

"I asked the boys what they would think if you and I were a couple."

"You did?" He sounded surprised, and she hoped the surprise would outweigh any anger or hurt he might still be feeling.

"I did."

"And what did they say?"

She let out a breath. "They wondered when you're going to come live with us."

"Oh. I don't ... That's not ..."

"Relax. I told them you and I are just getting to know each other, and sometimes that works out and sometimes it doesn't. That kind of thing."

He was silent for a moment, and she gave him time to absorb what she'd said. Clearly, he was flustered. She supposed she would be, too, under the same circumstances.

After a moment, he let out a breath. "Mrs. Foster told me you were trying to protect them from getting their hopes up, but I thought … Hell, I don't know what I thought. I guess she was right."

"Mrs. Foster?" Delilah said.

"Yeah, my neighbor."

"Why does your neighbor know about my kids' hopes?"

"She's a friend of Dolly's. She knows everything, apparently."

Delilah wasn't sure whether to be annoyed with Dolly. On one hand, Delilah didn't love the fact that her romantic relationship was being bandied about on Main Street. On the other, Dolly had been such a help since Delilah and the boys had arrived in Cambria, it was hard to be too upset with her about anything.

"Well … yes. Mrs. Foster was right. The boys took to you so strongly from the first moment they met you that I thought it would be devastating for them if they thought we were a thing and then suddenly we weren't a thing anymore." Privately, Delilah reflected that it wasn't just the boys who would be devastated if that happened.

Protecting her sons was important. Essential. But protecting herself mattered, too.

Still, if she didn't take a chance, how would she ever find something good to replace all the bad that had happened to her? How would she ever realize reward without risk?

"I get it," Quinn said. "I'm sorry I gave you a hard time about it. I get where you're coming from."

But that wasn't why she'd called, was it? She hadn't called to reinforce her position. She'd called to change it.

"Quinn?"

"Yeah?"

She steeled herself to say what she needed to say to him.

"If this is just fun for you, that's okay. It really is. But we need to end it now, before the boys get hurt." *And before I do.* "But if it might be more than that, potentially … well … I think it's time for us to be open about it with the boys."

"You do?"

"I do. I really do."

~

QUINN HAD SO many conflicting reactions to what Delilah was saying that he almost felt dizzy. He sat down on the edge of his sofa, the cell phone to his ear.

The sound of her saying the words *I do* made him feel vaguely sick —but not in a bad way. More like the way you felt when the bottom dropped out from under you in a carnival ride. You thought you might puke, but that didn't mean you wanted the ride to stop.

He'd been wanting her to tell the kids. He'd pushed her to do it. But now that she was giving him what he wanted, it also meant that he had to take a stand, here and now.

Either he thought this thing might become serious, or he didn't.

Suit up or go home.

"Quinn?"

It wasn't until she spoke that he realized he hadn't said anything.

"I'm in," he said.

"Really?"

"Yeah. Hell … yes. I'm all in."

He couldn't know this soon into the relationship whether things were going to become serious. But he knew he wanted to find out, and he knew he didn't want her to leave at the end of the month without him.

The idea of getting to January first and never seeing her again? Hell, never seeing Jesse and Gavin again? It was intolerable. It was a worst-case scenario that he couldn't let happen.

The whole thing felt a little bit like diving into a swimming pool without checking first to see if there was any water in it.

But, hell. He'd will the water into existence if he had to.

CHAPTER 26

Quinn and Delilah took the boys out for pizza at JJ's to talk about what it meant that they were, in fact, a couple.

They couched it in all sorts of disclaimers, saying they were just dating, it might not work out, they were just getting to know each other, etc. But it felt to Delilah like a momentous occasion —because it was.

Jesse reacted with unbridled excitement, leaping out of his seat, bouncing up and down on his toes, and exclaiming with enthusiasm. Gavin silently inserted his thumb into his mouth—a sure sign that something was bothering him.

"Gavin? Sweetheart, what are you thinking?" Delilah asked.

Wide-eyed, he pulled out the thumb just long enough to ask, "Does this mean Dad isn't our dad anymore?

Delilah's heart ached, and her throat grew thick with emotion. She wondered if all of this was a mistake.

"No, honey. No, it doesn't mean that. Your dad will always be your dad."

"Listen, big guy," Quinn said. "I don't want to take anybody's place, okay? I'm not trying to be your new dad—I know you already have one. I just want to get to know your mom better and maybe be your friend. Do you think you'd be okay with that?"

Gavin nodded, the thumb back in place.

"Does this mean you're going to live with us?" Jesse asked. "Are you gonna come to Connecticut when we go back there? Are you and Mom gonna get married?"

Jesse and Gavin had asked similar questions when she'd first brought up the subject of her relationship with Quinn. That had been awkward enough, but having the questions asked again with Quinn in attendance was worse.

Delilah's head swam with all of the questions, but she took them calmly, one by one.

"No, Quinn isn't going to live with us, but he is going to visit a lot. We haven't talked about what will happen when we move back to Connecticut. Yes, Quinn is my boyfriend. And it's far too soon to talk or even think about getting married, Jesse. Does that answer all of your questions?"

"I guess," he said. "Except, can we go hiking again?"

"Sure we can," Quinn said. "If your mom says yes."

"I'm sure we can make that happen," Delilah said.

~

LATER, when the boys were occupied with a board game in Jesse's room, Delilah and Quinn sat on the back patio and assessed how the conversation had gone.

"Gavin seemed really excited about the idea of the two of us when I brought it up with him before. But now … God. When he asked if Mitch won't be his father anymore? I almost lost it."

"I think you handled it well, though." Quinn took Delilah's hand as they sat side by side in Adirondack chairs facing the ocean.

"You did, too. Still. Did you see how he stuck his thumb in his mouth as soon as we started talking about it? He does that when he's anxious or upset. It started after Mitch left, and he'd been getting better about it. But then, there it was again." She let out a ragged sigh.

"Are they going to see their father at all at Christmas?" Quinn asked.

"No!" Delilah threw her free arm into the air in frustration. "Before we came here, when I was figuring out what to do, I begged him to come and visit them. But he can't be bothered. He's too busy with Celine." She said the name as though it belonged to a mythical beast that threatened to destroy humanity.

"Was the guy always an asshole, or is that a new development?"

Delilah considered the question. "You know, when he first told me he was leaving me, I'd have said it was a new development. But now, in retrospect … I guess he was always an asshole. I just didn't see it until it was flashing in neon letters."

"Yeah, I get that." He sank deeper into his chair, his long legs stretched out in front of him. "We all tend to see what we want to see, especially when there's so much at stake—your marriage, your kids' well-being. Your whole way of life."

"The way of life I can do without," she said. "But the kids and the way they feel about their lives? The way their sense of security was taken away from them? That's the hard part."

"I imagine it's all hard."

"Yes. It is."

Bringing a new man into the mix was probably going to make things even harder. But sitting here with Quinn, just talking with him, didn't feel hard at all. It felt like the easiest thing she'd done in a very long time.

~

SHORTLY AFTER THAT, Quinn started getting the phone calls.

The first one was from his younger brother, Jared.

"Why the hell are random people calling me asking about you?" He launched into it without the small talk that generally started a conversation.

"What random people?"

"How the hell should I know? That's why I'm asking you."

Quinn was at home, standing in his kitchen with his butt leaning against the countertop. It was early in the morning, and he hadn't had his coffee yet.

Quinn scrubbed at his face with his free hand. "Look. Can I call you back in ten minutes? I haven't had my coffee, and if you want me to know what the hell you're talking about, I'm gonna have to do that."

Talking with his asshole brother was unpleasant under the best of circumstances. Without caffeine, it would be unbearable.

~

WHEN QUINN'S coffee had been brewed and one good-sized mug had been consumed, he braced himself and called Jared back.

"It took you long enough." Jared inexplicably chose that as a greeting instead of the more traditional *hello* or *hi* or even *hey there*.

"Yeah, well. I'm here now."

"Great. Now tell me why some random fuckhead is calling me asking about you."

Quinn leaned against the kitchen counter and sighed. "Here's an idea. Why don't we pretend I have absolutely no idea what you mean. Because I don't. Can we maybe take it from the beginning and get me caught up?"

Obviously irritated, Jared went through it: how he'd gotten a phone call from a man he'd never heard of who peppered him with questions about Quinn—his romantic history, his financial history, his work history, his personality traits. Jared had refused to answer any of them and hung up.

Then the guy had visited Jared's office.

"I don't need that shit," he went on. "I don't need people coming to my work. It's not professional, and I don't need to lose this job. So you can just tell him—"

"I can't tell him anything. I don't know who it is or what he wants any more than you do."

"I need this job," Jared went on as though Quinn hadn't spoken. "I'm not like you, sitting on a big inheritance you didn't earn. Or, I guess you *were* sitting on it. What the hell happened, Quinn? Did you lose it all gambling or just being a dickhead, or what?"

If Quinn had been confused before, he was even more so now. "Again, I have to ask, what the hell are you talking about?"

"Well, I'm assuming the guy's a debt collector."

"A debt collector? Why would you assume that?"

"Because he said he's a private investigator. Why else would a private investigator want to know about you? Unless you're screwing someone's wife."

Quinn was struck silent by this piece of news. When he finally could form a response, he said, "You might have led with the part about the private investigator."

"Yeah? And you might kiss my ass."

Then Jared hung up on him.

~

THAT WAS JUST the beginning of the phone calls. He got more from his mother, his former employer, his former landlord, and Mrs. Foster. All of them were pretty much the same: Who was this guy who wanted to know about Quinn? And why did he want to know?

People who had a generally good impression of Quinn assumed it was some kind of security clearance for a job application. People who had a generally bad impression of him assumed he was in some kind of legal or financial trouble.

He wasn't in any legal trouble that he knew of, he had a healthy savings account, and he hadn't applied for a job. What the hell was this?

The whole thing was so unsettling, so strange. And so unexplainable.

Until he remembered one thing Jared had said to him: *unless you're screwing someone's wife.*

He wasn't. But he did have a relationship with someone's ex.

Delilah's ex-husband, as a lawyer, almost certainly worked with private investigators and had access to any number of them.

Could that be it?

He thought to ask her, but he wasn't ready to do that yet. Instead, he went to Mrs. Foster's house one day when he saw her car in the driveway.

"Oh, Quinn. It's lovely to see you. Come in, come in. I just bought some muffins at the Cookie Crock. They're chocolate chip. Would you like one?"

He was about to decline, but then he realized he liked chocolate chip muffins and he'd skipped lunch, so he was starving.

"That sounds great, actually. Thanks."

ONE MUFFIN, one cup of tea, and a lot of chitchat later, Quinn left Mrs. Foster's house with the phone number of the private investigator who'd been asking about him.

He went home, called the number, and got voice mail.

"This is Quinn Monroe," he said. "I assume I don't have to tell you what I want, because you already know more about me than either one of us is probably comfortable with. Call me." He left his number and hung up.

The guy never called back—either because he didn't want to tell Quinn who'd hired him or because he thought Quinn might hunt him down and kick his ass.

Or both.

When that didn't work, Quinn Googled *attorney Mitchell Ballard Paris*. Within minutes, he had an e-mail address for Delilah's ex.

Using it without talking to her first felt like a betrayal, so he didn't do that. He just hung onto the address while he thought about what to do.

If Quinn confronted him and the guy really didn't have anything to do with it, that would embarrass Delilah, and Quinn didn't want that.

All he could do, he decided, was wait to see what happened.

For a while, nothing did.

CHAPTER 27

Quinn, Delilah, Jesse, and Gavin spent Christmas Eve and Christmas Day together at Otter Bluff.

On Christmas Eve, they listened to Christmas carols, decorated the house with pine boughs and big red bows, baked cookies for Santa, watched *A Charlie Brown Christmas,* then set up Santa's plate of milk and cookies on a table near the fireplace.

It took a long time to get the boys settled down to sleep—along with several threats that Santa might not come if he knew the kids were still awake.

When the kids were finally asleep, Quinn and Delilah brought their stashes of wrapped presents out of a closet in Delilah's bedroom and placed them under the tree—putting the ones marked *From Santa* up front.

It made sense for Quinn to sleep over, since the boys would be up at the crack of dawn begging to open their gifts. It wouldn't be fair to make them wait for Quinn to get here, Delilah thought.

That was mostly an excuse. In truth, she just wanted him there.

Delilah and Quinn ate Santa's cookies and drank his milk, then they went to bed and made love quietly, so the boys wouldn't hear. They were getting good at it.

THE MORNING WAS a flurry of torn wrapping paper, gift boxes opened and thrown aside, and squeals of excitement from the boys as they unwrapped their gifts and revealed video games, books, board games, and art supplies.

Quinn had a goofy look of contentment on his face as he sat on the sofa in sweatpants and a T-shirt, sipping his first cup of coffee of the day and watching the boys.

That look scared Delilah when she glanced at him and saw it. That look hit her like a punch to the chest. Quinn was in love—with the boys, at least, if not with her.

Until now, she'd fooled herself that she could walk away from this on January first without anyone getting seriously hurt. But that look—the way Quinn was absorbed with happiness watching Jesse and Gavin—told her it was already too late for that.

Delilah opened gifts from the boys that they'd made with Dolly—a clay flowerpot full of herbs that Gavin had painted with a happy sun and lollipop-shaped trees, and a jar of lavender sugar scrub from Jesse.

Delilah exclaimed with pleasure at each one.

"Dolly helped me make it," Jesse said. "She's got a recipe. You can see the lavender in there. See?" Jesse pointed at the jar.

"I see it, honey." Delilah opened the lid and smelled the contents. "It smells wonderful."

"It's got trees," Gavin said, pointing to his flowerpot.

"It certainly does. They're lovely." Delilah scooped Gavin into her arms and gave him a squeeze.

When the boys were done opening their gifts, Delilah and Quinn exchanged theirs. She gave him a lightweight camping hammock he could string between two trees—an item he'd mentioned that he wanted the last time they'd gone hiking. He gave her a handmade scarf he'd seen in one of the boutiques on Main Street. The colors reminded him of her, he said.

Both of the gifts were chosen carefully, Delilah noticed. They were personal, but not too personal. They said, *I'm thinking about you,* but not *I love you.*

Right now, though, she felt considerably more for him than a travel hammock could express.

"I love my scarf." She leaned over to give him a kiss.

"I'm glad." He gestured toward the hammock, which was sitting on the sofa next to him. "You think this thing will hold two people?"

She grinned. "The box said it would."

His eyebrows rose. "That gives me ideas."

"What kind of ideas?" Jesse asked.

"Ideas for the naps we can take," Delilah put in quickly. The boys tended to resist naps, so she hoped that would put the conversation to rest.

Thankfully, it did.

THEY ATE a big breakfast of eggs, bacon, and toast, then Quinn and Delilah tidied up the living room while the boys played with their new things. Jesse wanted Quinn to see his new video game, so Quinn played it with him for a while after the cleanup was done.

After breakfast, they took a walk together on the beach, then they came back to Otter Bluff with sand in their shoes and seashells in their pockets.

Later, over a Christmas dinner of ham, scalloped potatoes, fresh rolls, salad, and pie, Delilah thought the day had seemed perfect.

Almost perfect.

The only thing marring it was the tick-tock of the timer they'd set on their relationship. They would have to decide where this thing was going—and soon.

But that wasn't what was on Delilah's mind as she sat in front of the Christmas tree after dinner, a fire crackling in the fireplace and a mug of hot cocoa in her hands. She was thinking that she finally had the kind of family life she'd always wanted for herself and her boys—

and she'd found it not with her husband, but with someone who might decide not to be with her past the next week.

Her eyes filled with tears and she wiped them away quickly, hoping Quinn wouldn't see.

He did see, though.

"Are you okay?" He'd been sitting on the carpet with Gavin, helping him assemble an indoor tent Quinn had bought him as a kind of clubhouse, but when he saw the look on Delilah's face, he got up and came to sit next to her.

"Yes." She took in a ragged breath. "Fine."

"You're leaking a little bit." He reached out and wiped a tear from her face with his thumb.

"Yeah, I guess I am." She laughed, blinked a few times, and willed herself to get her crap together. "It's just … thank you. The boys have had a wonderful Christmas, and it's because of you."

"Oh, I don't know about that. You put in a ton of work on this whole production. I'd say they owe their happy holiday to you."

"You don't get it." She shook her head.

"What don't I get?"

She glanced at the boys, who were so absorbed in their gifts that they likely weren't listening to them. She lowered her voice to keep what she was about to say just between herself and Quinn.

"What you don't get is … is that I was barely managing when you met me. I was trying to hold it together for the boys, but …" She shook her head. "I was a mess. I was miserable. And I was dreading Christmas because I thought … I thought it would be a reminder of the divorce, and the disaster of my marriage, and all of the things I couldn't give Jesse and Gavin now that their father is gone."

Damn it. There went the tears again.

"But," she went on. "You made me want to be happy again. Not just for them, but for me. You made me feel *hopeful*. And believe me, that's no small thing."

He took her face in his hands and kissed her until the boys yelled "Ew!" and "Gross!" and "Mom, that's embarrassing!" Then they pulled apart, laughing. Quinn grabbed a wadded-up piece of tissue paper from someone's gift box and threw it at Jesse. The tissue bounced lightly off his head.

~

QUINN HAD FELT the same way. He'd had no one to spend Christmas with, no one to buy gifts for, no one to make happy memories with. He'd wanted to forget that such things as holidays even existed.

But then he'd met Delilah, and all of that had changed. She and the boys weren't his family—not really—but they felt like it. Suddenly, he'd had things to look forward to. Suddenly, he'd been a part of something again.

"You know," he said, "we're going to have to figure this thing out sooner rather than later."

"I've been thinking about that." She shifted on the sofa to face him.

"You have?"

"Yes."

Nerves rattled around in his stomach as he waited for what she had to say. Whatever she said next—that she wanted to stay or that she wanted to go, possibly without him—would either send him soaring or crashing down to earth in a painful jumble of broken parts.

"Okay. What have you been thinking?"

She let out a breath and squared her shoulders, preparing herself. Okay, so it was something that required preparation.

"The boys and I have to leave Otter Bluff on January first. Our rental agreement will be up, and the house is booked to someone else after that."

"Yeah. Okay ..." He was starting to sweat a little.

"And I thought ..." She hesitated, almost like she was *trying* to mess with him. "I thought we'd look for another place here in Cambria. A long-term rental, maybe, until we can figure out a plan for what we're doing. I can look for a job, and I can enroll Jesse in kindergarten and Gavin in preschool, and you and I ... we can take our time. We won't be on a deadline anymore, and we can just ... just be together and see how it goes."

Quinn was so relieved that he felt dizzy. "You're staying."

"We're staying."

He swept her into his arms and let out a whoop of joy that had the boys coming over to see what was going on.

"What happened?" Jesse asked.

"Did you get another present?" Gavin asked his mother.

"I think I'm the one who got the gift," Quinn said. Probably the best one he'd ever received.

CHAPTER 28

Delilah should have known Mitch wouldn't let it go. She should have known he'd make trouble now that Delilah had found a way to be happy.

He dropped the bombshell two days after Christmas while Delilah was touring rental properties with a Realtor. Jesse and Gavin were having a guys' day out with Quinn—that's what they'd called it, a guys' day out. Delilah had thought that was adorable, but it had also hurt that her sons didn't have that with their father.

She was standing in the living room of a two-bedroom house on Happy Hill when the call came in.

"I thought I told you to stop seeing that Quinn Monroe person." Mitch launched into his attack as soon as she picked up the call.

Delilah instantly felt tension surge through her body.

"That's not your decision to make, Mitch."

"Yeah, well, you're half right."

"What does that mean?"

"It means, I might not have any control over what kind of random, questionable men you spend your time with, but I sure as hell have control over who you're bringing around my kids."

"Mitch. Quinn isn't random or questionable. You don't know anything about him."

"Oh, I know a lot," he said. "Probably more than you do."

Delilah felt cold dread as she thought about where this might be going. She told Mitch she would call him back, told the Realtor she had an emergency and would have to reschedule, then went out to her car, waited for the Realtor to leave, and called him back.

"Okay. I'm alone now. What's this about?"

Mitch told her a story she could hardly believe.

He told her he'd hired a private investigator to learn everything he could about Quinn. It was all for Jesse and Gavin's sake, he said. How could he just let them spend time around a strange man without Mitch determining it was safe? How could any good father do that?

The investigator learned that Quinn had received a sizable inheritance from his uncle—an inheritance that Quinn's two brothers had been shut out of.

"One of the brothers—guy by the name of Alexander Monroe—had a heart attack a year ago, which led to a two-week hospital stay. He couldn't pay his medical bills, and he was evicted from his home. All this while Quinn's sitting on a few hundred thousand that his brothers had as much right to as he did. Not only didn't your boyfriend help out with the medical bills—something he easily could have done—but the asshole didn't even visit his brother in the hospital."

Delilah sat in her car, frozen, not knowing what to think or what to do.

Finally, she said the only thing she could think of: "I'm sure there's some sort of explanation. Quinn wouldn't—"

"Yeah, well, he did. You want to keep seeing this guy? Be my guest. But if you do, I'm suing for custody. And I'll win. I'm pretty sure Jesse and Gavin will like Paris. What do you think?"

~

"CAN HE DO THAT?"

Delilah called her lawyer before anything else—before driving back to Otter Bluff, before asking herself if Mitch would really try such a thing, before even setting down her phone. His receptionist had tried to take a message, but the hysteria in Delilah's voice had persuaded her to put the call through.

Miles Lawrence had patiently listened to everything Mitch had said to Delilah, and now he pronounced his verdict. "No. No. Almost certainly, no."

"Miles, is it 'no'? Or is it 'almost certainly no'? Because one of those sounds pretty good, and the other one sounds like you're nervous."

Miles didn't answer for a moment, but she could hear him tapping the point of a pencil on his legal pad as he'd done every time they'd met. "Well, here's the thing. Suing for custody as a parent living outside of the minor's home country is ... problematic. However ..."

Delilah closed her eyes and waited for the *however*.

Miles went on, "Your ex-husband isn't a typical noncustodial parent. He's a highly skilled attorney with significant resources."

"So, what are you saying? Are you saying he'll win?"

"I'm saying he *shouldn't* win. My prediction is that he won't win. But ... in all honesty, anything could happen."

~

DELILAH DROVE BACK to Otter Bluff with tears in her eyes, wondering how much more Mitch planned to take from her.

He'd taken her home, her self-respect, her dignity. He'd taken her trust in him and had broken it into a thousand pieces. He'd taken her sense of security. And now he was poised to take her kids—or the man she loved.

She hadn't been sure she loved Quinn until Mitch had tried to force her to give him up. But now, in the face of that threat, she was sure.

She loved him.

But she loved her children more. The idea of losing them—of living here, half a world away, while they were in Paris with a woman they didn't know and a father who was too preoccupied to really parent them—was unthinkable.

Losing Quinn would devastate her, but losing Jesse and Gavin would kill her.

She came home to an empty house, because Quinn and the boys were still on their outing. Delilah didn't bother to turn on the lights or even take her purse off her shoulder. She just sat on the sofa with her hands pressed between her knees and stared at the floor, trying to process everything Mitch had said.

Delilah had never been an angry person. She'd been even-tempered from childhood, always taking things in stride, always expecting the best out of the people around her.

Until she'd experienced divorce.

Now, she had a well of anger within her that was so deep and so boiling hot that, for the first time in her life, she felt capable of murder. She felt like she could rip her ex into pieces with her bare hands if only he were here for her to do it.

Mother-bear instinct, she supposed.

Her thoughts bounced around from the impossibility of living without her children, to the constant, ongoing betrayal she was suffering at Mitch's hands, to the things he'd said about Quinn.

Disturbing things.

Had he really turned his back on his brother just when he'd needed Quinn most? Had he really put money above his love for his own family? Was that why he changed the subject whenever Delilah asked about his family? Was that why he'd been alone for the holidays until the Ballards came along?

She really didn't know Quinn that well, did she? She'd only met him a couple of months ago. If he was the kind of man who would put money above family, that made him … Well, that made him just like Mitch, didn't it?

Was it possible that she'd gotten entangled with another man who was like her ex? It didn't seem that way, but maybe that was just Delilah's poor judgment talking.

Maybe she was only seeing what she wanted to see.

When Quinn came in with the boys that afternoon, Delilah tried to put on a pleasant face for her children's sake.

"Mom! We went to Morro Bay and went in a boat and everything!" Jesse's eyes were wide with excitement.

"I got to steer it," Gavin said earnestly.

"Did you, honey? That's great." Delilah pressed a kiss to the top of his head.

"Yeah, we did one of those electric boat rentals," Quinn said. "We saw some harbor seals and a group of otters, didn't we, guys?"

"And then we got ice cream!" Jesse added.

"Gavin thought you might not want them to have ice cream," Quinn said, "but I thought—"

"Oh … that's fine." Delilah tried on a smile, but she felt it wobble on her face. "Thank you for doing this."

"Hey. Is everything okay?" Quinn peered at her with concern.

She would have to tell him what had happened, of course. But she couldn't do it right now—not with the boys here. She had vowed not to trash-talk her ex in front of her sons, and she wasn't about to go back on that now. It might feel good momentarily, but it would hurt Jesse and Gavin, and she simply wasn't going to do it.

Instead, she forced herself to offer him a more stable and convincing smile. "Yes, sure. Everything's fine. I just … I got some news today, and it's kind of thrown me."

He ran a hand down her upper arm. "You want to talk about it?"

"I will want to, yes. But not right now." She looked pointedly at Jesse and Gavin, who were talking to each other excitedly about all they'd done that day.

"Ah. Sure." Quinn nodded. "Listen. How about we order a pizza, and I'll—"

"I'm not really feeling up to it." Delilah shrugged apologetically. "If that's okay. The news I got … I think the guys and I just need to be alone tonight."

The disappointment on his face made Delilah feel guilty—even though none of this was her fault.

"Well … call me if you want to talk," he said. "Or if you need anything. I mean it. If you need *anything*."

The fact that he was willing to go—willing to take her word that she needed time and leave her alone—was another difference between Quinn and Mitch. If Mitch had wanted to know what she was thinking, he'd have badgered her like she was a witness in court. He'd have interrogated her until she cracked.

But Quinn trusted her to know what she needed, and that was a revelation.

It made the fact of what she'd learned about him even more painful.

He said goodbye to Jesse and Gavin, who protested, begging him to stay. Then he kissed Delilah goodbye and left, acting like all of this was just fine, like it was normal.

It wasn't fine, and it wasn't normal.

CHAPTER 29

Delilah had thought things would seem clearer after a good night's sleep. The problem was, sleep didn't come. She lay awake that night thinking about what Mitch had said. Had Quinn really chosen money over family? It was hard to believe, but they hadn't known each other that long. What if Delilah was wrong about what kind of man he was?

After obsessing about that, she switched to the question of custody. Could Mitch really take her sons away from her? If she stopped seeing Quinn, would Mitch back off? And what about next time? Would he pull this every time she met someone? What would her life look like then? He got to be happy with Celine, but was Delilah doomed to a life of loneliness until the boys reached adulthood?

It wasn't fair—none of it was. What was she supposed to do? How was she supposed to respond?

Delilah got up early, feeling exhausted and wrung-out. She made a strong pot of coffee while the kids slept and drank a cup on the back patio, watching the waves as she huddled under a thick blanket.

It was only six a.m. on the West Coast, but it was nine in Connecticut. Late enough to call Roxanne.

Delilah's sister picked up on the first ring, immediately launching into chatter about Christmas and which of the relatives drank too much and embarrassed themselves.

"But that's just like Sheila, isn't it? God, I don't know why Jim married her."

It took a while before Roxanne slowed down enough to realize Delilah was crying.

"Oh, God. What's going on? What happened?" she said when she finally understood Delilah hadn't called to chat.

Delilah told her everything Mitch had said, every thought that had tormented her while she'd tried—and failed—to sleep.

"The thing is, I was happy." Delilah dragged in a tearful breath. "I was really happy for the first time since I found out about Celine. I thought … I thought things were going to turn around for me. With Quinn. But now …" Her voice broke, and she squeezed her eyes shut with her free hand, willing herself not to lose her composure any more than she already had.

"That bastard. You can't let him get away with this. You've got a lawyer, right?"

"Yes."

"We'll get you a better one. We'll get you a team of them. That fucker is going to wish he was never born."

That was why Delilah loved her sister. Roxanne was always on Team Delilah, no matter what. If Delilah were to ask Roxanne to help her hide a body, Roxanne would start researching methods of corpse disposal before she'd even hung up the phone.

"Thank you," Delilah said, her voice shaky. "Really, thank you. I just … I just don't know what to do from here."

"Have you talked to Quinn about it?"

"Not yet. I wanted to get everything straight in my head first."

Roxanne's voice softened. "He might not have done what Mitch said he did. And if he did, he might have had a good reason. He deserves a chance to explain himself."

Overhead, a flock of gulls glided by. Down on the rocks, a sea lion barked.

"I know," Delilah said. "But that doesn't help me, does it? Whatever he did or didn't do, Mitch is going to make him sound awful in court, and I can't go through that. It's not fair to anyone—Jesse and Gavin, or Quinn. Or me."

"He's bluffing," Roxanne said. "He doesn't want to raise Jesse and Gavin. He never paid attention to them when you were married, and he doesn't want them complicating his nice Parisian life now."

Delilah had thought the same thing. But how sure was she? If she called his bluff and lost ...

"Maybe," she said. "You might be right. But ... he would take them, Roxanne. Even if he doesn't want them, he'd take them just to spite me. Just to prove he can."

~

LATER THAT DAY, while he was at home working on a new website project, Quinn got a text from Delilah.

It said, *We need to talk.*

All at once, he felt the earth open up beneath him. No good conversation with a woman had ever started with, *We need to talk.*

Might as well get it over with instead of spending his time worrying and wondering.

I'll come over, he responded.

Better if I call you. I don't want to get the kids excited and then disappoint them. Is this a good time?

So, the kids would be excited just to be disappointed, then. Terrific. She was definitely dumping him. The question was, why? And what could he do to stop it?

Because he knew he needed to stop it. The Ballard family was quickly becoming the center of his life, and he *liked* it. That had to mean something. That had to mean this relationship was worth fighting for.

He braced himself and typed, *Sure. Let's talk.*

Then he got ready to have his heart ripped out.

~

Delilah put on a movie for the boys—one she knew would absorb their attention completely. Then she went onto the patio to call Quinn.

She was not going to cry—that was her main goal. If she could just keep her composure, this whole thing would go so much more smoothly.

Unfortunately, her resolve crumbled as soon as she heard his voice, and a tear slipped down her cheek. At least he couldn't see that. Couldn't see how broken she was.

"Hi," she said.

"Hi."

From the sound of her voice, he knew this was going to be bad.

"So, Mitch called me yesterday." She took in a ragged breath and told him everything: the private investigator, the things Mitch had told her about Quinn, and the threat he'd made that if Delilah kept seeing Quinn, he'd sue for custody.

"He said you refused to help your brother with his medical bills even though you'd gotten a big inheritance, and even though he lost his house. Mitch said you didn't even visit him in the hospital."

"Alex had a heart attack? When? Is he okay?"

Delilah knew from his tone that he wasn't faking this—he really hadn't known.

"I'm not sure how he is," she said. "Mitch said it was a year ago, but he didn't tell me any details. You really didn't know?"

"I really didn't know. Jesus. They didn't tell me. And he lost his house?"

Delilah dried her eyes with her fingertips and steadied herself. "Quinn, what's going on with you and your family? Why didn't they tell you? And why don't you talk to them?"

She heard him moving around, maybe shifting his phone to the other ear or scrubbing at his face with his hand.

"Okay. Here's the story. I did get an inheritance a few years ago, from my uncle. Who was gay. And who was disowned by the rest of the family for it. My mother and my brothers judged the shit out of him, and for what? Because he didn't fit their idea of what a man should be? They told him he'd be welcomed back into the family *if* he quit his *lifestyle*. That's what they called it. A lifestyle."

He took in a breath and let it out in a ragged sigh. "I was the only one who stood by him, so, yeah, I was the one who got everything when he died. My brothers and my mother insisted that I split the money with them, and when I didn't, they cut me off. The only time I hear from them is when my mother calls to try to shame me into giving them all their share. She calls it 'their share,' as though they're entitled to it because of genetics. Because of blood."

"Quinn, that's awful." Mitch's report hadn't included any of those relevant details.

"But," Quinn went on, "I didn't know Alex was in the hospital. I didn't know he lost his house. Shit. I'd have tried to do … I don't know. Something. I would have been there, at least, if they'd let me in the door." He let out a weary groan. "So, that's what all of those phone calls were about."

He told her about hearing from Jared and a selection of other people from his past, all of them saying a man had been asking about him. Then he told her about getting the detective's number from Mrs. Foster and how Quinn had been unable to reach him.

Hearing all of it made Delilah more angry at Mitch than ever. What right did he have to poke around in Quinn's life?

"Quinn, I'm so sorry. About what Mitch did, and also about your family. About everything."

"Yeah, thanks. It's been shit, honestly. And I didn't tell you about it because … because things with you *aren't* shit. They're damned near perfect, and I just wanted to keep that part of my life away from this part, you know?"

She did know. She'd wanted to keep Quinn and Mitch as separate entities, planets with orbits that would never intersect. But things had a way of getting messy, didn't they?

"Mitch is saying … he's saying he'll sue for custody if you and I don't stop seeing each other. Because you're a bad influence on the kids. He says he'll take them to Paris."

She was starting to tear up again just thinking about the possibility. She wiped a stray tear from her cheek with her fingertips.

"This isn't about me," he said. "Not really. It's about him trying to control you, Delilah. And if you let him, he's going to do it again the next time you meet someone. And again the time after that."

"I know that."

"If you give in, you're never going to have your own life. You're never—"

"I know that, Quinn! Don't you think I know that?"

She'd raised her voice, which she hadn't meant to do, especially with the boys just on the other side of the sliding glass door.

"So, what do you plan to do?" he asked.

"I don't know."

"Do you have a lawyer lined up?"

"Yes."

"Well, that's good. Let's go see him, and maybe we can—"

"I have to handle this alone." She squeezed her eyes shut and fought to control her emotions, her breath. "I can't involve you any more than you're already in it."

"Delilah—"

"I can't risk it, Quinn. I can't risk having you be part of this until I have a plan. Until I know what I'm going to do. If he takes Jesse and Gavin … They're everything to me. They're everything." Her voice was a ragged whisper.

"I get that."

"You do?"

"Of course I do. If those boys were my sons, I'd crawl through hell to protect them."

If they were my sons.

Delilah had allowed herself to imagine just such a scenario. It had been so tempting. The idea had been so lovely—until Mitch had ruined it, the way he ruined everything.

"Then you understand why … why we have to stop seeing each other."

He didn't say anything for a long time. When he did, his tone was clipped. "You can't just lay down and let him do this to you, Delilah. To us."

But there couldn't be an *us*. Not anymore. Not if it meant losing her children.

"I'm sorry," she said, then disconnected the call.

CHAPTER 30

Quinn hadn't known what to expect when Delilah said she needed to talk. But it wasn't this.

She'd thought maybe he'd done something wrong that he didn't know about. He'd been a lunkhead guy, offending her in some way he hadn't realized.

That, he could have dealt with. He could have apologized. He could have learned from his mistakes and moved on.

But this? He couldn't fix this, and he wasn't sure it was even right to try. What if he convinced her to keep seeing him and then she lost her children?

He couldn't let that happen.

And this was one of the reasons he hadn't wanted to get involved with a single mother in the first place. He hadn't imagined this exact scenario, but he'd sure as hell imagined one in which her baggage complicated things.

Except, her kids didn't feel like baggage. They felt like wonderful people Quinn might never have the pleasure of seeing again.

He tried to go back to work on the website for his client, then pushed his keyboard aside.

He couldn't think.

And, shit, Alex.

A heart attack?

Alex was older than Quinn by about fifteen years—he'd been the result of a teen pregnancy, while Quinn and Jared had come along later, when his parents' lives were more stable. Still, Alex was young for a heart attack. He smoked, he never exercised, and he ate fatty foods, so Quinn guessed it wasn't out of the range of the probable.

Still, it came as a shock.

Alex might have died without Quinn ever seeing him again. Was the grudge so important to Alex—and to the rest of his family, for that matter—that he would shut out his brother on his damned death bed?

It wasn't his death bed, though. Alex had survived.

Which gave Quinn a second chance to work things out with his family, if he wanted to do it.

He just had to decide whether he wanted to do it.

DELILAH SPENT the next couple of days trying to act happy and normal for Gavin and Jesse.

They weren't fooled, though.

"What's wrong with your face?" Jesse asked one afternoon.

"My face?" She put a hand to her cheek. "What do you mean?"

"It's all weird and scrunchy," Gavin said.

Was it? Delilah guessed she hadn't been as good at hiding her emotions as she'd wanted to believe.

"I have allergies." At least that would explain her red-rimmed eyes. "There's something in the yard here, I guess."

QUINN NEEDED to be doing something about his situation. He just didn't know what.

He couldn't pressure Delilah, because she was under enough pressure already without him adding to it. And he couldn't fly to Paris and punch her asshole ex in the face.

That left him at home, puttering around, trying to work but not accomplishing much, and brooding about the fact that he'd been, essentially, dumped.

He hated this. He hated being without Delilah, hated knowing that she was hurting and there was nothing he could do about it. He hated being so ineffectual. And he sure as hell hated the fact that the asshole ex—a guy he'd never met—had this kind of control over his life.

He hated that Alex was so angry with him that he'd face death without ever telling Quinn about it.

Well, at least that was an area where Quinn could take some kind of action.

He sat at his desk, stared at the screen on his laptop without really seeing it, then got up and packed an overnight bag.

He didn't know if he was going to hug Alex or throw him out a window when he saw him. Given the man's recent health problems, the hug was probably more advisable.

He guessed they'd just have to see what happened.

~

DELILAH DIDN'T WANT to sit around and let her life get smashed to pieces, and she also didn't want to allow Mitch to be the guy holding the sledgehammer—again.

She needed to know how to react to his threat, and she needed to come up with a plan for her future.

She didn't know whether she and the boys were going to stay in Cambria, as planned, or return to Connecticut. But she did know one thing: she needed to take legal action now, proactively, instead of reacting later.

Delilah made an appointment for a video conference with her attorney a few days after Mitch's threat. It was going to cost her three hundred and fifty dollars an hour, but, hell. It was money that used to belong to Mitch, so that seemed appropriate.

Dolly agreed to take the boys during the call, not only because Delilah needed to focus, but also because she didn't want Jesse and Gavin to hear what she would be saying about their father.

It sucked to be the adult sometimes. It would be so much easier to rage against Mitch in front of any and all who cared to listen. But she had to be better than that. She had to think of her kids' feelings before her own.

After lunch, Delilah took the boys to Dolly's and called Miles Lawrence, whom she'd found through her parents.

Delilah wasn't used to making video calls on her laptop, so it took some fiddling with the program to make the thing work.

Just when she was worried that she might have to scrap the video call and just use the telephone, Miles's face appeared on the screen.

"There you are! Are you seeing me clearly, Delilah?" he asked.

Miles had come into Delilah's life after her parents had hired another, less bloodthirsty lawyer to draw up their wills. When Mitch had filed for divorce, they'd referred Delilah to their lawyer, who had sent her to Miles.

At first, she'd thought the older, portly, balding man—who came off as a grandfatherly type—wouldn't be aggressive enough to represent her against Mitch and his considerable resources. But he'd gotten her a settlement she would have thought impossible and that had allowed her to quit her job and spend two months at Otter Bluff without worrying about her finances.

"I'm here. I can see you," Delilah told him.

"Wonderful. Now, bring me up to speed on everything that's happening. Have you spoken to Mitch again since our phone call?"

Delilah and Miles talked about Mitch's threat, Quinn's issues with his family, and Mitch's relationship with his sons, until Miles was completely up to speed.

"It's true that I haven't known Quinn very long," Delilah went on. "But Mitch is making Quinn out to be some horrible influence, and it's just not true."

"Okay. This is more common than you might think." Miles jotted notes onto a yellow legal pad. "People often find it hard when their ex-spouse moves on to someone else."

"But he moved on to someone else first!"

Miles chuckled, but with no amusement in his voice. "Yes, well. There's no limit to the contradictions and complexities of the male ego."

Delilah ignored that bit of wisdom.

"The question is, can he do this? Should I worry?"

Miles steepled his hands on his desk and regarded her over his half-glasses. "It will be an uphill climb for him to win custody in court, but it's not impossible," Miles said. "And in matters of custody, I find that you should always, always worry."

THE WAY THEY LEFT IT, Miles agreed to do some "looking into" Delilah's case. Since Mitch hadn't actually filed anything yet, there was no formal work to do. But it paid to be prepared, Miles assured her, so he would do "a little checking"—whatever that amounted to—just in case it came to that.

Delilah felt better having talked to him, even though he hadn't given her the reassurance she'd hoped for.

It felt better to be doing something, anything.

Now she just had to decide what to do about Quinn. And about her living arrangements.

QUINN'S FAMILY lived in Flagstaff, Arizona, where Quinn had first learned to love the outdoors. He'd enjoyed hiking and fishing and camping with his brothers and his stepfather—and his uncle, who'd been an integral part of his family until he'd come out and everyone but Quinn had turned against him.

It was a ten-hour drive, and Quinn opted to do it all in one day. He was driving his van, so he'd be able to stop and take a nap if he got tired.

As it turned out, he didn't get tired.

He arrived in Flagstaff late, checked in at an RV park where he'd made a reservation, used the shower facilities, and turned in for the night.

He didn't sleep well, because he wasn't sure how his family was going to greet him when he saw them.

One thing seemed likely—they weren't going to throw him a party.

Well, that was fine. He didn't need one. He just needed to see that Alex was okay, and he needed to say what he had to say.

He could do that whether they wanted him to or not.

MITCH CALLED Jesse and Gavin again the next day. Under normal circumstances, Delilah would have considered that to be a good thing. But in this case, she knew he was just checking up on whether Delilah had broken it off with Quinn.

That was confirmed when Jesse returned Delilah's phone to her after the call.

"Dad asked if we've done any more stuff with Quinn," he said. "Where is Quinn? We went out on the boat that one day, and then he just went away."

"He didn't go anywhere," Delilah said, though she wasn't at all sure that was true. "He's just been busy."

"But he said he was gonna take us to the zoo. He said he was gonna ask you if it's okay. And then we didn't see him again. Did he even ask you?"

"There's no zoo around here, I don't think," she said, avoiding the question.

"Yes there is. There's a little one someplace nearby, he said, but there's a better one in Santa Barbara. That's the one he wanted to go to. The better one. I'll bet he didn't even ask."

"Oh, honey." Delilah ruffled Jesse's hair with her hand. "He's got a lot of work to do. Did you know he has three jobs?"

"He said he was gonna do it, though. He said."

"Does Quinn still like us?" Gavin asked, his eyes wide.

That, more than anything, was what made Delilah's heart tear into shreds.

"Of course he does, sweetheart." She knelt down and pulled Gavin into her arms. He let her hold him, his thumb plugged firmly in his mouth. "Quinn likes you both very much."

She weighed whether to tell them the truth, then opted to give them part of it—the part that didn't involve their father.

"I'm going to be honest with you guys." Delilah was still kneeling, facing both Jesse and Gavin, a hand resting on each child's arm. "Quinn hasn't come around lately because of me. Not because of you."

"Why? What did you do?" Jesse's look was already accusing, already angry.

"It's not that I did anything. It's just ... people have differences, Jesse."

Jesse pulled his arm out of Delilah's grasp. "You and dad had 'differences,' and we don't see him anymore. And now Quinn. Why do you keep making people leave?"

Before she could answer, he ran away from her and went into his room, slamming the door.

CHAPTER 31

When things had blown up between Quinn and his family over his inheritance, he'd sworn he wouldn't be the one to come running back, asking for forgiveness.

If they ever came to him and denounced their Neanderthal closed-minded ways, well, he could be the bigger man and they could talk.

But here he was, going back home without even a hint that anyone might want to see him. Without even a whisper that anyone might want to reconcile.

Well, it was one thing to stand on principle. But when one of your own was sick or God forbid dying, you at least needed to have a conversation with each other.

Quinn didn't have Alex's address—not since he'd lost the house—so he started at his mother's place.

Barbara and Carl, Quinn's stepfather, lived in a one-story wood frame ranch-style house on an acre of land off Route 180, north of town.

The siding was starting to peel and the place needed a coat of paint, but Quinn's mother had kept the garden perfectly tended, as usual. The shrubs lining the driveway had recently been trimmed, and the flowerbeds were tidy and sparse, awaiting the spring.

Quinn felt a tightness in his chest as he went up the front walk, stepped onto the porch, and knocked on the door.

Carl answered the door, blinking twice with his jaw slack as he saw his stepson standing there.

"Hi, Carl."

The older man was wearing a T-shirt and a pair of khakis that were past their prime. The pants were a little baggy, and he had them cinched at the waist with a leather belt.

If Quinn had thought he might be welcomed home with warmth and enthusiasm, he'd miscalculated. Carl didn't open the screen door that separated them.

"Can I come in?" It rankled that he had to ask, and he wondered if it had been a mistake to come here.

Carl pushed the screen open, yelled into the house, "Barb? Quinn's here." Then he walked away, leaving Quinn standing on the doormat.

"Quinn? Well, my goodness." Barbara emerged from somewhere in the back of the house looking vaguely stunned, as though she'd just emerged from total darkness into bright daylight.

Quinn, having given up on the idea that anyone might invite him into the house, stepped inside. "Hi, Mom."

His mother had never cut off communication with Quinn the way his brothers had. Her approach, instead, had been to nag him relentlessly, urging him to mend his relationship with herself and his brothers by giving them what they wanted. She'd taken sides, but she hadn't shut him out. He'd been the one to distance himself from her when she'd repeatedly refused to back off about Nate's money.

Now, she stepped toward him as though she might hug him, but she didn't. Instead, she stopped a few paces away and clasped her hands at her waist.

"Honey, it's good to see you." She looked frail, and he wondered if she'd lost weight. "Come on into the kitchen. I just put some coffee on." She bustled off into the rear of the house with Quinn following.

Barbara's Christmas decorations were still up—she never took them down until after January first—though the tree was starting to lose its needles. In the kitchen, the bulletin board next to the refrigerator was covered in Christmas cards affixed with push pins. A tiny ceramic nativity scene was arranged on the kitchen counter amid a garland of plastic pine boughs.

Barbara took mugs out of the cupboard and arranged them on the counter with a sugar bowl and a small carton of cream.

"Let me just take this to Carl." She poured a cup, added sugar and cream in the exact measurements Quinn's stepfather liked, then hurried off to the living room to give it to him.

When she came back, she put on a smile Quinn recognized as false. It was the smile she used for neighbors she didn't particularly like but who nonetheless had to be treated with courtesy for fear they might talk unkindly about her otherwise.

"You should have called and let us know you were coming. The house is a mess, and I haven't done the marketing yet."

"The house is fine."

She poured Quinn a cup and handed it to him.

"Mom, why didn't you tell me about Alex's heart attack?"

Her smile faltered, and she avoided looking at him as she fussed with her own mug, her own cream and sugar.

"Well, he asked me not to, and I figured it was his to tell, Quinn."

That was crap, obviously. Barbara had never kept a confidence in her life, and it made no sense that she would start now.

"You should have called me."

Her shoulders fell and her lips pursed, causing fine lines to fan out around her mouth. "I didn't call you because if you'd come out here, you and your brothers would have fought, and with Alex's heart …" She shook her head. "He needed rest. He needed calm. I was afraid if he got too upset, it might kill him." Her eyes were red and wet, and Quinn knew this—not the part about Alex's privacy—had been the truth.

"Well …" Quinn ran a hand through his hair. "I'm not stupid, Mom. I wouldn't have started anything with him while he was in his damned hospital bed."

"But he'd have started something with you as soon as he was able, and you wouldn't have backed down. You never have been able to walk away from a fight."

That part was true, too, he guessed.

"Yeah, okay. But still ... I want to know if somebody's sick or hurt or maybe dying, Mom. I want to know. Even if you tell me not to come. Even if you tell me to stay away to avoid making things worse. I still want to know."

Since when had Quinn's very presence been so upsetting, so traumatizing, that it might threaten someone's life? Just because he hadn't given his family shares of money that didn't belong to them? Just because he'd honored his uncle's dying wish?

"How is he now?" Quinn asked.

Barbara nodded, on surer footing now. "He's doing all right, I think. He's finally quit with the cigarettes, so that's something. Cheryl's been trying to get him to change his diet, and that's been hard. He doesn't want to give up his red meat."

Cheryl—Alex's wife—had certainly been part of the decision to keep Quinn out of the loop. He supposed he couldn't blame her. The whole thing had to have been hard for her. Probably still was.

"And the house?" Quinn said.

Barbara's face changed—it almost collapsed in on itself, deepening the lines between her brows—as she sank into a kitchen chair. "Oh, honey. The insurance didn't cover all of his medical costs. Not even close. And you know they were stretching to make the mortgage on that big place to begin with. Alex couldn't work, of course, while he was recovering." She shook her head. "Cheryl took a second job, but it wasn't enough."

"Mom." Quinn sat, too, so he could be at eye level with her. "The woman I'm seeing—her ex-husband is saying things about me. He's saying I'm unfit to be around her kids because I let Alex lose his house while I sat on some big inheritance. I didn't even know. How was I supposed to help him when I didn't even know?"

"Quinn ..."

"And I'm not sitting on some big inheritance, anyway. I spent it. I used it as a down payment on my house. You know that. You all know that. And yet you talked to the investigator anyway. You made me out to be some uncaring monster."

"Sweetheart, I didn't say those things. And neither did your brothers."

And then it became clear. "Cheryl did."

Barbara nodded, looking at the tabletop instead of at her son.

"She said that, even though nobody had told me what was happening? Is she so angry that she'd lie about me?"

"Don't be too hard on her, Quinn. She's been through a lot."

Now that it was all coming out, it made sense. Alex's wife had never liked Quinn, and some of that might have been Quinn's fault. Not all of it, but some of it. And, yeah, she was going through a lot.

That probably meant she wasn't going to welcome him when he showed up there. But he was going anyway.

"Where do they live now, Mom? I need the address."

WHEN MILES HAD SAID he was going to "look into" Delilah's potential custody case, she hadn't thought too deeply about what that might mean. She'd assumed he was going to look into international custody law in general, the statutes on the books, the precedents. That sort of thing.

What he actually did was employ the same kind of tactics Mitch had.

He called her on December 30—just as Delilah was packing up Otter Bluff—to give her some news.

"I don't think there's going to be a custody case, Delilah," Miles said, his face looking smug on the video feed. "I think we can make this thing go away."

"How are we going to do that?"

"I had someone take a look at Mitch's new live-in girlfriend. This Celine Mercier. What we found is something Mitch won't want getting out."

Delilah was speechless for a moment, then she gathered herself. "You sent a private detective after them? Like Mitch did to us?"

"Nothing that dramatic. I just had my researcher do a little Internet search. It didn't take much. Celine Mercier is a call girl."

Delilah was so surprised that she flinched. "She's *what?*"

"Well, she probably isn't anymore, now that she and Mitch are together. She was advertising her services—using an alias, of course—on a dark web site dedicated to such things, but she took down the ad around the time Mitch moved to Paris. Which either means that she's no longer in that line of work, or that she's only got the one client—if you get my meaning."

Delilah was stunned, processing all of the various repercussions of what Miles had told her. Yes, it probably meant Mitch's threat would go away, and that was good. But she felt vaguely sick at the idea of dragging another woman's name through the mud—even one who'd stolen her husband.

"I didn't ask you to do that. I didn't ask you to … to dig up dirt on Mitch's girlfriend."

"You didn't have to ask. I was doing the job you paid me to do. Now, if you'd like me to give him a call, make it clear to him what will be discussed in court if he pursues this …"

"No."

"Excuse me. No?"

"No," Delilah repeated. "I'll handle it."

"Are you sure? It might be best if I speak to him rather than you. Tempers can get heated, and we don't want—"

"I said I'll talk to him."

She ended the call feeling dirty, as though she'd sold herself just as much as Celine had.

CHAPTER 32

Quinn strategically planned his visit to his brother's house. Cheryl was a cashier at a local grocery store, and his mother had told him she worked the eight-to-five shift most days. So Quinn showed up midday, when Cheryl would be busy scanning six-packs of beer and Swanson's frozen dinners.

He walked up to the front door of the little two-bedroom place they were renting, knocked, and huddled in the cold, pulling his coat around him as he waited.

Alex had worked construction—hard, physical labor that was unsafe for a man with heart problems. He hadn't yet found a new, less taxing line of work, so he was still home, still unable to earn a paycheck, still seething, probably, with feelings of helplessness and the devastating blow to his pride that came from relying on his wife's employment for their livelihood.

When Alex opened the door, he looked thinner and paler than Quinn remembered.

"Well, shit." Alex looked at his brother through the screen door.

"Hi, Alex. Can I come in?"

Alex seemed to consider slamming the door in Quinn's face.

Instead, after a time that seemed far too long for comfort, he pushed open the screen door and stood back for Quinn to enter.

"If you're here to apologize …" Alex began.

"I'm not. I don't have shit to apologize for."

"Goddamn it, Quinn—"

"I'm here to find out how you are. To see for myself that you're up and around and doing okay. Since you never told me you had a goddamned heart attack, Alex."

They stood just inside the front door, a coat rack to Quinn's left and a side table holding a basket of keys, sunglasses, and other random items to his right. The fact that they hadn't gone farther into the house indicated to Quinn that he wasn't welcome here.

Alex looked at the floor and rubbed an eyebrow with his thumb—a gesture he'd used since his teen years whenever he was uncomfortable about something. "Yeah, well … it kind of seemed like you wouldn't much care."

"Ah, bullshit."

"Yeah, okay. You can just fuck off, then."

They both stood there seething, neither willing to back down. Finally, Quinn decided to be the bigger person. It was why he'd come, after all.

"Look. Can we just lower the temperature a bit? I didn't come here to fight with you. I came to see how you're doing. So can we maybe talk about that? And can I maybe come in instead of standing two steps inside your damned front door?"

Alex's expression was hard, and he still wasn't looking at Quinn. Then he shrugged, and his features relaxed. "Hell … I guess so. Sure. Come in. You want coffee?"

~

THEY SAT at the kitchen table, mugs in front of them, and talked. They kept it polite and superficial at first. Alex told Quinn about his latest doctor visit and the fact that his recovery had gone well. They talked about the new house—a rental, and much smaller than the old one—

which Cheryl had found for them. It was close to Cheryl's job, close to Cheryl's mother's place, so that was good.

They talked about what a bitch it was to stop smoking. Cheryl wanted Alex to give up burgers and bacon, but he'd already given up alcohol and Marlboros. What was the point in recovering if life wasn't worth living?

They talked about Christmas—who'd gone to whose house and who'd argued about what over the holiday dinner.

Through the archway into the living room, Quinn could see their tree still up. Past its prime and sparsely decorated, it reminded him a little of the tree in *A Charlie Brown Christmas*.

When all avenues of small talk had been exhausted, Quinn got to the point.

"You should have called me."

Alex shrugged. "You wouldn't have been able to do anything."

"Yeah, well ... that's not what Cheryl's been saying about me, is it?"

Alex tensed, then got up from the table and went to the sink to rinse his mug. He braced his hands against the counter and said, "What was that about, anyway? That detective? What did he want to know about you for?"

Quinn explained the situation: Delilah, her ex-husband, and his accusation that Quinn was a bad influence on Jesse and Gavin.

"She thinks she's going to lose her kids over this, Alex. Actually, she's already dumped me so she won't. And why, because you two said I refused to help you in your time of need? Kind of hard for me to do that when nobody even told me you were having a time of need in the first place."

"Quinn ..."

"Cheryl lied about me."

"No, she didn't." Alex rubbed his face with his hands, then sighed. "I'm the one who lied to her."

Quinn opened his mouth to respond, found that he was speechless, then closed it again.

"She told me to call you when all of the shit with the money started going down. She kept telling me, 'Call Quinn. Apologize. Do whatever you have to do. Just get him to loan us some money.' So I told her I had and that you'd shut me down. That stuff she told the detective? She thought it was true."

Quinn ran a hand through his hair. "But … why did you tell her that?"

"Because it was easier. Easier than swallowing my pride and telling you I was sorry. Easier than admitting I couldn't provide for my family. Easier than putting all of my problems on you, Quinn."

Quinn sat back in his chair and tried to absorb everything his brother was telling him. "You lied to get your wife off your back."

"Yes."

"And then the detective called."

"Yes."

"And she was pissed as hell because she thought I didn't care."

"That's … yeah. That's what happened."

At least it was all clear now—who'd done what and why. And it was clear that Alex was okay, and those two things were all Quinn had come for. He got up and faced his brother.

"For the record, I do care. Also for the record, the money's gone. Well, not gone, really, but I spent it on my house. I don't have it to give you."

"Quinn …"

"And finally. For the record. You hurt Nate. You all did. You treated him like shit, and that's why he left me the money and not you. I don't owe you an apology for that, and if Nate were here, he wouldn't, either."

Alex folded his arms over his chest. "Yeah. I guess."

"Have you changed your mind? About Nate, I mean? Do you still think his sexual orientation made him less of a man?"

Alex looked at some point well beyond Quinn, his face tight, and he nodded. "I guess I do."

"Then we've covered everything I came here to talk about. Take care of yourself, Alex." Quinn walked out of the house, got into his van, and drove away.

~

Delilah hadn't wanted to use the information she'd gotten about Celine. She'd thought that if she and Mitch could just have a rational conversation, the whole thing would go away.

She was wrong.

She called him the day after her conversation with Miles. She still didn't know where she and the kids were going to live, and January first had come and gone, so they were in a two-bedroom Airbnb until she could figure out what was going to happen between herself and Quinn.

Delilah gave the boys lunch, got them settled in at the kitchen table with a board game, then went onto the front porch to call her ex.

"We need to talk," she said.

"So talk."

From the tone of his voice, he hadn't backed down an inch on his stance.

"I've got a lawyer," she said. "He thinks we could win if you really do sue me for custody. But, Mitch, please don't do that." She felt herself starting to tear up. "Please. You know you're too busy to pay attention to the boys. Does Celine even want them to live with the two of you? Have you even talked about it?"

"Don't worry about Celine. She'll be fine. Are you still seeing the guy?"

"You've been talking to the boys. You should know I haven't seen him lately." She was hedging her answer. Just because she hadn't seen Quinn lately didn't mean she was resolved to never see him again.

She should have known Mitch would notice.

"You haven't seen him *lately*," he said. "Carefully worded to avoid the issue of whether you plan to see him in the future."

"Mitch ..."

"Have you broken it off with him? Does he know that you are out of his life for good? If the answer to those questions is yes, then you don't have anything to worry about."

God, he was infuriating. During their marriage, she'd overlooked his controlling nature, telling herself that a man in a high-powered career had to be that way. It was what drove his success, his achievement. But now she saw that it was dysfunctional and wrong. And what would his need to dominate, to dictate, do to Jesse and Gavin if they had to live with their father?

"Why do you even care?" Delilah demanded. "You don't want me anymore, but you don't want anyone else to have me, either?"

"It's not about that. It's about who you're bringing around my children."

"And who would *you* be bringing around our children if you get custody?"

There it was. She was going there. It didn't seem that she had any choice.

"What do you mean?"

"I know about Celine's line of work. Is that how you met her? Did you pay for that first date?"

He was silent, and she could almost feel the rage radiating through the airwaves.

"You had to have known it would come out, Mitch." Her voice was softer now. "It took my lawyer's researcher less than a day. You smear Quinn, we smear Celine, and what's the point? So you can control me? So you can micromanage my life from another continent?"

"Delilah, I swear to God—"

"Is it that important to you that I be unhappy?" She wiped a tear from her cheek. "Was all of this about seeing me suffer? Because it worked, Mitch. I'm suffering. How much pain is enough for you? How much misery is it going to take for you to feel like you've done your job?"

She hadn't meant to go off on him like that, but now that she had, it felt good. It felt like something she'd been holding back for a long time.

"You didn't answer my question," he said. "Are you still going to see that guy?"

At first, Delilah had thought it was a choice between Quinn and her sons. But it wasn't. It was a choice between standing up for her own freedom or letting her ex-husband dictate her life. If she didn't take him on now, she'd never be free of him.

"I will see him or anyone else I choose, and you'll have nothing to say about it. Because it's none of your goddamned business."

She hung up on him before he could say anything else.

CHAPTER 33

Quinn didn't stay in Flagstaff long enough to see his other brother, Jared, who was still an asshole, too.

Instead, he drove home and decided to confront Delilah.

Well, *confront* wasn't the right word. It was more accurate to say he wanted to talk things out. If she didn't want to be with him, he could live with that. He'd hate it, but he could live with it. What rankled the shit out of him was the idea that she'd stopped seeing him because her ex told her to.

Wasn't that why someone was an ex in the first place? So you didn't have to live your life according to their wants and needs anymore?

Yeah, she was afraid of losing her kids to that dickhead. But Quinn wouldn't let that happen. He didn't know how he might prevent it, but he'd make it his mission to try.

And anyway, if it wasn't this, it would be something else. The guy was clearly set on controlling Delilah, and he saw the kids as the perfect bargaining chip he could use to make it happen. If he wasn't haranguing her on who she was seeing, he'd be haranguing her on her parenting choices or her career choice—whatever it turned out to be—or spousal support, or some damned thing.

Quinn didn't know Mitch, but he knew his type. And that type never gave up control if they didn't have to. That type never quit taking as long as you continued to give.

So Delilah had to stop giving.

She had to dig her heels in—it was the only thing he'd understand.

The fact that Quinn would benefit from that strategy was a side bonus.

He planned what he was going to say to her as he made the long drive from Flagstaff back to Cambria. He mentally rehearsed his words under a clear blue sky as the highway stretched out ahead of him.

~

WHEN HE GOT BACK, it was too late to knock on her door. So he went home, tried to sleep, mostly failed, then got up early the next morning and fortified himself with strong coffee.

He weighed whether to call or text before going over there, then thought, *screw it*. He left the van in his driveway, got into the car he used around town, and went to Otter Bluff.

Delilah's car wasn't there, but an oldish gray Honda Civic was parked at the curb.

Quinn went to the front door and knocked, his heart pounding with the awareness that this might be a make-or-break moment for him with Delilah.

A middle-aged woman in jeans and a T-shirt opened the door. She had bright yellow rubber gloves on her hands, and her graying hair was tied back in a bandana.

"May I help you?"

"Ah … is Delilah here?"

"Who?" She squinted at him.

"Delilah Ballard. She's staying here with her two kids. Two boys. Is she around?" He peered around the woman to try to look into the house.

"There's nobody staying here right now." The woman put a gloved fist on her hip as though she thought he might be up to something and she wanted him to know she wasn't having it. "I'm cleaning it for the next guests."

Oh, shit. Was she gone?

Yes, it was past January first, and yes, he'd known she was supposed to leave Otter Bluff then. But she hadn't called or texted him to let him know, so he assumed she was still there. Surely she'd made a deal with the owner or something. It never entered his mind that she might leave without telling him where she'd gone.

"Do you know where she went?"

"They don't tell me anything about the renters. Sorry." She didn't sound sorry. "All I know is she left the place pretty nice, which isn't a given with some people. So if you see her, tell her Carol said thanks." Then she closed the door on him.

He walked back to his car feeling cold dread in his stomach.

He got behind the wheel and texted her.

You left Otter Bluff. Please tell me you're not in Connecticut. Please tell me you didn't leave without talking to me or without at least saying goodbye.

She texted back less than five minutes later.

Of course I didn't. I'm at 9835 Wharton Street on Happy Hill. Do you want to talk?

Damned right he did. He started the car and drove to Happy Hill.

~

DELILAH'S DIVORCE had left her unmoored. Without her marriage to anchor her, she hadn't known what she wanted, with whom she wanted it, or how she planned to get it. She hadn't known how she was going to construct a new life atop the ruins of the old one.

But her phone conversation with Mitch had clarified things. In the wake of it, she knew a few things for sure. One, she didn't want to live in fear of what Mitch might do. Two, she was tired of feeling hurt and traumatized by the way he had treated her. Three, she was ready to feel hope and joy again. And four, now that joy had presented itself, she knew she had to do what it took to keep it.

When she heard Quinn's car, she peeked out the front window and saw him park at the curb. She didn't wait. Instead, she walked out the front door to meet him.

~

QUINN HAD BEEN nervous as hell as he drove across town. Delilah had already told him she didn't want to see him anymore, so he supposed this couldn't be any worse.

But she hadn't left town, and that had planted a tiny seed of hope within him. Maybe she wasn't done with him completely. Maybe she could still be persuaded to let him be a part of her life.

He hadn't realized how scared he was—how much this whole thing had undone him—until he reached for the car door handle and saw that his hand was shaking.

Whatever happened, he had to be a man about it. He had to pull himself together and accept whatever she'd decided.

When she came out the front door, she was smiling, and he felt a surge of optimism and possibility. She wouldn't be smiling if she were going to cut him out of her life forever, would she?

Please let that smile be for me.

He got out of the car, headed up the front walk—and felt everything within him breathe again when she ran to him and threw herself into his arms.

~

DELILAH KISSED Quinn with everything she had, everything she was feeling. He tangled his hands in her hair and caressed her mouth with his.

What a wonder that she could feel like this after everything that had happened. What a miracle.

When he pulled back from her, she smiled up at him. "I talked to Mitch."

"Did you? I guess it went well."

"No, actually. It was awful." Her arms were still around him, and she relished the feeling of being held by him again.

"It did?"

"Yes. God." She shook her head. "He was terrible. And I essentially blackmailed him to drop it, and that was terrible, too. I don't know what's going to happen, but I know I can't let him dictate what I do with my life. I can't, Quinn. He decided everything I did while we were married. What I wore, what I did with my time, who my friends were ..." She started to get emotional, but she swallowed hard and tamped it down. "If I let him have his way on this, it's going to be like he never left. Like I was never free. I'd be letting him know that he doesn't have to treat me with respect. That he doesn't have to acknowledge me as a ... a thinking adult who can make her own choices."

He grinned. "Please say you told him to kiss your ass."

"I did. Not in those words, but essentially."

"Goddamn it, I'm proud of you." He kissed her again, hard and fast, to punctuate his words. "Back up a little, though. Blackmail?"

She shuddered. "I felt like I needed a shower."

"So, what dirt did you get on him? And how?"

"Not on him. On his girlfriend. That stuff he said about you? It's nothing compared to what I now know about her."

"Do I want the details?"

"You really don't."

He nodded, accepting that. They were still standing on the front walk, his hands clasped at the small of her back. "Does this mean you're staying in Cambria?"

"It means we should talk about it. About what you want, and what I want, and what's best for the boys. Without taking Mitch's opinions into account."

"We can do that."

Before they could go into it any further, Jesse spotted Quinn through the front window, and both boys came tumbling out of the house calling his name.

"Quinn! You're here! Where were you? Were you camping?" Jesse asked.

"I want to go to the zoo," Gavin said.

Quinn and Delilah walked into the house hand in hand.

THEY'D AGREED to talk about it, but they didn't do that right away. Quinn had, in fact, promised the kids a trip to the zoo if their mother said yes, and now, under the excited pleadings of her boys, Delilah agreed.

They drove down to Santa Barbara the following day under a blue sky dotted with puffy clouds. The drive was a long one, so by the time they parked, the boys practically exploded out of the car, releasing their pent-up energy.

"Guys. Guys! Stay with me. There are cars coming and going. You need to be careful." Delilah used her stern voice, corralling the kids while she filled a small backpack with jackets, water bottles, her cell phone, and her wallet.

They went to the front gate, paid, and emerged into the tidy, well-kept zoo, a map of the exhibits in Quinn's hand.

The boys began arguing about what they wanted to see first, so Quinn took the lead.

"You don't just go see your favorite animal first," he said.

"You don't?" Gavin looked up at him attentively.

"Oh, heck no. You've got to plan a route." He spread the map out on a bench. "See? We can start at the left with the snow leopards and the porcupines then continue around toward the elephants. Or, we can start at the right with the otters and the alligators and continue on toward the koalas. But it makes no sense to go straight for the giraffes, for example, because you'll just have to backtrack to see the stuff you missed, and you'll be walking all day."

Delilah grinned at him. "You've put a lot of thought into this."

"A thing that's worth doing is worth doing right."

"But we're still going to see the giraffes, right?" Jesse asked.

"Of course. I'm not an amateur," Quinn said. "I'm not going to plan a zoo trip that doesn't include giraffes."

Jesse, convinced, opted for the snow leopards, and Gavin agreed.

They headed off together on the route they'd chosen.

~

QUINN WAS FEELING PRETTY DAMNED good about himself and about life as he led the kids and Delilah from one exhibit to another. He'd thought he lost her over her ex's threats. He'd been prepared to fight for her, but only to a point. He knew she had to make her own decisions—especially after the way her ex had prevented her from doing just that during their marriage—and if she had decided to cut him loose, well, he would have had to accept that.

But, God, he hadn't wanted that to happen. Now that it looked like it wouldn't, he felt buoyed as he savored this feeling of being a part of something again—a part of a family.

They still needed to have The Talk, though—the discussion about what she would do next and what role he might play in that. There was still the potential for it all to go wrong, but he was determined not to let the worry of it ruin his day.

He bought the boys ice cream bars, and they ate them while exclaiming over the antics of the white handed gibbons. Quinn held Delilah's hand, smiling like an idiot. Or, smiling like a guy who'd finally found what he wanted.

CHAPTER 34

They had The Talk that night in bed, after they'd waited for the kids to go to sleep and then took a long, leisurely time to enjoy each other's bodies.

"So. Plans." Quinn was the one who brought it up. He'd waited as long as he could. Now, while they were both satisfied and relaxed, seemed as good a time as any.

"Right. Plans." Delilah rolled onto her side to face him. "Let me just preface this by saying it's awkward, because it's only been two months, and we shouldn't have to decide where this thing is going after two months."

"But, special circumstances," he said.

"Yes. Special circumstances." Delilah sat up in bed, pulling the sheet up to cover her breasts. "The way I see it, we have three choices: I stay in Cambria, I move back to Connecticut without you, or I move back to Connecticut with you."

"And there are choices within the choices," Quinn added. "For instance, if you move back to Connecticut without me, we can either let each other go or try a long-distance relationship." He'd said those things in the spirit of laying out all of the possible options. But he opposed this particular scenario so strongly he almost couldn't get the words out.

"I don't want us to let each other go."

He let out a breath and relaxed. "Okay, good. I don't want that, either."

"Okay." She nodded, grinning at him. "Okay, then. Next question: long-distance relationship, or do we stay close to each other?"

He sat up now, too, because this seemed like the kind of conversation you needed to be upright for.

"Long-distance relationships suck," he said. "I mean, I've never had one. But I imagine they suck. They'd have to."

"Agreed. We won't do that, then."

He pulled her into his arms and kissed her to seal the deal.

"I couldn't do that long-distance," he said.

"No. You couldn't. And I couldn't do this." She put her hand on his chest and started sliding it downward.

"Ah … as much as I love where you're going with that," he said, "we have to work out the rest."

Her hand stilled. "You're right. We do."

"Hold that thought, though."

She brought her hand to rest on his forearm—a much safer location.

"So. Do you stay here, or do I go there?"

That was the question. Quinn loved Cambria—he loved everything about it. He loved the small-town atmosphere, the beaches, the pines. He loved the locals who called out to him every time he went out on Main Street. He loved the community spirit, the farmer's market on Fridays in the vet's hall parking lot. He loved the proximity to Big Sur. He loved the annual town musical the longtime locals put on. Hell, he even loved the steady flow of tourists.

But he loved Delilah more.

"Do you want to go back to Connecticut?" he asked in a bid to get his thoughts off of himself and onto her. He was just one person, but she represented three people. It seemed to him that her vote should, therefore, have more weight.

DELILAH CONSIDERED the question carefully and deliberately.

Part of her never wanted to go back there again. The memories from her marriage and its ultimate collapse were too raw, too fresh. But there was more to consider than just herself.

"My family is there," she said. "My parents and my sister."

"Okay."

"Jesse and Gavin both have friends they'd be leaving behind."

He waited.

"But," she went on, "I think I need some distance from my family, especially right now. My mother hasn't accepted the divorce. She still thinks Mitch and I are going to get back together."

He nodded, still not speaking. She appreciated how he just listened, waiting for her to work through it on her own. Mitch never would have done that. Mitch would have had a hundred arguments to sway her in his direction.

"And," she said, "the boys are so young. Friendships at this age are so changeable. Kids can be best friends one day and refuse to talk to each other the next."

Still, he waited.

"I guess what I'm saying is … I think I want to stay here. With you."

"Are you sure that's what you want?"

She hesitated slightly, then nodded. "Yes. It is."

It wasn't until the smile spread across his face that she realized how tense he'd been waiting for her answer. "Thank God." He grabbed her and pulled her onto his lap, and she let out a subdued whoop at his sudden enthusiasm.

They kissed for a long time in this new place, this place where they'd both decided, at last, to be together.

When they finally broke the kiss, she brought up the rest of it. "I'll have to figure out what to do about a job. I have enough money from the settlement that I don't have to worry about it right now. But I'll have to worry about it eventually."

"Well, if you move in with me, you could save on rent. You could—"

"No." She put her hand on his chest and shook her head.

"No?"

"No. Or, at least, not now. The boys have been through too much change. I can't move in with you until I know you and I are forever. As much as anyone can know that. To move in and then have it not work out? I couldn't put Jesse and Gavin through that. I can't put myself through that."

And she needed to find out who she was when she wasn't living with a man. She thought that part but didn't say it. She'd let Mitch swallow her whole until there was no Delilah left. And it would be so easy to let Quinn do the same thing. She couldn't let that happen. She needed to be firmly herself long enough that when she and Quinn did decide to live together—or even get married—Delilah would be strong and firm and real enough that she wouldn't fade, even under the bright glare of her love for Quinn.

"Okay," he said. "Fair enough. So, we need to find you a place. Maybe one to buy this time, and not just a rental. If you want that."

Delilah felt a surge of excitement at the idea. She'd never bought her own house, not without Mitch. When they'd bought their house together, it had been all about him and his image of the way they should live. The thought of choosing what she wanted for the new life she was building made her almost giddy with pleasure.

"I'll want three bedrooms, and a big back yard for the boys to play in. And for the dog."

"The dog?"

"Of course we're going to get a dog," she said, almost without pausing. "And I want someplace bright, with a lot of natural light. Not too close to the water, I think. Too foggy. I love some of the places I've seen on Lodge Hill. They have so much character. And the kitchen …"

~

QUINN LISTENED to Delilah talk about the house she wanted, and he knew they'd made the right decision. If she'd been hesitant or scared at the idea of buying a house here, if she'd seemed to be pretending to be happy, he'd have worried that she was doing this for him and not because it was best for her.

But the joy he saw in her, the excitement—that didn't lie.

She wanted to be here.

And he wanted her here, today, tomorrow, next year, and the year after that.

He sat back and listened to her and felt a greater sense of happiness—of peace—than he'd felt in a long time. Maybe ever.

Everything was going his way.

Now, they just had to hope to hell that her asshole ex didn't screw with them any more than he already had.

CHAPTER 35

In the coming days, Delilah noticed an uptick in the number of calls Mitch made to the boys. He was perfunctory when Delilah answered the phone—*Hello, can I speak to my sons, please*—and Delilah sensed trouble.

Mitch had shown so little interest in the boys over the past year that this couldn't be about him trying to be a more attentive father. He had to be pumping Jesse and Gavin for information on Quinn.

She could have told them not to discuss Quinn with their father or, even worse, she could have told them to lie and say they hadn't seen Quinn. But Delilah didn't want to go down that road. It was simply bad mothering to encourage her kids to lie, and anyway, what was the point? She needed to be free—not to have the illusion of freedom because she'd managed to keep Mitch in the dark.

She and Quinn were a couple now, and the boys could say whatever they wanted about that to their father. Delilah would deal with the fallout.

She knew that fallout would come. She just didn't expect it to take the form it did.

DELILAH HAD plans to meet with a Realtor on a Wednesday morning in early January.

Quinn and the boys were planning to come with her as she began to look at houses for her new life in Cambria.

She was excited, and the whole thing had an air of festivity about it that rivaled what they'd all felt at Christmas. For the first time, Delilah would be choosing what she really wanted—what reflected her own personality, her own needs, her own vision about the life she was building for herself.

She was practically giddy with anticipation, bustling around the rental house getting ready for her day, when the doorbell rang.

Delilah thought it was Quinn—that's why she had a smile on her face as she opened the door. That was why she'd felt happy and relaxed.

But it wasn't Quinn.

Instead, Delilah's ex-husband stood on the front porch, looking tired and pinched and a little angry.

She gasped when she saw him, though she couldn't have said whether that was from fear or surprise.

"What are you doing here?"

If she'd had more time to come up with something to say, she might have been less confrontational, less hostile. But the words just popped out before she could form a strategy.

"Delilah, can we talk?"

Oh, God. This had to be about his plan to get custody. He was here to threaten her, or maybe to announce that he was filing the papers. Adrenaline shot through her. That, and stark terror.

"If you came to see the boys, you should have called first. How did you even know where to find us?"

He didn't answer, but he didn't have to. He might have found her in any number of ways. Her mother, for one. Delilah had no doubt her mother would hand over any information he wanted if she thought it meant she and Mitch might somehow repair their marriage.

"I didn't come to see them. I mean, I do want to. Of course. But mostly, I came to talk to you."

She folded her arms over her chest. "So talk."

"Can I come in?"

"No."

He wore jeans and a polo shirt—nothing fancy about that—but she knew from experience that no single item he wore cost less than two hundred dollars, probably including his socks.

He looked older than when she'd last seen him. He had the same medium blond hair, the same trim build, the same intense blue eyes. The same expensive haircut. But something about him—maybe his expression, maybe the way he held himself—suggested the kind of stress that wore on a person day after day. He looked five years older than when she'd last seen him.

"Delilah, come on."

Her intention to hold him off at the door was foiled when Jesse and Gavin, who'd been playing in Jesse's room, heard their father's voice. They poked their heads out tentatively at first, as though they dared not believe they'd heard what they thought they'd heard.

When they saw him, they exploded out of the room and down the hallway, running toward their father.

"Dad! Dad!" Jesse hurtled past Delilah and into his father's arms. Gavin, in his race to get there, tripped over his feet and fell to the floor. He got up and darted toward Mitch before Delilah could even react to his fall.

Gavin threw one arm around Mitch's legs, the thumb of his free hand plugged into his mouth.

"Hey, fellas." Mitch knelt down to the boys' level and wrapped one arm around each of his sons.

Jesse peppered him with questions. "Are you back? Do you live here now? Did you miss us on Christmas Day? Do you want to see what I got?"

Gavin simply clung to him without saying anything.

"Whoa there, Jesse. That's a lot of questions." But Mitch had a wistful smile on his face that Delilah rarely saw. His eyes reddened, and he cleared his throat before he spoke. If she didn't know better, she would think he really did miss the boys. Could that be true, or was it an act he was performing for her sake?

"Listen, guys. I have to talk to your mom in private for a bit. Then how about if I take you out for ice cream? Is that all right, Delilah?"

"It's nine a.m., Mitch."

"Well, breakfast, then. Pancakes. What do you say, boys?"

The kids erupted in excited agreement, so Delilah hardly had a choice in the matter.

"Fine," she said. It might be better if the boys didn't come on the house shopping expedition, anyway. They'd likely find it excruciatingly boring.

"Great. That's great." Mitch released his sons and stood up.

"Guys, can you go back into Jesse's room for a bit?" Delilah asked gently. "I need to talk to your dad, then he'll take you to the Redwood Cafe."

They went back down the hall, sneaking peeks back at Mitch as though he might vanish before they returned. Which, she thought, was a real possibility if their talk didn't go well.

"All right," she said when they were gone. "What do you want to talk about?"

"Can I come in now? The boys are going to wonder why you wouldn't let me past the front door."

He had a point. She stood back wordlessly to let him enter.

~

QUINN WAS LOOKING FORWARD to house shopping with Delilah. It wasn't his ideal scenario—that would have been if she and the boys had decided to move in with him.

But Delilah wasn't ready for it, and that was fine. As long as they were heading in that general direction, he could wait as long as it took.

He reminded himself not to take over as he had with the Christmas preparations. It was fine to do the man-in-control thing when cutting down a tree or planning a route at the zoo. It was entirely another to try it when a woman was choosing a home for herself. This was her decision, not his. He needed to be supportive, but he also needed to hang back and remember that this was about her and the boys, not his own opinions or desires.

Quinn went through his morning routine—coffee, shower, breakfast—planning what he might do when they were through with the Realtor. Maybe he'd take the Ballards to lunch. After that, they could see a movie if Delilah didn't have plans. There was a new Pixar movie out that the boys would love.

Feeling the joy and enthusiasm of a man whose life was going exactly to plan, he drove to Delilah's rental house anticipating kissing her.

He really liked kissing her.

When he saw an unfamiliar car parked in the driveway, he thought it had to be the Realtor. Was he late? He checked the clock in his car and saw that he wasn't. Maybe the Realtor was early.

He was actually whistling as he went up the front walk. He let himself in instead of knocking because Delilah had told him to do that. She'd told him he was on just-come-in status now.

He stopped short when he saw Delilah in the living room with a man whose face was familiar. He knew where he'd seen that face before: in the framed photos on Jesse and Gavin's bedside tables.

Oh, shit.

"What's going on?" he said. But that wasn't what he wanted to ask. He wanted to ask, *What the hell are you doing here? And when the fuck are you leaving?*

"Oh. Quinn." Delilah tried on a smile, but it was wobbly and unconvincing. "This is Mitch. Mitch, this is Quinn Monroe."

Quinn forced himself to walk over and extend his hand, but the asshole ex didn't take it.

"If you don't mind, I'm trying to have a private conversation with my wife."

"I'm not your wife," Delilah said. "Not anymore."

Mitch didn't acknowledge what Delilah had said. Instead, he

stared Quinn down the way he probably did with opponents at his law firm.

Quinn tried to assess the situation, but it was hard, given the undercurrents of tension and loathing flying through the room.

"Delilah? Are you okay?"

"Yes." She nodded. "Of course."

"Do you want me to go?"

"She just said she's fine. So, you can move along, sport." Mitch made a shooing motion with his hands.

Delilah got up, came to Quinn, and put a hand on his arm as she gently ushered him toward the door.

"He just showed up," she said, her voice low for privacy. "He said he wants to talk. If he's going to tell me he's suing for custody … Quinn, I need to talk him down, and I can't do that if you're here making him mad."

"I didn't do anything to make him mad. If he's mad, maybe it's because he's an asshole."

"Quinn, please."

The look in her eyes said she was begging him. Begging him to go.

"All right. I'll be right outside, in the car. If you need me, call me." He held up his cell phone to illustrate.

"I will."

"Delilah? You're safe, right?"

"Yes. Yes. It's okay. You can go." And she practically pushed him out the door.

~

QUINN'S sudden appearance had thrown things off, but Delilah composed herself and went into the living room to talk to her ex.

"Okay." She patted her thighs once, primly, with her hands. "You were about to tell me why you're here."

"That's the guy you're seeing? That guy?"

"That was Quinn, yes."

Mitch looked stricken, and Delilah tried to replicate his thought processes. The way Quinn looked—like some chiseled bust of a Roman god—probably was a threat to Mitch's manhood.

Mitch started to say something, stopped, then started again.

"That guy?"

"Can we move on, please? You came here to say something, and I have an appointment, so I don't have a lot of time. Please tell me what you wanted to talk about."

She knew this man's face as well as her own. As well as the sweet faces of her boys. So she knew he'd made a snap decision, a sudden change of course. She knew that whatever he was about to say wasn't what he'd planned to say.

"Delilah, I came here to ask you to take me back. Please. We can work things out, I know we can."

Whatever she'd planned to hear, it wasn't that. She stared at him as though he'd suddenly grown a third eye.

"Mitch, stop it."

"Stop what? Why? We're a family, you and me and the boys. We belong together." He'd softened his voice, and now he reached for her hand and held it in both of his. "Look, I know I put you through a lot. I know that. And I apologize for Celine, and … you know. For everything. But marriages go through rough spots. It happens."

"It happens? It happens?" Delilah yanked her hand away from him and stood up so she was looming over him. "Cheating on your wife doesn't just happen. Leaving me penniless until the settlement didn't just happen. You did those things. You did them intentionally and with no regard for your sons and how it made them feel. We were a family, yes, but you gave that up. You did that. You can't just come here and undo it now because … because Quinn made you feel insecure."

Now I've done it, Delilah thought. *Now he's going to go on the defensive, and he's going to lash out. And I'm screwed.*

Instead, he was silent, looking miserable. He raked his hands through his hair and looked at the carpet between his feet.

Feeling a sudden rush of sympathy, Delilah sat down again and spoke to him softly. "That isn't what you came to say, Mitch. What's really going on?"

He rubbed at his face with his hands, then shrugged, looking tired and defeated. "Hell. I don't know. I just ... Jesse and Gavin. The way they talk about that guy on the phone ... it's like he hung the goddamned moon. I'm losing them, Dee. The thing about custody ... I panicked. I just don't want to lose them."

From the sound of his voice, the way he held his body, she knew that after all of the posturing, all of the strategizing, she was finally hearing the truth.

She reached out and laid her hand on his arm. "They love you."

"They love him. That guy. Quinn."

"They needed a man in their lives and he was here. You weren't."

"That's why we should try again. That's why—"

"Mitch. Stop it." It was the same tone she might have used with one of her boys—the one that said the matter was decided and was not open for review.

"I fucked up. With them." He nodded toward the back of the house, where the boys were.

"Yes. You did."

"I missed Christmas with them. You know? I just ... I missed it. And for what? So I could go to a cocktail party with Celine's friends?" He shook his head, his face a mask of disgust.

"We can't get back together, Mitch. It's over. You made sure of that. But that doesn't mean you can't be a father to your sons."

"But, the custody agreement—"

"I'm not talking about the custody agreement. I'm talking about you and me and the boys. I never wanted to keep them from you. I want them to be happy, and seeing you more often will make them happy. But I can't make you do it if you're too busy running around Paris doing God knows what."

He nodded and looked at the floor again, his eyes red and wet. "Do you think it's too late?"

"You saw how they ran to you when you came to the door. You saw how happy they were to see you. How can it be too late?"

CHAPTER 36

Quinn sat in the car feeling so tense he thought the steering wheel might break under his grasp. Part of him wanted to barge in there and tell the asshole to get the hell out of Delilah's house. But he knew that would be the equivalent of peeing on his territory, and he urged himself to be better than that. Delilah wasn't his territory, and if she wasn't allowed to work this out herself—if he didn't give her the space she needed to take charge of her own life—there wouldn't be much point in them pursuing their relationship, anyway.

After a while, the asshole came out of the house with Jesse and Gavin, got into his car, and drove away.

The thing that struck Quinn about that—the thing that would stick with him—was how happy the boys looked in the company of their father. Yes, Gavin was sucking his thumb again—that stress-induced habit was back—but they both looked excited. Joyous, really. It occurred to Quinn that he would do just about anything, no matter how difficult, no matter how distasteful, to make them feel that way again.

He was still making his way up the front walk when the Realtor arrived, and that was lousy timing. He needed to talk to

Delilah. He needed to assess the situation, find out what happened.

"Oh, hello, Quinn!" The Realtor waved at him with enthusiasm. "Are you ready to see some houses?"

"You bet!" He flashed a thumbs-up and opened the front door for her like a gentleman.

THE TENSION WAS thick as they rode in the Realtor's car toward the first house Delilah would be seeing.

Delilah, sitting next to him in the back seat, flashed him a look of apology and squeezed his hand as the Realtor chattered about housing prices, kitchen layouts, and bedroom counts.

"I feel like a chauffeur up here. Ha, ha!" She threw a look over her shoulder toward her passengers.

"We need to talk," Quinn said quietly.

"I know. We will."

Delilah looked stressed and tense, but she didn't look distraught, the way she would have if Mitch had told her he was filing for custody. So, that was something.

THEY GOT the chance to talk while they were viewing the first house. The place wasn't right for Delilah—only two bedrooms and the back yard was too small—but she told Sue, their Realtor, that she and Quinn needed some time alone in the house to discuss it.

"Of course. Of course! I'll just be out on the back patio. You two take your time!" She clacked over to the sliding glass door on her high heels and went outside.

When they were alone, Delilah took Quinn by the hand and led him into the master bedroom.

There, in the privacy of the room filled with someone else's bed and lamps and shoes, she told Quinn what had happened.

"He asked you to *come back* to him?" Quinn tried not to raise his voice, but it was hard.

"He did. But I don't think he meant it. I think he's got a lot of things on his mind. For one thing, I don't think things are going well between him and Celine since I told him what I found out about her. For another, he misses the boys. Christmas hit him hard. Spending it without them. I didn't think he cared, but he does. Missing the holiday with them made him see what he's thrown away. And then, hearing the way the boys gushed about you—it scared him. He thinks he's losing them."

Quinn put his hands on his hips and let out a rough breath. "Well, he *is* going to lose them if he doesn't move his ass back from Paris and spend some damned time with them."

"That's what I told him."

Quinn rubbed the stubble on his chin and considered what she'd said. "And the thing he said about wanting to get back together with you?"

She wrapped her arms around his waist, went up on tiptoes, and pressed a kiss to his lips. "Not in a million years."

He grinned, feeling a release of more tension than he'd realized he was holding. "Really?"

"Really."

Sue called from the front room, "So, how's it coming in here?"

~

THEY LOOKED at three more houses: one in Marine Terrace, one in Pine Knolls, and another on Lodge Hill.

While they toured kitchens and bathrooms, spare rooms and garage space, Quinn began to form a plan.

It wasn't going to work if both Delilah and the asshole weren't on board, but if they were, it could be kind of great.

The plan might have seemed ridiculous or over the top to someone watching from the outside of the situation, but it actually made sense for a number of reasons: One, it might put the asshole at ease. If he decided Quinn wasn't a threat to him, he'd be more likely to back off and forget the idea of suing for custody. Two, it would position Quinn as the bigger man, which was convenient, because he really did want to be that bigger man. He wanted to rise above. Three, it would make the boys ridiculously happy.

In the end, reason three was the only one that mattered.

Quinn's father had left when Quinn was barely older than Jesse was now. Yeah, the guy had been a dick, but that didn't make Quinn love him or want him any less.

What would it have meant to Quinn if someone had done just what he was planning? How big a moment would that have been in his life?

He'd have never forgotten it, that was for sure.

He was in the position to give that to Jesse and Gavin.

How could he not?

~

HE RAN the idea past Delilah that night while they were sitting on the sofa after the boys were in bed. He laid out the idea, how they would accomplish it, and his reasons for doing it.

At first, she simply looked astonished, like she must have misheard him.

"You'd do that for Mitch?" she said.

"For him? Oh, hell no. But I'd do it for the boys."

She grinned and leaned over to kiss him. The kiss was long and leisurely and enthusiastic.

"I'm thinking that's a yes?" he asked.

"Have I mentioned to you yet that I love you?" she asked.

"You haven't. But no time like the present."

"I love you, Quinn."

He wrapped his arms around her and held her tight. "That's convenient for me, because I love you, too."

~

THE NEXT MORNING, Delilah called Mitch on his cell phone and told him the plan. He would be staying in town a couple of days to spend time with the boys, so there was no reason it shouldn't work out.

"Really?" he said.

"Yes, really. If you want to do it."

"That's unbelievably nice of you, Delilah. Given … you know. Everything."

"It was Quinn's idea."

"Jesus. Was it?"

"Yes. I hope you'll remember that before you treat him like crap again."

"Okay. Yeah, I get it."

Delilah felt a glimmer of excitement even as she fought the urge to hang up on him. "Six a.m. sharp. I swear to God, if you're late, or if you don't show up—"

"I'll be there. Hey, is there a toy store in town, or …?"

She sighed. "There's a toy store on Main Street, there's a Target in San Luis Obispo, and there's a Walmart in Paso Robles. You'll figure it out." And then she did hang up on him.

~

THE WHOLE THING took some preparation on Quinn and Delilah's part. They had most of what they needed, and what they didn't have, Quinn borrowed from Mrs. Foster.

They got up at four a.m. to put everything in place. Delilah had considered doing it the night before, after the boys were asleep, but she didn't want to risk somebody getting out of bed for a glass of water and spoiling the surprise.

Instead, they hauled themselves out of bed at an absurd hour and worked as silently as possible in the hours before dawn, like the Tooth Fairy.

Or like elves.

CHAPTER 37

When Jesse woke up the next morning, groggy from sleep and afflicted with bedhead, he froze, wide-eyed, in the hallway, staring at the display in the living room.

He looked as though he couldn't make sense of what he was seeing.

Christmas had come and gone weeks ago, but before him was a fully decorated tree, complete with wrapped gifts beneath it. And there was his father, wearing a Santa hat and smiling at him.

"Merry Christmas, big guy," Mitch said.

"But . . ." Jesse blinked a few times and rubbed his eyes. "We already had Christmas."

"Well, I wasn't here for it, so we're having it again."

Jesse's mouth hung open as he worked to recover from his shock. "Again?"

"Yeah, why not?" Delilah said. She smiled at Jesse, feeling his contagious excitement.

Mrs. Foster's artificial tree stood next to the fireplace, bearing the lights and ornaments Quinn and Delilah had bought for their first go-around with the holiday. Stockings for Jesse and Gavin, stuffed with small gifts, hung on the mantel. Artificial pine boughs—bought in the clearance section at Target—decorated the staircase banister. And

Christmas carols—from a CD picked up in the same clearance section —played on the stereo.

"You want to go wake up Gavin?" Quinn suggested.

That, finally, snapped Jesse out of his shock. He ran back down the hallway, yelling for his brother.

THE REST of the morning was a flurry of gifts, wrapping paper, hot cocoa, and pancakes in a scene remarkably similar to the Christmas celebration they'd enjoyed just weeks before.

The difference was, the boys now had all three of their favorite adults there to share it with them.

"Two Christmases. This is so great," Jesse said, looking drunk on gifts and cocoa. He was still wearing his pajamas, and his hands were sticky with the remnants of a clearance-section candy cane.

Gavin was sitting on Mitch's lap, his thumb nowhere near his mouth. "Are you going to live in Cambria now?" he asked his father.

"No, but I wanted to talk to you guys about that." Mitch patted the sofa next to him and gestured for Jesse to sit next to him. When they were all assembled, Mitch looked at first one boy, then the other. "You know how I moved to Paris for my job, right?"

That was the lie they'd settled on—that he'd moved for his job.

The boys nodded.

"Well, it didn't work out so well. So I thought maybe I'd come back to live in the United States again. New York. My law firm's there, and it's closer to you guys. If you come back to Connecticut—"

"We're not," Delilah said, keeping her voice neutral. "We're going to live here now, in Cambria. Permanently."

For just a moment, just a flash, Mitch looked as though he wanted to argue with her. Then he arranged his expression in a way that said pleasant, rational adult.

"Ah. Are you? Okay." He nodded. "Well, still. I can fly here to see you a lot more often. And when you guys come to the East Coast to see your grandparents and Aunt Roxanne, I can see you then. If that's okay with your mom."

"It is," Delilah said.

"The point is, guys, I'm going to do better. I promise."

Delilah had her doubts about whether he actually would. Mitch often made promises and had good intentions, and so often those promises led to nothing.

But maybe this time would be different.

Whether it was or it wasn't, she'd know she did her best to give her kids access to their father. She'd know she'd taken the high road, and she'd know she'd given her boys a memory to hold close even if their father was far away.

It wasn't everything, but it wasn't nothing, either.

~

QUINN WAS THERE for the second Christmas celebration—he hadn't wanted to miss it after he'd put all that work into it—but he'd held back, letting Mitch be the man of the hour.

He was standing in the kitchen, drinking a mug of coffee and trying to stay out of the way, when Mitch came to find him.

"Delilah says all this was your idea."

"It was, yeah." Quinn rubbed at the stubble on his chin.

"I guess I owe you a thank you, then." But he looked like it might actually kill him to offer it.

"Well ... don't strain yourself, man."

Mitch smiled ruefully. "Look. I was kind of a dick to you before."

"Yep. You were. And I don't expect us to hold hands and sing folk songs together now."

"I guess not," Mitch shrugged. "All I'm saying is that the kids seem happy. Delilah seems happy. And if you're part of that ..."

"I hope I am."

"Well ... I won't stand in your way, that's all."

"Big of you. But you couldn't stand in my way if you tried."

They glared at each other, sizing each other up. The option of pissing on the baseboards to establish dominance was still on the table.

"I guess we understand each other," Mitch said.

"I guess we do."

Mitch nodded a few times, his head bobbing. "If you hurt her, or them, I'll come after you."

"Same goes." Quinn stood with his arms crossed over his chest, trying his best to look imposing.

Mitch turned toward where the boys were sitting on the sofa, clapped his hands, and put on his best smile. "So, who needs more pancakes?"

~

THAT NIGHT, Quinn and Delilah put the boys to bed, then went to bed early themselves, but not to sleep.

They lay nude beneath the covers, facing each other, both of them wrapped up in the glow of the holiday spirit.

They'd made love twice—energetically the first time, with the urgency of two people who knew they'd found The One. Then again, more slowly, savoring every touch and taste.

Now, Delilah felt deeply relaxed and happy as she gazed at him in the pale moonlight coming through the window.

"Thank you for what you did. I don't know if Mitch—"

"Maybe we could not say his name while we're both naked," Quinn suggested.

"Right." She smiled. "I don't know if everyone who should have thanked you actually did. But I wanted you to know how much it meant to me and the boys."

He ran his hand down the glossy flow of her hair. "The person we're not mentioning—the one who should have thanked me—did. Sort of. As much as he could manage, anyway."

"Well, good. The boys had a wonderful time. And I did, too."

"I've got a bonus good time for you, if you want."

"I think you already gave it to me. Twice." She cuddled up to him, pressing her body against his.

Lying with Quinn, Delilah thought that he'd given her everything. Love. Hope. Joy.

And more than that, he'd given her some semblance of peace with her ex.

"What did you think of that house on Lodge Hill?" she asked him.

"The one with the big stone fireplace? I loved it."

"I did, too. I think I'm going to make an offer on it. If the boys like it."

"They will."

"And I was wondering ..." Delilah ran a finger along his bicep. "If maybe you might like it enough to live there with us one day."

"One day?"

"One day sooner rather than later. I'm not ready yet—and the boys aren't ready yet—but we're going to get there. If you want that."

He squeezed her a little tighter. "This is the Christmas that just keeps giving."

"Is that a yes?"

"That's a yes, absolutely. When you're ready."

Delilah drifted off to sleep in his arms, thinking that she felt happier and more at peace than she ever had at any point in her relationship with Mitch.

It would take a miracle for it to stay this good.

But if she was asking for a miracle, Christmastime—especially a Christmastime they'd manufactured themselves out of love and good will—seemed like as good a time as any.

Made in the USA
Columbia, SC
21 October 2021

47599054R00157